ABOMINATIONS

JASON HENDERSON

Illustrations by James W. Fry

BYRON PREISS MULTIMEDIA COMPANY, INC.
NEW YORK

BOULEVARD BOOKS,
NEW YORK

Special thanks to Ginjer Buchanan, Steve Roman, Stacy Gittelman, Mike Thomas, Steve Behling, John Conroy, Brad Foltz, and Carol D. Page.

THE INCREDIBLE HULK: ABOMINATIONS

A Boulevard Book
A Byron Preiss Multimedia Company, Inc. Book

PRINTING HISTORY
Boulevard paperback edition / July 1997

ISBN 1-57297-273-4

BOULEVARD
Boulevard Books are published by The Berkley Publishing Group,
200 Madison Avenue, New York, New York 10016.
BOULEVARD and its logo
are trademarks belonging to Berkley Publishing Corporation.

PRINTED IN THE UNITED STATES OF AMERICA

10 9 8 7 6 5 4 3 2 1

For Earnest Bell,
my Hero and my Grandpa.

For help with Russian customs and holidays, my thanks go out to Marina Frants, who was drafted to the cause by virtue of her marriage to Keith R.A. DeCandido, my editor, and who at least kept me from making a complete fool of myself. Whatever I still managed to get wrong is my own fault, of course. Thanks to Keith for his help and patience and more thanks for all the comics to get me up to speed.

Thanks to Pierce Askegren for co-creating Sean Morgan and letting me put him through hell.

Oh, and for inspiration, thanks to Toy Biz for the really cool Doctor Banner and Abomination figures. My wife is sick of me making fighting noises and throwing them around the home office, but I call it work.

There is grief.

Thank God there are heroes.

CHAPTER 1

Sometimes I wake up and time is moving backward.

It is just after the gamma blast. I am on my back, writhing, pinned to a sheet of green glass the size of a skating rink that a few moments before was hot New Mexico sand. My hand is still in front of my face, and I can see the bones underneath my flesh glowing green and fiery. The gamma wave is flying fast and backward, though, backward with time. Now the sudden-born rage snuffs out again; time is flying past the moment's birth.

Backward screams fly into my mouth and strips of clothing slap across my body as I fly off the green glass that turns brown and grainy. My feet go back into my shoes and hit the sand and my hand is still in front of my eyes as the wave rips past me and back to the opening flash.

Time careens backward and the flash is visible through my hand but now my hand is dropping. I see the beginning of the flash shrink down into the sand of the horizon, the gamma heat soaring back with the flash and leaving me standing in the New Mexico sand, beautiful, clouds moving backward.

Sometimes I wake up and it is before the gamma flash.

I am a man, my flesh is pink and always will be, my body is weak and always will be, my rage is human and controlled, like everyone else's. Everyone.

Sometimes I wake up and time moves backward and I am not tall, or angry, or strong, except in the ways I know and have seen a million times. My rage is safely hidden, it trudges through my mind unknown and unobtrusive. Sometimes I wake up and it is before the gamma flash and my life is small and I love it and hate it and am a normal man.

2

Sometimes I wake up and time moves backward and I am not green.

Damage followed the Hulk. The Hulk walked on the concrete road and killed it slowly, even as gingerly as he stepped. Despite his efforts, the concrete cracked, in tiny, inscrutable cracks taking years off the life of the thoroughfare. Step out at night, try to do some thinking, and what happens? Damage.

The Hulk walked the roads at night wondering why he was being watched when he heard the sound. Just after he heard the sound of the crash, that god-awful wailing metal sound, the Hulk reached the top of a hill and looked down on a highway of licking flames, scattering and worming through bubbling jelly and cracked glass, cooling into a frozen purple lake of fire.

But that was after.

Fact #1. The freeways are built for trucks. There is no secret about this. Save for some heavily travelled parts of densely populated towns, the freeway system that laces through North America is chiefly a thoroughfare for the tractor-trailer. Certainly, cars are allowed. In the daytime, the trucks share the roads and let everybody else drive, too, but none of them are happy about it. At night, the trucks rule the roads.

Fact #2. Songs about car wrecks jangle and careen across the airwaves like debris. There are a lot of them, and most of them are awful, in varieties of awful that change with the decades, from the sublimely morbid "Warm Leatherette" of the 1980s back to the mercilessly smarmy "Teen Angel" of the 1950s. Car wrecks are the stuff of songs that people really like to sing and dance to. No one can say exactly why.

Fact #3. The car radio plays the same songs as the radio at home.

There is an interchange just north of White Plains, New York, where Route 4, moving westward, swoops up and around to meet Interstate 365, and the exit from I-365 does the same in the opposite direction to get onto Route 4. Opposing vehicles pass one another on the curving ramp at the legal maximum speed of forty miles per hour. At forty, tons of metal careening into each other are already lethal, but forty is merely a *bon geste* on the part of the state of New York. Most cars make the interchange at fifty-five or sixty, sailing past their counterparts, usually separated by about ten feet of air and the perceived safety net of a sheet metal guardrail and, almost jokingly, a mesh of chain-link fencing.

At eleven p.m. on February 20th, Alex Deere travelled north on I-365 and prepared to exit onto Route 4. Deere drove an eighteen-wheel tractor-trailer, the kind that, as noted, rule the road. To say that he was preparing to make the interchange is not entirely correct. He was falling asleep, and looking for the interchange whenever he managed to wake up. Alex blinked and tried to focus on the road, thudded awake by the turtlelike bumps built for exactly that purpose. His eyes travelled from his knuckles on the steering wheel to the trip report suction-cupped to the dashboard. He shook his head. He had been driving for eighteen hours.

Alex took a deep breath and rolled down the window, allowing the slicing cold air to fly in. He blinked. *The hell with them. The hell with them and their Jumbo's Jelly and their deadlines. The hell with their pressure and their "Welcome to the Jumbo's Jelly family!" speeches. I don't need this.* ("Sorry, no, we need it by Thursday.")

Deere grabbed his radio and keyed the mike. "Breaker one-nine," he mumbled. "This is Jumbo Dog. Breaker one-nine for a radio check." He took off his cap and let the air blow his hair around. Sleep rumbled like a distant wave in the background, an animal frightened away from camp for a moment, but still there, lurking. Deere watched the road fly underneath his hood and thanked God the roads were clear. Three days ago this route was covered in snow. Now the ice and snow had been pushed onto the side of the road so the trucks could get through, so people everywhere could get their peanuts and popcorn and Jumbo's Jelly.

The radio crackled. A voice popped out of the night and rasped through the wires. "Loud and clear, Jumbo Dog," came the answer. "This is Backpack. What's your twenty?"

Deere looked out. *God. Someone to talk to. Even for a second.* The animal sleep growled and slunk back a bit more. "Three-sixty-five North, Backpack. About three miles to Route 4."

"Hell," came the response. "We're neighbors. I'm on 365 too, passed 4 a while back, must have passed you just a few minutes ago."

"Welcome," said Alex. The disembodied voice was moving in the opposite direction. For a moment Deere considered that he and the party on the other end had been about twenty feet from one another a few minutes ago, travelling in opposite directions. It didn't mean much, but it just struck him funny.

"Right," said the radio. "You sound beat, Jumbo. Whassamatter, you been eatin' too much o' that jelly? Need a nap?"

Deere laughed. "Hell. Just a little tired." Then he yawned, despite himself, as he keyed off the mike.

Backpack came back. "How long ya been out, Jumbo Dog?"

"Eight—eighteen hours."

There was a pause, and Deere watched the road, which had gotten shiny. A few wet specks struck the windshield and he grimaced. It was starting to rain. After a few seconds Backpack came on again and said, "That's a little long, Jumbo. Not right you should be out that long."

"I know."

"There's rules."

"Yeah. But the company, you know."

Pause. Somewhere out there, Deere knew, Backpack was shaking his head, blinking awake, looking at his own trip report, watching the road. "Yeah," said Backpack. "I know."

"Yeah," Deere repeated. The animal growled near the camp, hanging back. Deere turned on the wipers and watched the water roll across the windshield, and for a second it all went dark. Now and again the animal swallowed him, just jumped up and grabbed him, sucked him down, and then he'd blink out, and the animal sleep would wander away, watching.

"Take care, Jumbo. My daughter, man, she does love that jelly."

"Heh. Mine too," said Deere. He put the mike back and realized his face was getting wet, and rolled up the window. He turned on the radio.

(Teen Angel, can you hear me?)

"Hey, man, don't fall asleep on me." David Morgan turned up the radio and shifted his foot. Ted Chamberlain moved a bit in his sleep and looked up at the driver of the small Ford Escort from underneath a mess of black hair that had fallen over his face. David was getting tired of depressing the gas pedal, but the Escort was not legendary for its accelerating prowess, and he had to stay pretty heavy on the gas to maintain a good speed. They were travelling east on Route 4.

Ted blinked a few times and rubbed his eyes. "It's raining."

"Yeah," said David. "Cut me some slack and talk to me."

"What are we listening to?"

"Oldies," David said with a grimace. He felt filthy. They had been driving for hours since the last stop. Not long now. He ran his fingers through his red hair and felt like washing his hand afterwards. He was drenched in the kind of dry sweat that comes from sitting all day.

Ted reached down to the floorboard and rummaged through the mess of candy wrappers and crumpled fast food boxes to find the portable stereo. He lifted it to his knee and popped the cassette drive open. "What do you want to hear?"

"Anything," David said, as he indignantly flipped the car stereo off.

"Eureka," Ted said coolly. He held a tape under David's nose. "Aerosmith."

"Fair enough." David watched the white lines disappearing under the hood as he listened to Ted popping the tape in and punching the play button. After a moment Steve Tyler's wailing voice pierced the air with "Walk this Way"—briefly, because Tyler was immediately struck by an electronic seizure that warped his voice and dwindled it down to something that might have come from the mouth of Mr. Ed.

"Um."

David shook his head "What did I say? Hm?"

"I don't have the faintest—"

"What did I say? Alkaline. Buy alkaline. House brand batteries, 'no, those are just as good, David, they'll last us 'til we get there.' Hm? And I said—"

"They were cheaper."

"Just so long," said David, "as you know I was right."

"Right you were, oh wise one," said Ted, putting the stereo out of its misery. The long-haired student looked out the window and back at his red-haired friend. "So. How long 'til we get there?"

"Oh," said David, "about an hour. Maybe an hour and a half."

"Think your Mom'll be up?"

"She'll get up. You know her. Soon as we hit the house, she'll have a full-fledged barbecue ready in a quarter of an hour."

"Think she'll be ticked that we took a three-day weekend?"

"As long as I get the grades, I can do what I want. You'll see."

"Cool."

"She is cool. Not the slightest bit like my dad."

"I'll take your word for it. What does he do?"

"You don't want to know," said David, which was what he usually said, and it tended to suffice as an answer. Fact was, he wasn't completely sure what his dad did, and he didn't much care. Dad was a distant person who tried really hard and sent money and just wasn't around that much. And he could live with that.

They were driving to the Hamptons on a sort of musical whim. David had decided on Wednesday during Romantic & Victorian Poetry that Friday's class wasn't so important, after all. He had decided this because his mom had sent him a letter, the usual care-package-and-a-check, and she had included a clipping from the local paper advertising a two-day Horror Fest-o-Rama at the art theater down the street from a community college where Mom took art classes. Mario Bava, the Italian horror-meister of the 1960s, was to be showcased. "I'm not sure why," the woman had scrawled, "but I thought you might be interested."

"You bet I'm interested," David had said, almost screaming it aloud while Professor Gregory chanted on about the neurotic Percy Shelley. "Hell, yeah," he had answered to Ted's incredulous questions. "Mario Bava! Babes in black and smoky crypts! Billowing smoke and vampires! And you should see the women at these things, man. Slender, dressed in slinky black, like refugees from *Black Sunday*. Suicidal-looking, but distinctly cool.''

That was good enough for Ted. So here they were. They had gotten off late on Thursday and hadn't left Davis College until late afternoon, despite all intentions. But now they were nearly there.

"Not a problem," David said again. "We crash, we eat well tomorrow, we hit the Fest-o-Rama tomorrow night, and we ogle the suicidal babes." That was three minutes before they hit the jelly truck.

Three minutes is a long time. Alex Deere was still awake. Three minutes later on the curve, the animal sleep had pounced and devoured.

Alex Deere heard the hollow crunch of the guardrail ripping at the bumper and the snapping of the posts on which the railing stood. Above the grating of the chainlink fence grinding against the radiator grille he made out two sounds, like shotgun blasts: the tires blowing. He realized he had been sleeping and was already fighting the wheel.

In a highway accident, time becomes syrup. It is thin in parts and melted, and then the cooler parts grab you and stick to you. Deere saw his hands streaking like arcs of light on the wheel, saw a glint of metal from the front of a Ford Escort, saw two white hands down there, way down there in the Escort, a world away, fighting a steering wheel. He saw two eyes, the driver's eyes, looking out from under shoulder-length red hair. Alex watched and for a thousandth of a second felt like he was in the Escort, the dorky little zero-to-sixty-in-three-minutes Escort and he was a long-haired kid trying to steer out of the way of a tractor-trailer coming like a locomotive over a flimsy sheet-metal guardrail, the fence twisting and rolling underneath.

(And yoooouuuu went running baaaack . . .)

Crunch and munch. Like candy, like foil on the candy bar and Alex was eating it without taking the foil off, foil grinding into the chocolate and scraping Alex's teeth and making his nerves sing with agony. Crunch and grind, and Alex tore the truck back in the direction of the highway toward his side of the guardrail even as the Escort was coming under the bumper. The flat wheels snagged the twisted guardrail. Time snapped thin and thick. The passenger side of the Escort slammed against the edge of the tractor, the shredded tractor wheels glancing off the ruined guardrail and getting wrapped up in the chain-link mesh.

Alex felt a great thrust from behind and realized the trailer had taken on a life of its own, bucking like a bronco, trying to throw him, trying to come through the back of the tractor and giving up and going around instead. The trailer twisted on its gigantic hitch and headed over the guardrail as Alex watched the windshield.

(Slip the juice to me, Bruce!)

The Escort wrapped around and wedged itself into the open seam between tractor and trailer and the two vehicles crunched on the slick concrete, tumbling in a long somersault off the ramp.

Freeze it. A moment in time like any other. Alex Deere is staring out the wet windshield looking up at the stars. The view out of the busted Escort windshield is of a narrow V between tractor and trailer. Two vehicles have become one, and they are frozen as they tumble through the air. Someone on a hill nearby is watching, and the concrete is exploding beneath his feet as he begins to run.

David Morgan thought: *Streamers.* He saw streamers in a dream once, after a pileup he narrowly escaped way off on Gulf Freeway coming out of Galveston, and he dreamt of it for months. In the dream, there were hundreds of cars crunching into one another like a soul train, and there were people hanging out of the cars, waving their arms, standing by the side of the freeway baking in the Texas sun, and off their arms and heads flew red streamers, long red ribbons whipping in the wind, trailing off the arms and heads and feet and out of mouths and off the jagged teeth of gaping windshields, *streamers*! And now he saw streamers and heard distant popping and felt mass and bone and metal and plastic moving together.

(Warm . . . leatherette. Warm . . . leatherette.)

And again something else, not the exploding concrete under the feet of the giant man who hadn't made it there yet, something else, a new sound, a screaming that meshed and chewed in with the screaming people, a sizzle of fire and gas lines bursting and pouring down.

And something else again: the thin metal of the trailer tearing open like a cookie box, and out of it begin to pour a million jars of grape jelly.

Crunch and sizzle, and now a *whoosh*, air and gasoline and fire, ripping through the gas tank of the tractor. A million jars of jelly raining down on and around the wreckage onto the asphalt. Glass jars busting and grape jelly flying through the air with bits of glass, streaming across the asphalt and mixing with gasoline.

Nothing you could write down, not a *krak* like a mortar or a *blam* like a firecracker, nothing you could describe unless you were there, pinned under the wreckage, nothing could put a word to the sudden, sharp, lacerating explosive sound of compressed tanks and gasoline making themselves known to the world at large.

Robert Bruce Banner's feet hit the highway as a wave of flame seared past him and the sweat on his chest erupted in steam. He felt something hot and sticky against his bare feet.

The highway was aflame, gloriously garish. Grape and glass burned and exploded from the jars. As soon as it hit the ground, the wave of glass cooled to the touch of the wet asphalt and hardened into a giant sheet of purple, flaming jelly. The Hulk felt himself slip on the lake of jelly and go sliding for an instant. He righted himself and kept moving toward the massive flaming wreckage. The night sounded like a war zone, jelly jars popping every second.

Through a curtain of fire and popping glass the Hulk could see a little car, streaming with something dark and on fire and someone was in there screaming.

(Won't come back from Dead Man's Cuuuurve. . . .)

The Hulk reached the wreck and was putting his hands on the hot metal of the underside of the trailer when he stopped. Flipping everything over wouldn't solve anything—he looked over at the crumpled Escort and realized any more twisting would finally crush whatever was left intact inside. He heard a honking and the screeching sound of rubber and looked over his shoulder to see a Mercedes just reaching the lake of jelly glass. The Mercedes valiantly fought the spin but succumbed, careening over gas and glass towards the wreckage. The Hulk watched the German box spinning towards him and thought, *Airbags*. He slammed his heels into the still-hot glass and felt traction where the sheet cracked.

As the Mercedes reached arm's length the Hulk bent down and grabbed the front bumper, slinging the car sideways toward the side of the road, as gingerly as one could reasonably sling an out-of-control Mercedes.

Screams.

In the distance, he could hear the sound of sirens. Someone had reported the crash. The Hulk looked up at the wedged-in Escort and hopped over the wreck to the other side, getting a clearer view of the windshield.

Two people. One of them was moving, beating at the dashboard, pinned, the other slumped over the wheel.

Robert Bruce Banner owned several doctorates, none of them medical, but he knew that moving people before the paramedics arrived was, in the abstract, a bad idea. Then a rumble and sizzle reported from the tractor, a tank still full and beginning to shake. The Hulk cursed loudly. The hell with the abstract, he had to move them.

The Hulk reached up his giant green arms and grabbed

either side of the V in which the Escort lay wedged between the tractor and trailer. He began to push the edges apart, careful not to move too fast.

Moving giant objects for the Hulk could be like surgery for a normal human. Anyone can take a knife and rip a torso in half—the trick is to deny your strength, hone it and wield it carefully. The Hulk pushed the entwined metal apart as a surgeon would separate tissue and winced when the Escort began to move inside the V. Gas trickled faster, and as the Hulk pushed the V open wider he let the car move gently down, tumbling almost softly upon his knees. The Hulk grabbed the metal of the car door with one hand and pushed the tractor-trailer back, then began to step away.

The truck began to come with them. The two vehicles had joined one another, were determined to die together, and they had taken their last few moments to wrap as many little arms of metal around one another as they could. Flames began to snap and rise, and the last tank began to change color. The Hulk grimaced as he found he had to tug and twist the car a bit to dislodge it, until finally there was only some resistance, and then, when what the Hulk thought was the rear axle of the Escort finally tore away, the Escort jerked towards him. A scream shot out of the Escort and the Hulk saw the kid inside, staring at this giant mass of green muscle carrying the car away.

Through the flames and grape jelly, not leaping but stepping very fast and very carefully, so as not to slip on the hot glass, the Hulk moved off to the far edge of the shoulder and prepared to pry the Escort open. An eighth of a mile away, the fire trucks had begun to arrive. The ambulances were back there too, and they were not getting in.

There is an apparatus called the jaws of life. It is a large machine, basically a big wrench used to rip a car open to extract whatever soft bodies might be inside. The jaws are a favorite tool of firefighters and emergency medical teams. The Hulk, who had travelled to distant planets and beaten up sundry weird aliens and world-devouring cosmic beings, found himself momentarily horrified at the thought that for this Escort, he was the jaws of life. He looked over his shoulder and saw the V where the Escort had lain, disappear behind a curtain of fire in the middle of the jelly lake.

The Hulk peered through the driver's side window and tried to ignore the blood and screams. The Escort resembled not so much a car as a deformed taco shell, the front and back twisted up, the hood crumpled. Mercifully, it was the underside of the Escort that had been in the vise grip of the V, and the roof, while damaged, had not been crushed. The real damage, the Hulk shuddered to think, would have come from the seats themselves, and the dashboard and floorboards.

Overhead the Hulk heard the sound of a helicopter. LifeFlight. *Thank God.*

Banner grabbed the roof of the car with one hand and pressed down on the bottom of the driver's side window with the other. The metal protested. As if peeling the top off a sardine can, he tore the metal back, until he pressed the roof down behind the car. He leaned over and put one hand on the driver's side window and the other on the far window. This meant his arm barely brushed against the dark-haired kid in the passenger seat. The kid wasn't screaming anymore, and if he was in pain, he didn't show it. The Hulk could not tell how badly damaged the kid's legs were.

An awful, terrible noise came with the widening of the car as the Hulk gingerly pressed the two sides apart, just a bit. Just enough to see the kid's legs. If they were too badly trapped he would do no more; he would wait like a good little physicist for the real doctors to get here and do their thing.

The Hulk almost cried out in joy, considering. When

he pushed the car door away he saw a wonderful sight: the legs were indeed broken, but they were not trapped or impaled or imbedded. The Hulk reached down and picked up what appeared to be a wallet and stuck it in his pocket, and in an instant lifted the dark-haired, bloodied kid into his arms and began to carry him.

"*Stop!*" came an amplified voice from overhead as a searchlight struck the Hulk's eyes. The helicopter came around and dropped to a height just about equal to the Hulk's eyes, not twenty feet in front of him. "*Stop what you are doing.*"

The Hulk stood still, ignoring the bright light. He knew what was going on. He knew what he looked like, a giant, green monster holding a bloody kid in his arms. He knew they were scared to death. After a moment the Hulk nodded to the pilot and waited for the searchlight to dim, and he could see the pilot's eyes. He held his gaze for a long time, not shouting, because no one would hear, and he would appear to be roaring. He held his emerald gaze and hoped that he could convey enough to say, *This boy is in trouble. Come get him.* The Hulk gestured with his head for the helicopter to set down. The pilot stared at him from beneath a shiny helmet and then, slowly, did as the Hulk suggested.

In less than six seconds two paramedics jumped from the grounded helicopter and ran to the green giant and lay a stretcher on the ground. In his arms, the kid moved, mumbled something. "David . . ."

The paramedics stopped a few feet short. One of them was a young kid, not more than twenty-two, and he pointed at the stretcher. *They don't know I can talk,* thought the Hulk. "I don't mean any harm," he heard himself say, and he winced at the sound of it because he sounded like Michael Rennie in *The Day the Earth Stood Still.* They shot Michael Rennie.

"There's no time," said the paramedic, shaking his head. "Help us get him on the stretcher."

As the Hulk lay the kid on the stretcher the paramedic began to strap him in. "Any others?"

The Hulk shrugged. "Driver of the truck is dead. No question."

The paramedic frowned, looked back at the freeway where the smoking truck lay, then at the Escort. "He keeps asking for someone. Was there someone else in the car?"

"Yeah," the Hulk nodded. "Yeah."

The paramedic nodded again and his partner signaled to the helicopter, which lit and began to move toward the chopper. When it was overhead the paramedics ran the lines from the stretcher to the chopper's underbelly. The other paramedic scrambled up a ladder and the younger one turned to go, then looked at the Hulk. "You did good, mister." In a moment the paramedic was in the cockpit and signalling with his thumb to the pilot.

The freeway was a nightmare of lights and sound, fire trucks and ambulances and a gathering crowd of onlookers. The Hulk stepped toward the shadows, toward the feeder road, and stepping under the underpass he fished the wallet out of his pocket. He opened the wallet and found a license.

David Morgan. The Hulk sat in the shadows under the overpass, staring at the wallet. He read the address several times. When he was sure he was not mistaken, he shook his head in shame. After a long moment he looked up, peered out from under the overpass, across the freeway to the hill on the other side. There, a man stood, with a pair of binoculars. Watching him. The Hulk was not surprised.

Worse and worse. Worse and worse by day and night.

CHAPTER 2

ourning, the people were saying, became the hell out of Nadia Dornova. Nadia thought about the phrase and smiled to herself as she made her way to her dressing room behind the Langley Theater. It was one of those phrases that starts on some clever critic's lips and ends up in a column, and then, because it was short and clever, started getting said everywhere. The Americans, especially the "educated" types that frequented Broadway, were as captivated by the appearance of cleverness as they were with art, and so anything clever became conventional wisdom (conventional cleverness?) and got repeated. It didn't even matter that Nadia wasn't playing Electra but Antigone—in a revival of Jean Anouilh's *Antigone*, no less—the phrase stuck because it was terribly clever, or seemed to be. (Nadia reminded herself that the Americans were captivated with saying "Where's the beef?" for years.) She knew without doubt that her producer laughed every time he heard the *Electra* phrase, and in his head, if she could listen, would be that distinct *ka-ching* sound that cash registers used to make.

Nadia Dornova, the actress walking through the cavernous hallways behind the Langley, the blonde Russian with the voice and eyes of Dame Judith and the legs of Brigitte Bardot, was on the rise. She stepped through the corridors with more authority than she had in years, watching with a hint of concealed amusement as people looping cables backstage got out of her way as if she were on fire. *Antigone* was into its fourth straight sold-out month and going strong. People could just keep on being clever.

Nadia turned a corner and felt her face flush. Her dressing room door was open, and standing in the hall, lit by the yellow lights from the room, were three men. They were speaking in hushed tones and looking up and down the corridor as they talked. She knew two of them. One was her director, Richard March, and he was nervous, because he kept rubbing his back at the lumbar region, a reminder to all that he had aches he wouldn't talk about. (Everyone in the theater was chronically dramatic.) The next man wore a charcoal gray suit that seemed to encase him like a coffin, and he had a face of stone. Though some of the murmurs came from his mouth, his face barely moved when he spoke. That, Nadia felt sure, was a cop, and if she were at home, she would have called him KGB.

The third man was a breath of fresh air. "Greg?" Nadia tilted her head as she walked and tried to make the name ask all the questions. Greg Vranjesevic was nodding and had his hand on the shoulder of the cop when he looked up and caught her eye. He smiled, and she felt her stomach twist despite herself, professional that she was.

Greg was not the quintessential Russian politician. The simple gray suit that he wore betrayed a lean, muscular frame, the frame of a man who had been handpicked to grow up to be a medal-earning Soviet gymnast before a nasty car accident put his career on hold. The story went that he had been studying all along, anything he could get his hands on, just in case he went down for the count. When the time came, he petitioned for removal to the state department. It was a demotion, a terrible shame. His family was horrified at their loss and practically mourned him. By the time he made Ambassador to the United States, he was thirty-three, and the gymnast thing was nearly forgotten—except that try as he might, he would never look the part of a Russian politician, having forsaken the role of a walking testament to vodka and cigarettes for the look of a new breed. He also had a great smile.

Greg took Nadia's hands in his and kissed her cheek, still smiling, but she could see the concern in his brown eyes. She had seen that look before. Her late husband

Emil used to have that look. He would kiss her and smile charmingly and then go out and someone would nearly kill him. Then he would come back and kiss her and smile again, repeated until, finally, he didn't come back. Men lied with their mouths but their eyes were oracles.

He said, "Nadia! How is my favorite defector?"

"Something I should know?" Nadia asked, tilting her head to make the question sound almost casual.

Greg's smile lingered for a moment and then exited stage left. "I've been talking to Richard. . . ."

"I called him," said March. "He said to call him if there was another."

"Another?" Nadia frowned. "Another message."

"Ms. Dornova," said the coffin man, "do you know if there might be someone upset with you? I mean, someone who might want to—frighten you?"

Nadia felt her eyes flash. "I don't frighten easily, Mr.—?"

"Timm."

Nadia breathed and said cooly, "I don't know you, Mr. Timm."

Greg chuckled. "They're the same in every country, aren't they? Mr. Timm doesn't like to talk much, he prefers to ask questions. He doesn't like to talk about who he's with. But he's been very helpful." His voice was cool, his English perfect, with a useful trace of Russian accent about it, which Nadia suspected he left there intentionally.

Nadia raised an eyebrow and smiled wryly. "None I can think of," she said, in answer to the question.

"Well, you know," said March, "I've seen this before, someone becomes a star and there's bound to be a few fans who've gone 'round the bend."

"What was it?" Nadia asked.

Greg softly grasped her shoulder. "Why don't we go for a walk?"

"I think she should see it," said Timm, as if this were a topic already long running.

"See what?" Nadia turned to go in the dressing room door, but Greg stopped her.

"I wanted to erase it, tell you about it later."

"I agree," said March.

Nadia nodded again and stepped inside, heels clacking on the linoleum. She looked around for an instant at the cheap chairs, the mountain of expensive flowers and cards. After a moment the mirror caught her eye and she almost gasped. Almost.

"But I thought you should see it," came the voice of Mr. Timm.

There was green putty, or makeup, on the mirror. Scrawled in huge, block letters was one word: HAUGHTY.

"Haughty?"

"Does that mean anything to you, Ms. Dornova?"

"Oh, come on," said March, "that's like asking if *proud* means anything to her."

Nadia continued to stare at the word and felt for the chair behind her and sat down, never taking her eyes off of the smudgy letters. For the longest time she kept reading it, as if it were some terribly significant name to which she had forgotten the face. "I don't know," she said, finally.

Greg said, "I guess it's not much." He was behind her, hands on her shoulders.

Timm stood in front of the mirror, the word HAUGHTY hanging over his shoulder like a caption. "It could mean anything."

"Anything it means, anyway," said Nadia. "So people think I'm haughty now?"

Greg said, "No one could think that."

"Very helpful, Greg," she laughed, putting her hands to her forehead. It was a nervous laugh. After a moment she said, "I think you men are scaring me more than this."

"It's not the first message," said Timm.

This was true. There had been a few notes before, small things that at first Nadia had almost completely ignored. Little notes left in places where she would find them, on her marks on the stage. She had pointed them out to Greg when one appeared in her mailbox at home. Sometimes they went on for paragraphs, in long strings of impossible-to-understand symbols and disconnected words. Sometimes they were short.

"People fixate on Ms. Dornova," said March. "Fixation becomes Ms. Dornova's audience, I guess."

Nadia felt her composure slipping, a distant early warning blinking on the horizon, telling her her hand was shaking, and she calmly bit the edge of her finger. She had been fixated upon, indeed. She had been kidnapped, even, a few years ago. A mad mistake of nature known as the Abomination had scooped her up and taken her below ground and then, as quickly, had released her.

As if reading her mind, Greg asked, "Could it be the Abomination?"

"You're asking me?" Nadia shrugged. "That monster wanted—" she stopped, staring at the mirror. "He wanted my company. He was like a child that watches television and wants the people on the programs to come live with him. I called him a monster, but he was never angry. He let me go." She heard a scratching sound and looked up to see Mr. Timm scratching notes with a plastic wand on a handheld computer. It was long, like a notepad, with a hinged black cover that hung down from the top.

"Just the same," said Greg, "we can't be too careful."

"What I want to know is how did he get in my dressing room, whoever he was?"

"I don't know," said March, shaking his head and staring at the floor, hand working the lumbar region. "The security—"

"Your security," interrupted Mr. Timm, "leaves a lot

to be desired, if I may say so. He could have broken in in the middle of the night, even slipped by with a press pass in the daytime. There are hundreds of people working on this show, Mr. March. People can slip by; security can slip up."

March nodded sourly. "I agree. We'll double it. Anything for the star, eh?"

"Wouldn't hurt," said Timm.

Greg rubbed his chin. "Mr. Timm, I appreciate your concern. I'm aware that you would not be so concerned if not for Ms. Dornova's—connection with me. Is there anything you can recommend?"

Timm's mouth barely moved, but there was a shrug in the voice, at least: "Honestly? Right now I'd say Ms. Dornova should keep acting, and keep thinking, and call if she thinks of anything, or if anything else happens."

"Call me?" Greg asked.

A card appeared in Timm's hand, outstretched toward Nadia in a motion that was almost impossible to follow with the eye. "Call me."

Nadia took the card almost warily and glanced at it before putting it away. It said: JULIUS TIMM. SPECIAL AGENT. STRATEGIC ACTION FOR EMERGENCIES. Under it was printed a simple logo bearing the acronym SAFE, and under that was a local phone number. She nodded and put the card in her breast pocket. She sighed, and smiled, looking to each of the three men. "Well."

"That's the 'Get-the-hell-out-of-my-dressing-room' well, folks."

"Fine," said Timm, slapping the computer closed. It was an almost comical movement, as if someone had put the hinge on there to make the agents feel like they still had old spiral notepads instead of liquid crystal displays. "I hope all goes well, Ms. Dornova. I'm sure it will."

"I'm sure," she responded. "But I do have a performance to prepare for. Thank you very kindly for your time."

When they were gone she realized that no one had yet scraped the word off. And all through her makeup session, she stared at the word. Haughty.

Eyes, thought the Abomination. *Haughty eyes.* In the darkness above the theater, in the rafters, the keyboard clacked beneath long, green nails. If anyone had chanced to look up above the chandelier, the person might possibly have seen the odd creature sitting there cross-legged, back against a post, scaly hands lit by the glowing LCD. The unlucky spectator might have seen the face lit up there, a face more like an amphibious reptile than that of a man, a face with hard, green, thick skin and fins that puckered and splayed with every breath.

The Abomination flexed his fins and looked around the heights of the Langley. No one was watching. No one heard the clacking keys.

Every eye in the theater was on Nadia Dornova far below, and he could hear that voice rising through the air, commanding and defiant. The performance was going well. Antigone was having it out with Creon, the king and her uncle, who swore to execute anyone who gave a proper burial to Antigone's dead brother. The defiant Antigone had stolen into the night to scatter dust on the baking, rotting flesh, a ceremonial burial to appease the gods. And now Creon knew of her defiance, and the house was enrapt as he announced that she was going to die.

"It's true," says Creon, "we are not a very loving family."

And Oh! Nadia was brilliant. More brilliant than she had ever been before. She was on fire, and the Abomination's nostrils and fins flared as he thought of those eyes of hers, and the fire he had once felt in her arms, all those years ago. Those eyes, those haughty eyes.

Yes, haughty indeed! Full of pride that she had become this angel of the theater to these snivelling masses, reflecting the haughtiness of all those who stared at her.

The audience, the Abomination knew, stared at her with pride, because they felt they owned her. They paid their money and they got to watch her, got to hear that voice that should have been his alone and watch that body that should have been his *alone*.

Breath rasped and bubbled within the Abomination's mouth, which hung open slightly as he concentrated on entering the memorized codes. He squinted his demonic eyes and cursed at the bulk of his claws, which required him to be extra careful not to crush the keyboard, much less enter the wrong code. One slip and his claw would punch right through the liquid crystal display, and the Abomination watched the image for a moment in his mind, the glowing crystal oozing from the sliced fabric. Later. That would amuse him later.

He tapped the keyboard again, and something about ten feet away clicked twice and hummed. The Abomination listened as he tapped a few more times. *Klik-klik-humm*, from various parts of the rafters throughout the building. His allies had done good work. It pleased him that they were willing to help him as much as he helped them. With each click and hum, a small jet dislodged from its cradle and lowered itself a couple of feet, titling downward. The sound multiplied itself a hundred times, throughout the theater, like a rainstorm of barely audible clicks, until at last each jet lay in its proper position.

Haughty indeed! They would learn haughtiness. The Abomination tapped another entry code into the keyboard and heard a new humming sound, saw the rubber hoses snaking through the rafters whip as the gas came online and travelled to the jets, ready.

The Abomination's vision shifted in focus and he peered down to look on Nadia once more. Something in his gills hissed angrily as he looked at her, not anger at her, not at himself, but at whatever demon forced him into this. There she was, supple and tall, slender like a gymnast, like that gymnast bureaucrat Vranjesevic she was carrying on with. He changed his mind—he was angry with her after all. Angry that because she was beautiful and soft he could not see her, could not talk to her, because for every soft curve of her body he had scales, and rocklike green flesh, and where her eyes were soft and radiant, his radiated hatred and glowed like rubies. What had she called him? Like a child? A *child*?

All of them would pay, every last haughty one of them, laughing at Anouilh's clever witticisms and laughing at their good fortune to be the Beautiful People, the happy people, the worst of the whole lot of these Americans who rape and pillage the entire Earth because they feel entitled to it. They looked at Nadia and heard her velvet voice and their eyes travelled over her body. They laughed and smiled because they owned her and she owned them, and when one owns something beautiful one surely became beautiful. That was what they thought, the Abomination was sure, and they would all learn; they were abominations just as he was *the* Abomination, and by the living Lord he would surely teach them.

The computer beeped twice and a timer flashed on the LCD. Fifteen seconds, it said, counting down. The Abomination smiled as best his warped mouth could manage, and he felt the slime stretch between his lips, bubbling as he breathed. He watched the seconds tick away, as he stared down at the theater, at all those heads, all those haughty eyes, and finally at Nadia.

And Nadia was looking at him. For a moment he froze, felt the gamma-irradiated blood chill in his hardened veins. It was an illusion, of course, just a freezing of time, a snapshot of her looking up at him by chance, not seeing him at all. Nadia was deep in her part, and he watched that faraway look and dove into her eyes, and rode them back to their youth.

God, my God, Nadia, you were so beautiful. God, my God, Nadia, how I loved you.

And they were young again and disgustingly happy,

as he recalled, and she sat by the fire as he brought in
more wood. She laughed at the furry cap he wore, because
it was his father's and must have been a hundred years
old and should have been taken out and buried, she said,
and she would take off his cap and she would kiss him.
The Abomination watched those eyes, felt those eyes
looking on him with love, with simple love, and he felt
his throat gurgling. Somewhere in the back of his mind
the timer beeped away, and he held the vision a moment
longer, almost reaching out a scaly claw as if to touch
her.

Beep. The Abomination looked at the keyboard and at
the vision and thought, *No*. He reached through the vision
and tapped a code quickly, and one, specially aimed jet
went offline, clicking and humming back into its cradle.

Haughty were her eyes, it was true. She was an abomination. But it would be enough, he decided, for her to
watch.

Beep. A hundred rubber hoses pumped and whipped
in the rafters, and something began to spray. In a moment,
the Abomination heard screams, and he sat still, listening,
clawing the liquid crystal, and letting the glowing green-
ish-blue fluid run down his fingers.

Nadia heard the first scream as she was delivering a line
that always gave her trouble, and she found she had to
step out of character for a microsecond in order to remember how the line went. And then the line disappeared
entirely from her mind, and she struggled to grasp it, chas-
ing the white rabbit of a lost line, trying to ignore the
sound of *screaming*? The line, the play, vanished. She
stared out into the audience and heard a rumble of voices,
questions being hurriedly whispered, and the spotlight was
so bright that the audience looked as if it were on the
other side of a cloud. After a moment the lights seemed
to dim, or else Nadia's vision adjusted, and she heard a
scream again and looked out and saw a woman, in about

the tenth row. She was middle-aged and wore a smashing evening gown, and she was rubbing, no, *clawing* at her eyes. A man next to her stood, to help her, Nadia thought, but no, he too was tearing at his eyes, rocking on his legs with his fists in his hands.

Nadia gasped now, not because of the woman, exactly, but because she saw the green cloud for the first time, and marvelled that she had not seen it before. A green mist hung in the air, floating down, and the air glowed with iridescent sparkles as the lights pierced through a billion droplets of green liquid. More murmurs, still just that one woman, screaming, and then another scream lit the air, and another. Nadia looked around in horror and saw more people howling in pain and tearing at their eyes, rubbing violently, and someone was screaming from the back, "Please, get it out!"

Nadia backed away, numb, tripped over a prop lamp and fell to the floorboards, and she looked over at the man playing Creon. He was backing off the stage. Nadia propped herself up too hurriedly, and saw a man running towards the stage, a stranger to her, running blind with his face in his hands. The man hit the stage and fell over. She watched his hands reach the stage as he clawed to get up on to it. Time froze for a second as she saw the man's bald head top the edge, and slowly lift, and then she saw his eyes.

Fused, hideously fused eyes glowing green and bubbly, and the man was screaming in terror and running blind and she could not take it and screamed herself. Her scream mixed with those of the man and the thousand in the theater and she looked out and saw them all, the whole of the audience, on the floor and in the balcony, crawling over one another, blind, eyes fused, hands tearing at one another and at their own faces. They resembled a large mound of worms, people without minds, squirming, irrational masses of green-glowing terror. Nadia saw the man get closer to her and she found her feet and ran.

Across the stage, off and into the corridors she ran. She felt the edge of a desk tear at her leg, heard cloth rip away, and the sound of howling terror eased as she ran, but it was still back there. She saw her dressing room door and ran for it, thinking all the while that she should turn, head out onto the street. Someone said her name and touched her shoulder. She shook furiously and ran on, and heard again, "*Nadia!*" She found her dressing room door and whipped it open.

She was just running inside when something caught her, hands on her shoulders, turning her around. She cried and screamed and looked in his eyes, and saw Greg Vranjesevic. Greg shook his head and held her as she shook violently and wept onto his chest. After what seemed like an eternity the shaking dwindled to a tremble, she opened her eyes and blinked as Greg asked again and again if she were all right. She knew that she was. And then she looked in the dressing room and saw the mirror and began to shake and scream again, because the message there had been lengthened by one word.

It said, HAUGHTY EYES.

Michael Cross watched the Hulk through a pair of field glasses. The glasses recorded everything he saw, feeding into the SAFE databank miles overhead in the agency's Helicarrier. Cross stood about fifty yards from where he had parked his car. He had considered himself lucky— this was the first night the Hulk had stirred from his nest in White Plains, and Cross had followed at a safe distance, watching everything. So Cross had been in perfect position to see the fugitive gamma giant desperately try to rescue the parties to one of the grisliest accidents Cross had ever seen. Cross's call to EMS brought the trucks and helicopters by the time the Hulk was doing his jaws of life act. Now Cross stood, his jacket flapping in the wind, binoculars pressing a crease into his face, and below him the highway still smoked and burned with wreckage and jelly.

Cross spoke softly, the binoculars picking up the sound of his voice. "Look at that. Look at that. This is the Hulk, ladies and gents. This is the guy who rips tanks apart, that's him, handing an injured kid over to the paramedics like he's the Green Samaritan."

Cross watched the Hulk walk away from the paramedics for a while and look around him. For a moment, as the Hulk stepped under a shadowy overpass, the green giant gazed around, and Cross sucked in air as the gamma creature seemed to focus up on the hill, directly toward Cross himself. But after a moment, Cross saw the Hulk look away, and slink into the shadows.

The SAFE agent watched the shadowy patch of the underpass for a long while. After a quarter of an hour had passed he saw no more movement and cursed softly. The Hulk must have disappeared out the other side. Cross decided to go back to his car; he could chase the rabbit a bit before parking again.

God, what an assignment. SAFE didn't pay well enough for this. Half the time Cross's quarry hung out at home, the other half, he could suddenly leap way the hell off into the southwest, leaving Cross at the mercy of other authorities to tip him off. Sometimes it was hopeless and he could do nothing but wait for the Hulk to reappear at his home base. Sometimes he didn't reappear; that was whenever he and Mrs. Banner moved, and then it could be weeks before intel got caught up. SAFE was very good at its job. But the Hulk was a hard man to follow.

Cross looked up in the sky. If all went well, it would all be a lot easier very soon. They'd never have to lose the Hulk again.

Cross sighed and turned as he clicked the binoculars onto his belt and walked toward his car. He shook his head, thinking of the accident—how remarkable, that this was what it took to get a little action out of the reclusive

Hulk. How lucky that the Hulk had decided to go for a walk. Life was funny.

Cross sighed as he got closer to the black sedan parked by a shadowy walnut tree at the side of the road. It was just so—identifiable. There was something bright neon obnoxious about the black suits and black cars that agency men and women utilized. Cross suspected there might be something deliberate there, in fact. Sean Morgan, SAFE's less-than-jovial boss, was a clever man, and he knew a little intimidation, even a little encouraged paranoia, could go a long way. So they followed people in big black sedans and wore black raincoats and Elvis Costello sunglasses, just like in the movies. It all worked to the right effect.

Of course, Cross thought, perhaps the heroes were different, and perhaps they should be dealt with differently. The Hulk was not some crooked numbers runner you want to notice the black car parked a block up. With the Hulk, it really was a better idea to keep pretty clear.

Cross opened his car door, sliding into the front seat. He was about to put the key in the ignition when he remembered he hadn't noted his itinerary in at least an hour. If the Hulk was out of sight now, another twenty seconds wouldn't matter. Hell, with the Hulk, he could almost pack it in for the next week once the gamma giant was out of sight. Cross retrieved his notepad and pen device from his coat pocket, flipped the cover of the pad back, and began to scribble a few notes on the LCD. Typical stuff. *Here, going there. Big crash, Hulk heroics. Can't wait for GammaTrac to render me obsolete, yadda yadda yadda.*

The SAFE agent flipped the pad closed and dropped it and the pen device back in his coat pocket. He placed the key in the ignition and heard the eight-cylinder engine turn over and begin to purr—Morgan insisted that all machinery be kept in top condition, from pocket pads to the engines in the cars. "We're on a budget here," Morgan kept saying, "and there's no way we're letting what we have go to waste."

Cross was about to put the car in reverse when he reached up to adjust the rear-view mirror and saw a hand-scrawled note stuck to the glass: BEHIND YOU.

Cross dropped three inches in his seat and drew his gun as he fell sideways and twisted to peer between the seats and see:

Nothing. Cross breathed for a second, rising in the seat to peer over. No one was there. He allowed his eyes to adjust and he saw what he was looking for: there was a hole in the rear passenger-side door, where something large had ripped out the lock. Something not unaccustomed to acting like a jaws of—

Crunch. Something that sounded like a freight train landed on the hood of the sedan and Cross whipped around again, staring forward. In the darkness he saw light from the highway reflected off dark green skin, sweat glistening over green veins and muscles. As Cross drew his gun, he saw two giant, green arms reach down, saw ten green fingers clutch the windshield itself and tear it all away in one chunk, which the creature let fly. The windshield sailed into the distance and Cross stared at the disappearing glass. Then he felt the jaws of life grab him by the lapels and drag him through the front of the sedan.

"Drop the gun," came a deep voice.

Cross didn't move. He held onto the gun, just as he felt knuckles the size of plums bruising his breastbone. He looked down to see his feet dangling over the hood, and a few feet below that, the Hulk's own legs, impressed in the hood of the car as if it were a papasan chair.

"You don't seem to grasp," said the Hulk, pulling Cross close, "that resistance is beyond futile."

There was a human in there, thought Cross. He was eye to eye with the Hulk and he could see it, the red-veined eyes, the lack of sleep so evident. He knew all along that he was dealing with a mutated Robert Bruce

Banner, brilliant guy, but it could be so easy to forget. But the eyes locking with his now were scary, not because they were those of a beast, but because they were those of a very smart, very dangerous man.

Cross dropped the gun.

"I'm not going to ask you why you're following me," said the Hulk. "You've followed me everywhere since New York. I'm sick of it. I want it to stop. Do you understand?"

Cross opened his mouth and closed it. He nodded, slowly.

"Did you see the accident?"

"What?" Cross shook his head. Was the Hulk interrogating him?

The Hulk shook his head and stepped off the hood of the sedan, setting Cross down on the front of the hood. Cross winced as his coccyx collided with the crumpled metal. "Did you see the accident?"

"How could I miss it?" Cross stared. He could run, maybe. *Yeah. Right.*

The Hulk scratched his chin, looking over the hill where Cross could still see the dancing lights from the emergency vehicles. "It's just so . . . Have you heard of Galactus?"

"Who?"

"Galactus. Big guy. Huge. Eats planets."

"Galactus. Yes." Cross spoke slowly, having no idea where this was going.

"I mean *planets*. The whole thing. And there was the Beyonder: a guy the size of the cosmos, no real limits at all. I've been whisked to the other side of the world because he wanted me to be. He could destroy the world. Like that!" The Hulk brought up a mammoth green arm and curled his fingers, about to snap them. Cross d——
He had heard that being too close to one of those snaps could be deadly. The Hulk seemed to rememb——

and stopped his hand before the thumb and finger collided. "You get the idea."

"I'm sorry, but . . ."

"You're supposed to watch me, right?"

"Ah . . . yes."

"Right, then. Shut up."

"Okay."

"So here's the clincher. The Fantastic Four, they beat Galactus with the regularity of the Super Bowl. The FF save the universe all the time. *I* helped beat the Beyonder. And we all rejoiced, because we used these amazing powers to stop these mega-beings. Do you begin to follow me?"

Cross opened his mouth. *You told me to shut up.* This was turning weird.

"The point is, Galactus *makes sense to me*! Isn't that rich? I'm *accustomed* to that. The Beyonder wanted to erase the world, or whatever. I can deal with that." The Hulk turned towards the flashing lights in the distance, placed his fists on his hips. "This I can't—I can't figure it."

"It was an accident."

"Wait a minute. Did you call EMS?"

Cross said, "Yes."

The Hulk nodded, his mouth turned downward. "Good. Good."

Good? You wrecked my car!

"Listen," said the Hulk, turning back to look at Cross. He fished in the front pocket of his giant black Dockers and pulled out what appeared in the darkness to be a wallet. It was dark leather, but Cross was pretty sure there were blood stains on it. "Morgan's the same way. There are things that make sense to him. Budgets make sense to him, so do national security threats. This isn't gonna make any sense to him." The Hulk flipped the wallet to Cross, who caught it and opened it up. There was a driver's license inside, and it belonged to a red-headed kid called David Morgan.

"Oh, no."

"Did you know Morgan had a son?"

"No." Why would he? The boss of SAFE was a very businesslike man, to put it kindly.

"I knew because I knew. No big deal. But that's him. That . . . was him." The Hulk brushed at his eyes, his voice rumbling. "He didn't make it."

"You . . . I saw you get one . . ."

"The passenger. He was lucky. He wasn't impaled on the handle brake."

"You pulled him out."

"Right." The Hulk stared at the horizon. "Who cares? Just one of those things. Galactus makes sense to me, here I'm just a wrench." The Hulk put his giant green hands in his pockets and slumped for a moment. "So you go, Agent Cross. I gave you that wallet for a reason, so that someone other than the police can get the news to Morgan first. Do you understand? Does that make sense to someone like you or me? No national security threat here, just a really, really bad thing. And all we get to do is open doors and carry messages. Can you handle that?"

Cross folded the wallet and put it in his pocket. "I can handle that."

The Hulk sniffed. His face was mottled with soot. "And stop following me. If Morgan wants to talk, tell him to give me a ring. But I'm sick of being shadowed. Tell SAFE you'll just waste more vehicles and someone could get hurt." The Hulk was already walking away, leaving Cross on the crushed hood of his car. Cross pulled out his cell phone and distinctly heard the Hulk grumble as he leapt into the air, "I want to be left alone."

CHAPTER 3

The voice rumbled through the dank tunnel, reverberating through the sludgy walls and dripping pipes:

"O Lord God of my salvation, I have cried night and day before thee . . ."

The creature that was once called Emil Blonsky knelt on a scarlet rug in his inner sanctum, pouring the eighty-eighth Psalm out of his heart and his wretched, Abominable mouth.

"Let my prayer come before thee, incline thine ear unto my cry."

Once he had been a man, a man of Georgia and the Soviet Union, a soldier and a spy. And now he was *this*. The singer of the Psalm, cut off from the world above by his new shape and his new voice.

"For my soul is full of troubles, and my life draweth nigh unto the grave."

In his mind flashed images, one after the other, and he rocked on his scaly knees and tried to send the demon images away, singing out the Psalm, becoming one with the Psalmist:

"I am counted with them that go down into the pit; as a man that hath no strength."

Flashing images in the gamma-irradiated mind, scattering salamanders and crickets chirping, echoing the Psalm, and there before him, Nadia, and Georgian fields, and the Western beast called the Hulk. And all around him, beyond the sanctum, stagnant pools and smells of death and decay.

"Free among the dead, like the slain that lie in the tomb, whom thou rememberest no more, and I am cut off from thy hand."

It was true, all true, and the creature rocked on his

knees and wailed out the words, hearing them gurgle in the dripping sludge. Forgotten.

"Thou hast laid me in the lowest pit! In darkness! In the deeps!"

Forgotten by Nadia, forgotten by humanity, forgotten by his country, forgotten by God himself!

"Thy wrath lies hard upon me, and thou hast afflicted me with thy waves!"

The Hulk, that beast, and those weapons, all of them, and the one gamma gun, and he had stepped before it as his superiors told him, seeking power *for them*, seeking revenge *for them*, and what had he become? Forgotten! Forsaken!

"Thou hast put my acquaintance far from me . . ."

Nadia! Mother! Father! Russia! And what was he now, what did they call him, far above, where the world did not stink and salamanders did not root and he had no place?

"Thou hast made me an Abomination unto them!

"An Abomination!"

The word roared from the Abomination's mouth, tearing through the caverns below the city and bouncing off the bricks and pipes, frightening secret unmentionable crawling things into the cracks, and he rocked violently on his knees, claws before his chest. The creature threw out his hands to his sides, and cried out, gurgling and cacophonous:

"An *Abomination* I shall *be*!"

For what seemed like an eternity, the Abomination sat, claws dangling at his sides, leaning back where he knelt. He listened to his breath slowing and the delicate timing of the drips from the pipes. As his own subsided he heard breath from elsewhere in the sanctum and opened his glimmering red eyes. "Who is there?"

A figure stepped from the shadows, and in the dimness the Abomination could see the trim figure of a woman, black hair pulled back to reveal a gaunt, serious face. She answered, "Sarah Josef, comrade."

His words came slowly. "You have been watching me." It was neither a question nor an accusation, merely an observation.

"The eighty-eighth Psalm, yes?" The woman stepped closer and dropped down, sitting on her haunches. "The Psalm of the forsaken Abomination?" She tilted her head and he rose in his place, and even though she stood up he still towered over her by at least a meter.

"Yes."

"Good news. *We* have not forsaken you."

The Abomination made an expression approximating a sneer and nodded, and walked over to a large console built into a grungy wall. The console seemed to be an organic part of the underground itself, a dark tumorous piece of technology. The Abomination sat on the stool that seemed to grow from a dark, metallic arm jutting from the dripping wall. He tapped the keyboard and the monitor came to life. "No, you have not, my friend."

Sarah ran a finger along the edge of the console and regarded the dripping walls. "Your—sanctum—is to your liking?"

"Yes."

"So lonely," she said, with a strong note of care in her voice.

"Not always," said the Abomination. "Once there was a city here, in the tunnels. A city of the lost and forgotten, the huddled refuse of the world above. And I was their comrade and their protector. I told them stories and they accepted me as a man and a brother." More images flashed in his head, the unmistakable sound of gunfire echoing in the tunnels, bodies slapping against the wet concrete, screams of innocents. "I was used by enemies above as an excuse to clean the tunnels out. Even the Hulk had a hand in it, an act I would likely have thought below Bruce Banner, who never had the stomach for slaughter. All of them," he whispered, "young and old, women and men. My family. Torn by bullets from crooked police in riot gear. No, it was not lonely then. But now it is a tomb."

"All of them?"

He looked up. "Some of them survived. Scattered deeper in the tunnels. I do not think we will ever be together again. People learn lessons when they feel pain. The lesson my underground family learned was not to trust. Not to feel safe." The green lip curled. "But I will have my revenge."

She shook her head, and the barest hint of a smile appeared. "I think you need a little light."

"My time for light, my dear," said the Abomination, as he read the files that scrolled past his eyes, "is past."

"At URSA we believe the past can come around again."

"Who knows? You may be right," said the Abomination. Who knew, indeed? It had been Sarah who had approached the Abomination. When she found him below the streets and spoke to him in Russian, he took one look at her and her standard-issue sidearms and nearly squashed her like the tadpoles he expected to feed her to. But she identified herself, not as KGB, but URSA. URSA was a new group, made up of KGB refugees and political discontents hellbent on a familiar ideal: a return to the strong-military, Communist, West-hating Soviet Union of old.

"Bah," the Abomination had said to her then. "The Soviets hung me out to dry. What do I want with a return to that regime?"

"Not that regime," Sarah had replied after she found her breath and began to explain herself. She had recovered from nearly being strangled. The Abomination found her refreshing, and that is why he let her talk. "A new regime, a purer Communism."

"I am not interested."

"Listen to me and tell me again when I'm finished," she responded. "It is at great expense that URSA has located you and I will not return until we have talked."

The Abomination looked around, as if he had other things to be doing. "Talk."

The agent composed herself before beginning. She wore a gray jumpsuit and she stood with her hands on her hips, an authoritative stance. "Bad deals happen," she said, "when only one side benefits. The other side feels used, cheated, and finally refuses to cooperate."

"Yes."

"*Good* deals happen when both sides benefit, multiple party deals when all sides are satisfied. URSA understands this and wishes to make a deal with you. As a gesture, shall we say, for the old regime's mistreatment of such an agent as Emil Blonsky."

The Abomination tilted his head and stared at her. "What you may have heard in some seminar could not possibly even hint at the truth."

She stared at him, and the Abomination detected the slightest tremble in her voice. "I think you are wrong about that."

"Go on, little girl."

"It is our understanding that you bear something of a grudge against the United States and especially against the Hulk."

"You are underinformed. I bear a grudge against almost everybody. I find it easier that way to keep them all straight."

"All right, then," she said. "Then at least we'll share a common enemy or two. URSA would like to see a little chaos here. You enjoy chaos, I understand. Something you said a while back about bringing it all down around their ears."

"I did say that."

"We can help you. Whatever you want. I'm in charge

of the American theater and you, Emil Blonsky, promise to be my most powerful ally."

"You've got to be joking."

There it was again. A tremble, faint, hidden back there, a personal stake hiding behind the austere mask, every agent's Achilles' heel. "Why do you say that?"

The Abomination strode over to stand before her and he crouched so that he could look her in the eyes. She barely flinched when she was struck by the rank breath that flew across her face. "You want me to be an agent? For you? You and this URSA of yours? I am through with serving masters, and I do not see anything here that is about to change my mind."

"We can help you," she said, suddenly more vulnerable. "Helping one another, we both benefit."

"Yes, yes, you said that. Very nice speech, little sister, but what is it, why are you here? What is going on? You're not afraid of me, I can tell that." He studied her carefully. "You think highly enough of yourself to feel confident you could escape me if I tried to kill you again and I don't think you frighten easily, so what is it? So I answer no, and you ask again, and still I say no, and you go away and that's that. Yet here you are, trembling."

It was true. She was. She averted her eyes like a junior officer being dressed down.

"You want me to join you—why? Why me," the breath blasted in her face, "really?"

"Because you and I—"

"What? You and I *what*?" The Abomination waited for a second and looked at her. He had had enough torturing of this girl for one day. "Go home, little girl. Go tell your masters that a resurrected Soviet state would do me as much good as the old one did, and I am not interested."

She slumped only slightly and turned, and maneuvered out from the space between the Abomination and the wall. Sarah moved away, towards the ladder leading up to the world of light. The Abomination turned and sat on a pipe, contemplating the dank water.

Her hand was on the first rung and she was swinging herself up to the ladder when he muttered, "Sarah. . . ."

She stopped and hung there, looking back at him.

"Sarah *Josef*, did you say?"

She hung there still, staring at him, only the white knuckles showing her edginess. "Yes."

"Come back, Sarah." She dropped to the ground and the dank water splatted out around her feet.

"I see," he said. So long, so very long, but if he reached back, yes, there was still pain there, too. So many other pains abounded, but yes, it did still ache a bit, didn't it? "We do share a bond. It is revenge you want."

"Yes," she said, looking up at him. It seemed to him she was looking at him like an uncle. "Revenge I think we both would like very much. Every side benefits."

The Abomination nodded his massive, scaly demon's head. "Very well, Sarah Josef," said the gamma creature. "Tell me more about this URSA. And tell me about yourself."

And that was the beginning of their curious relationship. Indeed, URSA had taken good care of Sarah Josef's new charge—they had set up his sanctum below New York exactly as he had requested, had even helped him set his own plans to work, beginning with the assault on the Langley Theater.

"The Langley assault proceeded to your liking?"

"Perfectly," said the Abomination. "The equipment was marvelous."

Sarah looked at him and reached into a zippered pocket and retrieved a disk, and laid it on the console. "My employers want me to reiterate that we hope you will have as much success holding up your end of the bargain with us."

The red eyes flashed as the Abomination slid the disk into a drive and began to tap at the keys. "Tell them you have nothing to worry about, Sarah. I am grateful for your help, and find it serendipitous that so many of our goals coincide.'' He looked at her carefully. She was young, really, as young as Nadia had been when they had gotten married, as young as he had been, all those years ago, in Istanbul, when his career had begun its downward trajectory. ''We both have something personal in this.''

''You will have a new home, Emil. You can come home when the new order is set up, and—''

''Let me tell you,'' he hissed, as a series of names and addresses began to flash across the screen. ''Let me tell you what kind of home I would like to return to. I would like to see a Georgia that recalls its rich past. I would like to see a Russia that remembers Alexander Nevsky as much as it does the Prague Spring. A Russia that looks and sounds more like the land of the firebird than it does like the land that lost millions of troops for nothing in the sands of Afghanistan. Perhaps the dream of URSA, perhaps this renewed enmity with the United States will help your dream, but that dream is not mine. I will not return until my home is what it was.''

''But—''

''Yes. You know what that means. I will not return. I will help you and you will help me, but I am *this* now, just as Russia is *this* now. Stop talking to me about dreams of a new Soviet system. I am the *Abomination*. I have my own destiny.'' He hissed again and tapped the keyboard and it went dark, and the sanctum plunged into dimness again. ''Go. I have heard your message and you have nothing to worry about.''

After a moment, Sarah nodded. Her eyes, he felt sure, spoke paragraphs of almost unbecoming warmth: *No, uncle, there is new hope.* ''Very well.''

As she left he said, ''Your father was a good man, Sarah Josef.''

The creature that had once been Emil Blonsky turned back to his console and began to draft a series of letters.

He had URSA to thank for the complete list of proper recipients.

Betty Gaynor tapped on her lectern as she looked at her notes for a brief moment and looked up again. "So what do we know about the end of the world?" She stepped away from the lectern, sweeping her gaze over the students. About half of them were daydreaming or scribbling on paper; perhaps some of those were taking notes. She was pleased to see the other half actually seemed interested.

"Hm?" she continued. "Genesis 6:6. 'The Lord was *grieved* that he had made man, and his heart was filled with pain.' *Grieved*. The almighty makes the earth in five days and likes it. He makes man on the sixth, rests on the seventh, and out of all the things He creates, He comes to regret man. He looks down on us and *grieves*. Think of that. What does it mean to grieve? Generally, we feel a great loss. We grieve our lost loved ones because they are no longer there, we're missing the past—" she looked around "—and we miss the future that might have been. But for God to feel grief? His heart is filled with pain, why?" She paused, flicking her wrists to indicate she'd like a response.

None came. Betty put her finger to her lips and scanned the selection of students who were paying attention, half-enjoying the deer-caught-in-the-headlights look that came over an entire class in fear of being called upon. She considered calling on a Victim, one of the unfortunate students who had not been paying attention and only now were looking up, out of sheer nervousness about the sudden silence. But truth be known, that wasn't really all that fun. Well, maybe the first couple of times, but after she had gotten that out of her system, she preferred a decent discussion.

She decided to pick one of the Mouthers. That was her word for students who sat there, mouths slightly open, words waiting to come out, but kept back by—what? The same force, obviously, that caused a lot of the Mouthers' hands to lift just centimeters off their desks, but denied them the ability to lift their arms any further. One like . . .

"Clara?"

Clara Luici coughed and a flutter of mild laughter swept the room. She looked back at Betty, half relieved at being called and half imploring God to make it not so. Betty waited a moment, watching Clara and her librarianesque blouse and large glasses. *Amazing*, she thought. *I'm looking at myself. Strip off a few years and a whole universe of trouble, and it's me.*

"Ma'am?"

"I'll rephrase," said Betty. "The chronicler says that the Hebrew God was *grieved* about making man. Not regretful, but grieved. How does that make sense?"

"Um." Clara stared, and Betty could see the wheels turning. "He can grieve if He wants to, right?" Laughter. A flash of personal grief rolled over the student's face, fear that the professor might not appreciate a bit of wit. "I mean, you can grieve someone who's not gone."

Good. Betty tilted her head. "What do you mean?"

"Like you said. We grieve people who are lost—but the real pain, or maybe a lot of it, is the loss of opportunity. God is grieving over what humanity could have been."

"Before the fall, you mean?"

"He got over that," responded Clara, leaning forward and sweeping her hand. She was gaining momentum and confidence before Betty's eyes and it was a joy to behold. "Kicked Adam out of the garden and changed the program. One disappointment doesn't have to ruin your future. God is grieving because no matter what, people kept going in the wrong direction. I think if you opened up the mind of God in Genesis 6 you'd see plans, gigantic plans, all the wonderful things He hoped for. The way you might plan to have someone around forever, and you play out little fantasies, right? And maybe something happens. And they die, or maybe worse, maybe they change, or you change. But those plans, all those fantasies, those are still knocking around in your head. And you look at what you have and you look at what might have been and—yeah, you grieve.''

Betty smiled. The room was hushed. She almost wanted to applaud. She looked at the clock and was pleased to see her quiet student had just about lectured them to the end of the hour. A few minutes. She considered calling on someone else and squelched that.

What the hell. Bring it on home, Clara. ''So what's the difference, here? That's humanity you just described, and the creator here in Genesis 6 is a lot like humanity. What's the difference?''

Clara looked around her, putting it together. She was on top of it. ''The difference is that God grieves for his lost plans and then sends the flood and just *erases* the world. He destroys it, and starts over,'' Clara said. ''And we, um—we can't do that.''

Four o'clock. Chairs began to rumble. Betty nodded and only partially smiled. *No, we can't.* ''Thank you.'' She looked at the whole class as it rose as one beast and made its way for the door. ''Check your syllabus, guys! Tomorrow I want to get through the flood and start the Greek flood as well!'' Fat chance, that. But she liked to entertain the thought that someone might read ahead for once.

Betty Gaynor sorted her books and notes into her bag and out of the corner of her eye saw Clara Luici approaching. She was glad, too, because she had just at that instant made a decision. ''Excellent points, Clara.''

Clara stood by the lectern with her hands clasped in front of her, once again a mirror image of once-Betty. ''Um. Thanks.''

Betty laughed. ''Why do you do that?''

''Ma'am?''

"You start almost every sentence with 'um,' " Betty said, pulling her brown leather bag over her shoulder. She pulled back her hair and clasped it with a scrunchy as she talked. "It's not my place to notice, so don't take it the wrong way."

"Uh—" Clara blinked. The shame was palpable, and Betty felt monstrous instantly. "No, ma'am."

"Nervous habit, right? A lot of people say verbal tics like that are stalling tactics while we're trying to think of what to say."

There was a pause where an "um" should have been. "Could be."

"But if that were the case I wouldn't bug you about it. I'm mentioning it because I think you almost always know what it is you want to say and you take an extra second to summon up the courage."

Clara stared. Betty felt as if she could jump into the girl's head and see out, filled with awe at the clairvoyance of someone who knows the tactics of a shy-but-getting-by student. "I don't know what to respond to *that*," Clara said, and she laughed, a bit nervously.

"Well," said Betty. "Work on it. You scored one for courage today. Meantime I have a proposition for you."

"A proposition?"

"The instructors get these notices all the time from various journals, here and otherwise. Anyway, the religious studies department is looking for papers. I thought if you were interested you could explore this topic we were on today some more. I'd be glad to help. I admit the Richards College journals aren't tops in their class, but it's a start, and maybe we could look for other places for it if it works out well."

Clara stared. "But I . . . how long a paper are we talking about?"

"Yeesh. Always it's 'how long.' Long enough to be worthwhile." Betty smiled. God, she loved this job. "And it's worth a credit if you can do it by Christmas. That's three months, and it'll be good for the writing requirement."

Clara was nodding, the wheels churning away. "I . . . I can do that."

"I've read your essays in class; I *know* you can do that."

Clara's face mirrored every emotion she held, just like Betty's once did, and now the face flushed. "Thank you."

"*De nada.* Anyway," Betty looked at the clock. A few students from the next class in the lecture hall had begun to wander in. "I have office hours tomorrow. Come by, we'll talk more."

"When do you want an outline?"

Eager, too. "If you want to do something, just work up a preliminary list of sources, and we'll talk. Tomorrow." Betty shrugged, indicating the time. "Gotta go."

"Right. Me, too." Clara headed for the door. "Thank you!"

"You're the one who's gonna do the work, Clara," said Betty. "Now don't forget to read tomorrow's assignment!" But Clara was gone. *Doesn't matter. Kid reads ahead, dollars to donuts.*

Betty rode the commuter train home trying to read her own notes and spending as much time looking out the window. Four-forty-five was the beginning of the afternoon commute, still on the cusp between the day riders and the professionals, who rarely showed up on the trains until the early evening. She stared out the window at the passing tunnels and ignored the diverse group around her, punks and old folks and the odd hooky playing lawyer or two. She repeated the thought: *I love this job.*

In the last several years, she had been everything from a pilot to a telephone operator, even spent time away from her husband trying to become a nun. And when a few strings—strings about which she preferred to know as little about as possible—were pulled to get Betty Banner, fugitive, into the faculty at Richards, complete with fake verified *curriculum vitae* and all manner of letters of recommendation for the hitherto-nonexistent Betty Gaynor, she had no idea it would suit her this much. But it did. And after two months she knew that the next move was going to break her heart.

Betty got off the train at White Plains and walked the mile and a half to the Gaynor's condominium. Taking cabs was expensive and she had found of late that she liked the exercise of the walk—even through what had been called by some "the most boring place in America," perhaps an unfair nomenclature. It was serene enough, in any case.

When she had her key in the door she found herself listening for signs of Bruce, and heard the keyboard all the way from the study. Inside, she snickered at Bruce's insistence on calling an unused bedroom with a desk a "study." He had wanted to call it a War Room, for some reason, but it hadn't stuck. At least he was home.

The condo was dark, every shade pulled. Betty hated to admit it but her heart sank whenever she walked in, just a little. The place stayed dark out of necessity, since they couldn't very well have neighbors peeking in to see her seven-foot-tall, green-skinned husband. To make matters worse, Bruce had taken to wandering around with the lights off, and it made their home feel somehow funereal. She dropped her bag by the door and stepped softly down the hall, toward the blue glow that emanated from the study, following the rapid hammering on the steel keyboard Bruce used. The tapping stopped and Betty heard the sound of a modem connecting. Bruce was consulting again, and it meant a lot of faxing, and, thankfully, a great deal of money. Betty reached the door and slid it back a few inches to lean in. He knew she was there. The man had hearing like a junkyard dog.

Betty's face softened when she saw him. Bruce was sitting in his gigantic chair, hunched over the steel desk in the dark. The bulk of his torso hid the lower half of the monitor, but his great, blockish head was perfectly silhouetted against the bright screen. So much green. The green shoulders and neck, the green tousled close-cropped hair, all lit up with the electric glow of the screen. He sat still, watching the status bar on the screen ebb away as the fax went out. If Bruce had his way, Betty thought, she would spend years talking to the back of his head. She blinked, hearing Clara, hearing herself in Clara: *We can't do that. We can't erase it. God can grieve and start over. We just grieve.* That wasn't right, was it?

"You didn't come home last night," Betty said, breaking the silence. The green head moved slightly and she saw Bruce's three-quarter silhouette. He was not frowning. He was just blank.

The Hulk suddenly snapped alive, as if having needed a few seconds to translate her English before he could move. He rubbed his eyes and leaned forward on his elbows, still looking at the screen. "I'm sorry."

"You're lucky I'm not the jealous type. If the only gamma female around weren't your first cousin, I'd think you were having an affair." She was still leaning on the study door and moved forward when he granted her a short laugh.

He scratched his chin loudly, as only the Hulk could. "It was . . . a hard night."

Betty moved forward and stood behind him, leaning in, hands on his shoulders. It was impossible to tell if he were tense by touch. Her husband the Hulk weighed a ton and felt like slightly padded steel to the touch. "C'mon, Bruce. Clue me in. Make me a partner, okay?"

He nodded slightly, tipping his head toward the chair next to his. He needed her; he showed it in a thousand ways. One of the most dangerously powerful gentle men on earth and he needed her. She sat and leaned over, nuzzling her head against his torso.

"It's hard to explain," Bruce said. "Sometimes I wish

I could just dump my brain into yours and you could know what I'm thinking without having to explain, to catch up.''

Betty nodded. She wished the same thing, a thousand times. So much didn't get said because it just took so much *effort*.

''And then I think no one wants what's in my head.''

''Don't do that,'' she said, sitting up, looking at him sternly and softly at once. ''Not with me. You can pity yourself to your heart's content but I signed on this marriage for a reason, and it wasn't to be spared your pain. Clue me in.''

Bruce nodded again. When they were first married he was so distant, and yes, she had been pretty distant herself sometimes. It was amazing to feel how far they'd come. Despite the fact that they had so far to go. ''I was walking last night. You know, I like that. I can get out on the side of the road and blend into the grass pretty well. I can think.'' His voice was low, almost a whisper, although it was so deep it made her spine shiver.

Betty wanted to say, *Why do you need to leave? Why can't you stay here, talk to me all the time?* But she kept that, for now.

''There was an accident. Worst accident I've ever seen up close. A semi went into oncoming traffic and hit a car head-on. A blazing mess.''

''I read about it on the train this morning.'' She left out: *Although I barely paid attention to the paper since I was so mad at you for not coming home. Want to see the paper? You won't see any tear-stains. I was too annoyed to cry, and nearly cried over that in itself.* She said none of that.

''So, did I make the paper?'' When she shook her head, Bruce muttered, ''Just as well. I . . . couldn't . . .'' he stopped, shaking his giant head, his lower lip trembling. ''I ripped the car apart and got to one of those kids. But the other . . . and there was nothing . . . *nothing.* . . .''

"Hey," she whispered. "Hey, Bruce. I read about it. They said it was a miracle that the one kid survived, okay? By all rights he shouldn't have, just like the driver of the truck."

"By all *rights?*" He whispered, almost angrily, but it was clear that Bruce didn't want to be mad, and she could see on his face he instantly regretted the tinge of anger. This thing in him, this Hulk-gamma thing, God, what it did to him and his emotions, and God, how he struggled. "I can leap a mile. I can tear tanks apart with my bare hands, and have with regularity. And do you know what? It amounts to nothing."

"You're upset that you couldn't save them both?" She whispered, "What could you do, watch the road and keep the accident from happening?"

"I don't . . . I don't know, Betty." And he didn't, that was clear. "It's just so . . . *wrong*. I felt so helpless, so underqualified. Why was I there and not Dr. Strange or some clairvoyant? Why has—" he waved his hands, indicating the green color, "—*this* happened if I don't do anyone any good, and it ruins my life for nothing, and it ruins *your* life, for *nothing!*"

Betty asked, "Why were you there instead of no one at all? Then they all would've ended up dead."

There was a long silence. The tiniest part of her wanted to accuse him of just feeling sorry for himself, but this was really hurting him. It took a lot to hurt the Hulk; it deserved attention. Finally he looked up and breathed. "Morgan's son was the kid who died."

She blinked. "Sean Morgan, the SAFE guy?"

"Yeah."

"They didn't give a name in the paper."

"That makes sense," Bruce said slowly. "There was a SAFE agent on the scene."

"How?"

"Ah, well, there's the other thing. He was following

me. Been following me since that little to-do with SAFE and Spider-Man in New York.''

''Oh.'' The syllable came out weak, childlike, and Betty felt her stomach ball up and twist. ''Oh.''

''Now, Betty, don't, please . . .''

''I love this job, Bruce,'' she was shaking her head, her eyes already welling up. ''Please don't do thi— Please don't let this be true.'' She had almost said. *Please don't do this to me*, and there was no rescuing it. ''Please. I love it. Really. I'm so *sick* of moving around. God, Bruce, please. . . .''

''Honey.'' Bruce held up a hand, but he was shaking his head. ''I know. I know. I haven't decided yet what we're—''

''Don't you even talk about *deciding* what *we* are going to do.''

''I don't want you to have to move, either, Betty,'' he said. Their eyes locked for a long moment.

''What does that mean?''

''I guess I haven't decided yet . . . what *I'm* going to do.''

She breathed, slowly and heavily, several times, clasping her fists to her forehead, eyes closed. She felt as if her insides had been lined with lead and she wanted to lie down. After a moment Betty opened her eyes and shook her head. ''I don't know . . . I don't . . . let's go to sleep.'' It came out of her mouth at once, as if it would fix things. An idiotic thing to say, she knew.

''Betty, it's six o'clock in the evening.''

''I know. I just . . . did you sleep?''

He rubbed his green face. ''No.''

''I don't want to talk about this right now, okay? But I don't want to be . . . *away* from you.'' Betty stared, imploring. Fine, if his emotions didn't have to make complete sense, hers didn't have to either, right? ''So, come to bed. Let's sleep. Come to bed with me, okay?''

He nodded. "Okay. You go on, then, and I promise I'll be there in a minute."

"Really? Do you mean that?"

"I do. I want to finish something real quick and I'll be there."

Betty nodded. She stood up and kissed him on the forehead, this green forehead that was once pink and burned with the slightest hint of sunlight, the forehead of a scrawny genius she fell in love with. She kissed his green forehead and stepped toward the door. "Bruce?"

"Betty?"

"Listen to me," she said. "Before we talk about what's going to happen I want to tell you this."

He looked at her, patiently. "Yes?"

"You're upset that you couldn't do enough with your strength, whatever. I just want you to remember: It was Bruce Banner, not the Hulk, that was a hero from the start. All those years ago when you saw that kid out there on the testing ground, it was Bruce Banner who ran out there unprotected to get the kid to safety. *You* did that. Not an alien or an Olympic athlete or some mutant or other. You. And you've been hurting ever since for what you did. But I'll never forget that the hero . . . my hero . . . is Bruce Banner. And whatever comes, I want you to hold onto that. Remember that. Okay?"

Bruce actually smiled. "Okay."

Betty went to bed and cried.

The message had been blinking on Bruce's computer screen for at least three or four minutes. Bruce brought up the second half of the file he had been working on—another engine design, God love'em—and faxed it off, and turned to the e-mail with a scowl. It was from an anonymous user, but Bruce knew immediately it was the same anonymous user who had already contacted him once. The first message had simply attached a Reuters report of the bizarre attack on the Langley Theater. Nadia

Dornova had escaped unharmed, but she was at home resting, possibly under sedation. The whole audience had been blinded with a low-level gamma-irradiated gas. None of this made Bruce any happier than he had been already.

The second message was personal.

DR. BANNER—

IN ALL THE TIME WE HAVE KNOWN ONE ANOTHER WE HAVE IN FACT MET, WHAT, SIX OR SEVEN TIMES? SIX OR SEVEN. WHO RECALLS THESE THINGS?

WE MUST BE, IN THE END, WHAT WE ARE. WHAT ARE YOU?

DEAR NADIA HAD HAUGHTY EYES.

NOW SHE SEES ONLY PAIN.

WHAT DO YOU HAVE, DR. BANNER?

WHAT WILL I MAKE YOU SEE?

        —OLD FRIEND

Bruce frowned and shook his head. The Abomination was making no attempt to hide himself. The anonymous account was just a gag. But could it really be Emil? Emil was smart, but not this level of smart. Was he?

What do you have?

Bruce ground his teeth. He was tired. He had a beautiful wife waiting for him. (What if Emil had help?)

What will I make you see?

The incredible Hulk shuddered despite himself. He flipped a switch and the screen went dark. In darkness he went to bed.

He found Betty there, still awake. It had been six minutes since she had left, and when he lay beside her, she was still crying, but she smiled.

CHAPTER 4

asily the size of a city block, the vessel that held the mobile headquarters for SAFE was a contraption of remarkable engineering, although some whispered that it seemed a bit overdone. It resembled nothing so much as a fully enclosed aircraft carrier held aloft by antigravity engines and two rotor blades the length of football fields. There were only a handful of them in the world, and most people were glad of that fact. It was called the Helicarrier.

Deep in the bowels of the armored, floating beast, Tom Hampton became aware of someone standing over his shoulder by instinct alone, and turned around slowly in his swiveling chair. Immediately he signed, "Morgan."

The man standing before the technician was tall and lean, but not gawky in any sense. He had fair hair, cut close like any bureaucrat's. In sharp contrast to the unique body-sock-leather-strap, faintly s&m-inspired uniform that all non-undercover SAFE agents, including Tom, wore, Sean Morgan opted for a conservative, dark blue wool. The athletic cut swept dramatically from a broad pair of shoulders to a narrow waist hidden by double-breasted coat. There wasn't a square centimeter that didn't scream *professional*. Morgan was the endless butt of jokes and impressions from hard-used new recruits. He knew that. But Tom also knew that time and time again, Morgan was also the object of unquestionable loyalty from the same men and women who liked to try to master impressions of him.

Morgan's hands flashed. "Agent Hampton. Progress?"

Tom nodded, tipped his head back at the station behind him, and signed, "The GammaTrac is fully calibrated, sir." This was big news. It had taken six weeks

60

from the placement in orbit of the GammaTrac satellite to get the satellite and the computers at headquarters to talk to one another. Morgan ran the risk of great embarrassment if the expensive project had been a failure from the start, but Tom had vowed he could get it running.

Morgan seemed pleased. "So we were the root of the evil, huh?"

"It seems that way," Tom responded. Morgan was an expert signer, and it was refreshing not to have to rely completely on lipreading. He especially disliked using the voice-modulator that interpreted his own signing into "words" for the nonsigners to understand. The modulator was not uncomfortable, hanging as it did in its own pouch on the front of Tom's uniform, except that the inevitable tiny vibration on his chest annoyed him. Thank God for signers. "There was never a problem with the satellite itself," Tom continued. "The long and short of it is our engines were interfering with the receiver here." He indicated the station again. "But we found that if we isolated—"

"Spare me," signed Morgan. "I'll read your report. So what do we have now?"

Tom nodded. Morgan was being a little short today, or maybe it was Tom's imagination. But generally the technician was fairly skilled at feeling people out, and Morgan was distracted. "Ah. You wanted New York for starters, correct?"

"That's right," said Jo Carlin, aloud, and Tom did not hear her. But he saw Morgan look up and Tom turned to see Agent Carlin, the Gamma Threat Specialist, approaching. Carlin signed for Tom's benefit, although her question was directed at Morgan. "So we're up and running?"

"Apparently," Morgan signed. Tom enjoyed the fact that for a brief moment the two hearings were signing at one another for no reason except to keep him abreast. That took training. He could not number the conversations he had only received a third of because the hearings would talk to one another and then try to catch him up. But signing was hard, especially if it wasn't a necessity for the signer, and it took far more effort than just flapping your jaw.

Jo looked at the station. She had voiced her enthusiasm for the GammaTrac as much as he had, the way anyone rhapsodizes about a piece of machinery that will make her job easier. "Could you patch in to Conference Room Twenty-Seven? We can get comfortable," signed Jo.

In five minutes the three had relocated to one of the countless conference rooms scattered up and down the plush, carpeted halls of the Helicarrier. Tom shook his head as he sat in a high-backed leather chair across from Morgan, and Jo slid in at the end of the table. Thankfully, this was one of the more intimate conference tables, built for four or five, tops. All along the walls were evenly spaced, recessed lights, which lent a soft, pleasant glow to the scarlet walls. This was all Morgan. "Just because it's called a 'carrier, doesn't mean it has to look or smell like one." Consequently, it looked like a law firm. Nice place to work.

Tom tapped the keypad on the table and gestured toward the screen on the wall. A map of the United States came up instantly, a band of green light seeping across it from the center, like a radar screen. A few more taps and he zoomed into New York, Manhattan in the center. He picked up a remote pointer and then held up a hand, remembering his own pointer. After a moment he had it fastened to his collar and continued signing, while the pointer followed the direction of his head, a light blue arrow dancing on the screen.

"As you're aware," he signed, "augmented folks seem to gather here. Gamma subjects get around more, it seems, but they tend to come back fairly often."

Jo Carlin nodded. She was the expert on this, she didn't need the introduction. "How many right now?"

"See for yourself," he signed. "This green spot over here in Westchester—that's probably the Hulk."

"No question," Morgan signed. Tom saw the man sigh, and for a moment he seemed distant again. Even the slightest such distance was out of character for him.

Jo signed, "At least we won't have to send any more agents out to tail him."

"I agree," Morgan's hands flashed. "I'm getting tired of commissioning new cars for Mike Cross."

Jo smiled and then wiped her smile away. Tom suddenly became sure that there was something he did not know. Jo went on, "He knows we know he's there. Wonder how long he'll stay?"

Tom shrugged. "Wherever he ends up we can track him now. The GammaTrac will pick up any large concentration of gamma radiation, even more inert manifestations like the gamma mutants."

"That's the idea," signed Morgan.

"Right," Tom continued. "This other spot is the only one left here." The arrow flew to a green spot near the park. As he spoke the green line circled around the map. Suddenly the spot disappeared.

Morgan raised an eyebrow. "Where'd it go?"

"It'll be back," signed Tom. "I've been watching this guy for a day now. I think he goes underground."

Carlin leaned back in her chair. "The Abomination is back," she signed, finally.

"If you say so. I just watch the maps."

Morgan turned to Jo but continued signing, wanting to keep Tom included. "The Langley thing. Tell me about it." He was tired, Tom could tell. The man had circles under his eyes, and he was pale enough that they practically glowed blue.

"Someone who knew a lot about gamma radiation did a very bad thing," signed Jo. "There's about six hundred people from the front row back with heavy damage to the eyes."

"I know what happened, Agent Carlin. I want to know your thoughts. Who is it?"

"Well, it could be the Leader. That's sort of his style, I suppose. But he hasn't been around in a while, and we think he may be dead."

Morgan snorted. "No one stays dead. Could it be Blonsky?"

"The Abomination tends more towards tearing things apart. But, with Nadia Dornova there, with the notes on her dressing room mirror, and all the rest—yeah, I think it could be."

Morgan put his chin on his palm and watched the green hand sweep around the map. "He's not keeping himself secret, then. He signed this work. How long until we get to see him again?"

"It could be hours," Tom responded.

Morgan sighed. "The Abomination made some pretty serious threats the last time he turned up. I have a lousy feeling that this isn't over."

"I'm on it," said Jo. "If we can find him, we will. As far as capturing him, even though he's right below us. . . ."

"We need to go outside," signed Morgan.

"Outside?"

Morgan nodded again. "Keep me posted if you think of anything, but I think I need to get involved here." He studied her face for a second. "It's no reflection on your team, Jo. But to catch a thief, I think we need a thief."

Jo dared to sound sarcastic. "Really. You're talking about hiring the Hulk."

Morgan chewed his lip. "I am. I think it's time to call in a few favors."

"They're gathering," said David Chase, and he lowered his field glasses to look at the woman beside him.

Darlene shook her head. The blonde woman bent over the wall inside the small pocket in the tunnels, and looked out on a section of tunneling the size of a subway station. Like David, she had forsaken the world above for a more unique life in the underground. One used to go west to run away. Now, you could only go under.

David peered over the wall at the four or five men who had already shown up in the dark, dank section. He knew them all. Every one of them was a cop, every one of them he had worked with. Until that night. In the back of David's mind visions flashed again of bullets flying, blood spattering the walls.

The sewer massacre had been a police fiasco. Lieutenant David Chase had been one of the many boys in blue to report to the mouth of the sewer tunnels, dressed in riot gear and helmets. David remembered putting on the vest, holding the tall shield in front of him, and even then, before he went below, visions of Kent State were already dancing in his head.

The official story was that there were thieves and muggers and rapists down there, hanging out and waiting to attack the good people of New York. And a monster, too: the Abomination. Everyone said he was plotting a massive surge of chaos and violence. So they went on down and did what good people do. They shot them all to hell, and the city rejoiced.

The truth was this, and David knew it even when he went down there, even though he didn't want to admit it. The people down there were just living. Maybe some made a mistake or two. Maybe most had. And the Abomination was there, too. (This he learned about later, from the denizens themselves, those left alive.) The Abomination sat down there with the denizens of the underground and told stories and lived a gentle life. But there was a man named Christopher, a wealthy, devious soul of a man who wanted to use the tunnels for his own purposes. And he got the cops to go down and shoot the people to hell.

But that wasn't the worst part, was it? (Stones flying, smacking into helmets, cops with stones cutting their chins, the only exposed part.) The worst part was that they went down there on their own power and lined up to look at a bunch of scared people armed with rocks. And they threatened and howled and the people got scared. And someone threw rocks, was that it? He couldn't remember now, exactly. No one could. But they backed those desperate people into a corner and David looked in their eyes and could *tell*, could *tell*, right then, that he had no business being there. Backed them into a corner and they exploded with fear.

(Shots.) He could have walked away at any time. (Blood.) He could have thrown down his badge. (All those sounds, screaming, God, and the one, rageful howl of the Abomination, rising to protect his family.) The Abomination tore into them and they scattered, but not before they practically wiped out the underground.

And then David did walk away. Threw the badge down and stayed there. The Abomination disappeared after that, maybe afraid if he stuck around, he'd get everyone else killed, too. And David Chase and the denizens of the underground moved to other parts of the system, abandoning their old territory. Maybe Christopher was using those tunnels now and maybe he wasn't, no one knew. No one really talked about it. The old sections were off limits.

There was plenty to go around.

But here David was, with Darlene, back in the old section, because someone had managed to send him a letter. David saw the cops below, lit by one torch right under the ladder from above. They gathered near the ladder to unfold pieces of paper they fished from their pockets, and David retrieved his own. A kid had brought it to him, having run into a dark figure that told him to find David Chase and deliver the note.

It told him to gather here, at this place of death, for a meeting. The note had come with a few copies of documents David thought had been expunged long ago. If he were living above ground, that would have been an effective threat, but it didn't matter anymore. He was dead to the world. But it made him curious enough to want to see this "meeting."

"We shouldn't be here," said Darlene. She twisted the hem of her ragged dress nervously. "This is off limits."

"I helped put it off limits, hon, I know," he said." I just want to see."

"Clarence is going to be doing reruns tonight. *The Munsters*, he said. Come on, let's go. Leave it, David." She put her hands on his shoulders and he smiled. Clarence could do excellent voice impressions. It was worth hearing.

"Just a while more," whispered David. Down below there were about fifteen men. That about did it, too. The rest had been killed by the Abomination back at the massacre. He was looking at the vestiges of a murderous crew.

"Gentlemen." A deep, rasping voice cut the dank air in the room below and everyone looked around, unsure where the echoing voice came from.

Someone found his voice and called out, "Who's there?" Some of them drew weapons, the steel flashing in the dim light.

"Innocent blood has been shed here," came the voice, slithering and rasping.

David backed up. "We'd better go."

The voice spoke once more. "But not *tonight*."

All at once the torch went out, and the room was bathed in slick, wet darkness.

"Come on, Rick. It's the numbers. You know how this works."

"He's a putz." Rick Jones paced in his dressing room. They had thirty, forty minutes before they went live, and the last thing he wanted to be doing was arguing with the producer about changing questions.

"Senator Hill will bring in some good ratings," Mack Stocker said. Stocker was the executive producer of *Keeping Up with the Joneses*, the program that Rick and Marlo Jones hosted, day in and day out. It was a talk show with a fairly local bent and, Rick liked to think, something of an edge—or at least more of an edge than most of his competitors.

"Since when," Rick asked, "are people interested in seeing politicians on talk shows?"

"But he's so controversial," said Stocker, practically slobbering over the word.

"Oh, I agree. And that's why I let him on the show. But Mack, Marlo and I have worked up some great stuff. We have the research on the mob ties, this Wulf Christopher guy . . ."

Mac shook his head. "He'll storm right off the set, Rick. He told me so himself."

"Then what the hell's the point?" Rick sat down in his chair because the makeup artist had just come in. He continued gesturing even after she had put a sheet over his hands and silently began applying base.

"The point is you let him talk and let the audience yell at him."

"They ought to yell at him," agreed Rick. "That ridiculous campaign slogan of his: 'My eyes on the stars, my feet on the ground.' He's a reactionary and he's dangerous and he's crooked. People should know that."

"Then let him hang himself. But you keep your questions, ah, . . ."

"Cheesy?"

"Exactly. Hey, it's not for two days. Think it over, okay?"

"Rick?" The assistant director, Laura Hutchins, stuck her head around the doorway. "Phone call."

"Now?"

"Says it's important. A doctor, Indian name."

Rick looked at her. "Indian?"

"Um." She popped her gum and tried to recall it. "Uh—Dormammu?"

Rick mouthed the name back. "Dr. Dormammu. Huh." He looked at Mack and at the sheet hanging from his neck. The silent makeup artist looked at her watch and raised an eyebrow. "I better take this. Be right back, I promise."

"Rick," said Stocker.

"You're the boss, Mack, whatever you say," he said, getting up and moving out, the white sheet flowing around him. Whatever. Maybe he could sneak a few double meanings in or something. Marlo would be livid. *Dormammu?*

Down the hall the phone lay off the hook on a high stool and Rick picked it up. "Dormammu?"

"The Dread one himself," came the familiar voice on the other end.

"Couldn't pick something less—"

"Dreadful?" Bruce always called with a fake name. Lately he had been having fun with it. For a week or two Rick kept getting phone calls from a guy named Uatu.

"What's up, Doc?" Rick grinned. "I'm already in makeup."

There was a pause, and Rick felt the frivolity slip away. The deep voice on the other end said, "Rick?"

"Doc?"

"How are things?"

"Bruce—"

"Okay, okay."

Rick looked around. *What now?* "You okay, Doc? Betty okay?"

"Yeah. We're fine for now, I think. I just wanted to ... ah ..."

"Uh, Doc, really—"

"I just wanted to say that if I were out there in New Mexico on the base, and you went driving out there with your harmonica and your jeep ..."

Rick nodded. Where this could go he had a few ideas. He could never forget that he had been the cause of Bruce Banner's exposure to the full blast of a gamma bomb. "Yeah?"

"I know how you feel about it, Rick. And I just wanted to say that if it happened again, if I could go back?" He paused.

"Yeah?"

"I'd still do it."

Rick felt a tingle of absolution run down his spine. "I know that, Bruce."

"I just wanted to say that."

"Okay," said Rick. "Thank you . . . for that. Are you sure everything's okay?"

"For now, yeah." The Hulk was lying through his teeth. "I gotta go."

"Okay, Doc. You take care. Uh, maybe we can do something this weekend, you and Betty and me and Marlo."

"I don't know how much longer I'm going to be in town."

Rick had heard that before. "Then we better make it a date. Keep in touch."

"I will."

"So long, Doc."

"So long, Rick. See ya soon."

Rick hung up the phone and walked back to the dressing room. The makeup artist gave him a look and set right to work.

The Hulk and Betty retired early again for the second night in a row. At eleven o'clock Bruce lay awake, staring at the ceiling. They had been walking around the house like zombies, doing everything to avoid making plans. And now, in the haven of the dark bedroom, Bruce found that every time he closed his eyes he thought of jelly and glass and fire.

Something bright flickered on the far wall and caught Bruce's eye and he tilted his head up. It happened again, and in the tiny dust particles he saw that the light on the wall came from a beam that swept over the curtains, occasionally cutting through spaces. He looked at the thick curtains and confirmed it. Someone was shining a light on the window. The beam swept slowly back and forth, as if scanning. Presently he became aware of a strange, low hum.

"Betty," he whispered.

"Hunh?"

Bruce turned over and took the curtain in one hand, and pulled it to one side, a few inches, to peer out. It was dark outside, a moonless night, and he could see nothing. The beam had been shut off. "Get down," he said.

Betty flickered to life and looked at him for a second. "What?"

"Get *down*." As Betty rolled off the bed and crouched next to it, Bruce got on his knees, causing the reinforced frame to whine tortuously. All at once the Hulk hurled the curtains wide and the lights came on again.

Very big lights. Bruce held up his hand and felt his eyes adjusting and saw a hovercraft light up outside the window, two great, hard white beams shining in. The craft now swam with lights, in fact. Well, well. SAFE. And they were lighting up like a Christmas tree on purpose.

A man stood on the deck of the hovercraft in a topcoat and suit. He held up a megaphone. "Dr. Banner?"

The Hulk snarled and nodded contemptuously. *Morgan*.

"Why don't we go somewhere we can talk?"

In less than a minute the Hulk was on the hovercraft and the lights had been doused again. The vessel floated high over the condo, and Bruce wondered how many people had seen it shining outside his window. Luckily, even Westchester New Yorkers tended to mind their own business.

The hovercraft was one of the larger models, big enough to fit a large SWAT team, and Morgan told his two guards to hang back up front with the pilot while he and the Hulk moved to the aft section. The Hulk put his hands on the railing and looked down at the streets.

"Well, you did say to contact you."

"I said to give me a *ring*," Bruce snarled.

"If you'd be more comfortable we could go up to the Helicarrier," said Morgan.

"I feel fine right here."

Morgan nodded, leaning on the rail. The Hulk looked down at the fair-haired man and said, "You're taking a lot for granted, Morgan. Your guards couldn't get to you if I chose to throw you over the side."

Morgan folded his arms. "The thought had occurred to me. I'm willing to take that chance."

The Hulk frowned. He was tired of playing around. "I'm sorry," he said. "I'm sorry about your son."

Morgan bit his lip and shook his head. "It's a madhouse with my ex-wife. Madhouse. And there's not a lot of time to take care of things." The Director of SAFE was talking to himself and letting the Hulk listen. "He was a sophomore, you know."

"I did what . . . what . . .?"

"Don't," snapped Morgan. "I'm not here to talk about that. I don't know what to think about *your* involvement in David's death."

My involvement? "It had already happened when I got there—" the Hulk started.

"That's not what I mean," Morgan said curtly.

"But—"

"Drop it. Now. We have work to do." Morgan's face was a stone.

"It's the Abomination, isn't it?"

"We think so."

"I guarantee it. But I'm not going to do this again," said the Hulk, shaking his head. "Every time I work with

SAFE or S.H.I.E.L.D. I end up with more trouble than I started with.''

"There's a big difference between us and S.H.I.E.L.D., I like to think. Big difference between Nick Fury and me.''

"Oh, absolutely. You shave.''

"The Abomination blinded an entire theater audience—look at this.'' Morgan fished a manila envelope out of his coat and opened the flap, let a contact sheet come out in his hand. There were about twenty photos there, taken at the hospital. "Look at this. This is a little girl here, see that?'' He stabbed at the photo. There she was, too, a nameless girl with dark hair and a hideous strand of green, puss-bearing welts on and between her eyes. The eyes themselves seemed to be fused.

God, Emil. The Hulk shook his head again. "That's terrible. But what do you want?''

"We want you to help us bring him in and hand him over.''

"And that's the rub, Morgan. If I can stop Emil I will, but I don't want to go around capturing prisoners for the government.''

"What,'' snapped Morgan, "afraid of what it'll do to your sterling reputation?''

"Get serious. You work for a very powerful organization. Don't you think I know how valuable a gamma mutant, dead or alive, would be to you and your labs? I'll just bet there are teams of scientists salivating over the chance to get at our DNA alone.''

"He's dangerous, Dr. Banner.''

"I agree. But I'm not going to give him to you.''

Morgan sighed through tightly pursed lips. "Really. Then let me ask this. What are you prepared to lose?''

Bruce threw Morgan a suspicious glance. "What do you mean?''

Morgan turned around and leaned on the rail, facing the same direction as the Hulk. He clasped his hands and rubbed them. "How does Betty like her job?"

Bruce gritted his teeth. "You bastard."

"Watch your language, son," said Morgan. "She likes it, then?"

"She loves it. Best thing that ever happened to her. A final hint of normalcy."

"I hear she is held in some regard."

"Yes," Bruce responded. "I figured you had some hand in that."

"We helped. We owed you for helping us against Hildebrandt in New York."

Bruce nodded. "So it was a trap to get me back here."

"We're not Hydra, Dr. Banner. This was strictly SAFE, and no one shared this information. We did it purely out of the goodness of our hearts."

"Wow."

"Now," Morgan rubbed his hands again. "I want you to pay very close attention. We have very tight security, but information can leak. And I don't want to think what could happen if Richards College figures out that Betty Gaynor isn't who she says she is. Indeed, when they figure out who she *really* is."

The Hulk whispered. "You people are all alike, you know that?"

"Don't I ever," said Morgan. He stood up a little straighter and said, "Look. Honest, Dr. Banner. I'm not a bad guy. I don't want to see that happen either."

"But?"

"But I really need some help here."

The craft passed over Route 4, and both of the men stopped to watch the mangled guardrail go by. The Hulk said, after a while, "So I help you bring in Emil and then what? I go home, vulnerable to blackmail as ever?"

Morgan sniffed. "We can be of some help to you, actually," he said. "There are certain folks at the KGB who would very much like to talk to Blonsky. And they are willing to trade a great deal for him. Something about

Blonsky's involvement in some Russian rebel group.''

"Go on."

"You deliver the Abomination into our hands and I can see to it that your record is wiped. You'll still have your reputation to contend with, but I mean *clean*. No more tanks to crush.''

The Hulk gave out a short laugh. "I think I've heard that before.''

"I'll do it," said Morgan. The Hulk made eye contact with him and somewhere in there it looked like he might just be telling the truth. "A clean delivery and I'll do it.''

The Hulk folded his arms, watching the freeway go by. "The stranger comes bearing a gift in one hand and pain in the other, and he says, 'choose.' "

"That's right."

"God, I loathe you agency guys."

"A wise choice. We loathe our very selves."

"All right," said the Hulk with an annoyed sigh. "Where do we start?"

"He's underground again," said Morgan. "We start there.''

CHAPTER 5

Time?"

Jo Carlin extended a leather-strapped arm and consulted her watch. "Eleven hundred hours, Dr. Banner."

For an augmented human who ostensibly fared badly with teams, the Hulk had certainly worked with a number of them. Even in his purple-panted, Hulk-smash-puny-missile-silo monosyllabic days, the Hulk had found himself allied with teams of all ilk: the Avengers, the Defenders, the Titans Three. Odd, Bruce reflected, as the hovercraft holding Jo Carlin's Gamma Team sped toward the park, that since his brain had come back the teams he worked with had become less colorful, more corporate. For a time he had taken up with the Pantheon, an augmented security force and occasionally renegade paramilitary outfit. And now, for the second time, he was working with SAFE, of all people. Working with SAFE seemed a short step away from going ahead and working for the Army. The thought made his stomach turn. He had not worked for the Army since the gamma bomb explosion. Generally, he had run from them (occasional tank-stompings aside).

As they neared the park, the Hulk turned to Morgan and pointed out a sewer cover near a bench. "Let's start there."

He turned to the rest and looked them over. Seven SAFE agents, including the leader, Jo Carlin, looked up at him, each one wearing the distinctive close-fitting uniform, with a patch on the shoulder pronouncing their status with Gamma Team. The only one without the patch was Morgan, although for once Morgan was actually wearing a field outfit. The Hulk was impressed with how well the bureaucrat fit the roll of field agent. Still, it seemed odd that Morgan would want to come along on this particular mission. There didn't seem to be anything here that Gamma Team and Jo Carlin couldn't do alone, especially with Bruce's help. But for some reason Morgan wanted in on the action. "Hey," Jo Carlin had said, in a brief moment when the Hulk had asked her about that, "he knows what he's doing."

Gamma Team eyed Bruce warily, as if they expected him to suddenly start trashing the hovercraft and they'd have to turn their weapons on him. It was not lost on Banner that working with this team would provide them with valuable information should they ever decide to come after him; after all, that was what they were created for.

Each member of Gamma Team carried distinctive weaponry of his or her own. The Hulk recognized one as a heavy netgun, developed by Stark Enterprises, designed, Bruce presumed, to capture the Hulk. He doubted it would work on either himself or the Abomination, but Tony Stark's capitalist willingness to provide toys to all sides never ceased to amaze him. Some carried tranquilizer guns that would pierce a helicarrier's hide—that might work. Jo Carlin carried a trank rifle with a mounted light guaranteed to blind anything that looked at it. To be sure, the rest were just guns with large-calibre titanium bullets, designed strictly to slow the gamma beasties down. That was pretty much all you could do. Slow him down. Knock him out. Tie him up. Every one of those was almost a fantasy. Amazing how simple things could get when the quarry got powerful enough.

"All right," said the Hulk, as the pilot began to lower the hovercraft toward the sidewalk. The craft stopped about seven feet off the ground. A few joggers gave it a second look and went on about their regimen. This was the town where the Fantastic Four, the Avengers, and Spider-Man made their homes, after all. "When I met the

Abomination last, this is where we went in, so I figure we ought to start here.''

Morgan spoke to Jo Carlin. "Jo, it's your team."

"Down below," Jo called, "you will follow the orders of Dr. Banner, and Colonel Morgan will be second in command. Now, I know some of you might have a bit of trepidation about Dr. Banner. Cool it. We're all on the same team here. Understood?"

The Hulk heard the not-entirely-unenthusiastic, "Yes, ma'am," from the team and grinned a bit. Carlin obviously treated her team with respect, and in the past few hours, going over plans at the Helicarrier, he had seen that she had a mind like a trap. She was a valuable asset to SAFE, and it was apparent that Morgan knew it.

"Turn on your comlinks," said Jo, tapping the unit that wrapped around her neck and ran from ear to mouth. The Hulk had worn a more sophisticated version of this in his Pantheon days. He switched his on, as did the others. Next came the upper half of the headset, which held a tiny but powerful halogen beam at each temple.

"Let's go," said the Hulk, and he hopped over the side, followed by Gamma Team. One of the heavy gun wielders ran to the sewer cover as the hovercraft raised up and zipped away. In a moment the cover had been pulled back. For another moment the agent shone a strong, forearm-mounted light down the hole—to check and see if anything were waiting below, Bruce supposed.

"Looks okay," crackled the agent in Bruce's ear. The agent disappeared down the hole.

Twenty seconds later they were lined up in the tunnel and the Hulk took the lead. "This way," he said. He was tempted to walk funny and had to keep from chuckling into his comlink. *No sudden laughter, Bruce. They're already scared of you; that would probably freak them all out pretty good. No use wasting ammo.*

The sound of water dripping on the pipes was almost musical, and when the cover had been drawn back into its place it seemed to the Hulk as if the sounds of the tunnel lit up, the way a lighted match will illuminate a completely dark cavern. The tunnel walls danced with the swimming headlights, white beams zipping up and down the dripping concrete and lead, the odd sedimentation giving off shimmering reflections.

The comlink crackled with Jo Carlin's whisper. "Dr. Banner, where should we start?"

"Emil used to have his 'family meetings' in a series of tunnels a little east of here. There are a number of large areas. If he's set up down here, he's bound to use one of those. That is, if he's sentimental enough to come straight back to where he left."

"Well," she whispered, "if not, we'll keep looking."

"That's the spirit," Bruce muttered. Encouragement. They taught that in leadership training, undoubtedly. She was doing her best to treat him as one of her team, and to show that behavior to the other members. He listened to the sound of their boots sloshing in the stagnant water around them.

He had just turned a corner when he heard the voice.

When the team came around Bruce held up a hand and they lined up and got quiet. Echoing through the tunnels came a voice as familiar as his own, by now: the rasping, ragged deep voice of the creature known as the Abomination.

"Morgan, you hear that?"

"Yes. Dawson, augment that, could you?"

An agent in the back of the line shouldered a heavy gun and pulled out a pocket computer. "Okay, guys, I'm gonna try to isolate that sound and bring it in cleaner."

"Won't that confuse us when we get closer to it?" the Hulk asked. The comlink crackled.

"Yes, Doctor. It might. So I'll monitor the true sound on a different mike and switch the augment off if it gets too close."

Carlin nodded. "Switch us over at your discretion."

Dawson held up a thumb. "Okay. Here she blows."

There was another, sharper crackle and suddenly the distant voice came in as clearly as if the speaker were on a headset of his own. Bruce trudged on, watching the headlights dance and listening to the Abomination's sermon. No, not a sermon: more like a song, or a meditation. The rasping words were being moaned out, or sung, like a priest at mass.

"The sacrifice of the wicked," came the voice in the Hulk's ear, "is an Abomination."

The Hulk looked back at Morgan, a hand to his ear. "Is that a Bible verse?"

"The way of the wicked is an Abomination unto the Lord: but he loveth him that follow the path of righteousness."

There was another corner up ahead about twenty paces. Bruce said, "There's a wide room around that turn. The first of them."

"Where the police line met the underground," said Morgan.

"Yeah."

The voice continued: "The thoughts of the wicked are an Abomination unto the Lord . . ."

"Here we go," whispered Dawson. "Shutting off, guys, he's close."

"But the words of the pure are pleasant to him . . ."

The sound dropped from the Hulk's headset and picked up in true sound. The Hulk stuck to the corner and Morgan, Carlin, and Gamma Team fell in line behind him. He held up a hand. "Okay. Let's go. Slowly."

The Hulk went around the corner and crouched. He peered in the darkness, watching his headlights dance around. He could see nothing. The room appeared empty. Empty but for the dripping, and the recitation.

"Everyone that is proud in heart . . ." The voice echoed so much, and yet was so faint, so raggedly whispered, that it was impossible to trace.

Gamma Team came around the corner and fell in again in the room, lining up on one wall, crouched. The room was about thirty feet across by twenty feet long, and at the other end the tunnel continued. On the wall to their left was another exit, but this one had what appeared to be a makeshift gate in front of it, or else a crude door.

". . . is an Abomination to the Lord."

"Can anyone tell where that's coming from?" Morgan looked around.

The Hulk looked around, and brought up his hand to widen the scope of his headlights. "Hello," he said.

"What?"

"I think this is new," he said. Stretching across the dark ceiling, illuminated only by the suddenly attentive headlights, was a heavy iron chain, rusted but still strong. At one end of the ceiling it looped over a pulley. Bruce followed the chain to the other end with his lights and saw that it disappeared through a mousehole in the top of the wooden door.

The words were echoing louder now, more deliberate: "Abomination to the Lord, Abomination to the Lord . . ."

The Hulk listened and stared. There was a gamma beast inside of him that would not be here. He would know enough not to come here. "This is bad, guys," said the Hulk, just as the door began to creak.

"Check that door," Carlin said.

"Though *hand* . . ."

The door began to swing, opening into the room, and there was another sound, the chain beginning to roll on the pulleys, the voice of the Abomination growing louder: " . . . join in *hand* . . ."

"Holy—" said the Hulk, and every weapon came up, but they could do nothing but stare as the chain rattled and something came out on a hook. Several somethings. (. . . *join in hand, join in hand, join in hand* . . .)

Somewhere, the Abomination screamed, with a cry like a sucking wound, "He shall not be *unpunished*!" The chain cried out, rattling, as they emerged from the door, one after the other, feet bound at the ankles and slung over the chain, one after the other, dead men trussed like calves at the slaughterhouse.

"Oh my God," Morgan whispered.

The Hulk just stared, taking in the carnage. *Oh, Emil, what are you doing?*

(. . . though hand join in hand . . . in hand . . . in hand . . .)

Blood splattered on the floor below the men and Bruce heard Jo cry, "Their hands . . ."

He hadn't noticed that, but now a wave of nausea came over the gamma giant as he followed the length of the torn and trussed bodies down to the swinging arms, and he realized that every single one was waving in vain.

Because they had no hands.

"Somehow," said Morgan, "I think we were expected."

"This isn't for our benefit," whispered the Hulk.

"What do you mean?"

"This is art."

"And art," came a hiss, "needs its audience!"

"The door!" Morgan spat. It was hanging open, the chain protruding from it, the view of the doorway blocked by the haphazardly nailed lumber.

Something moved, a dark green blur, an animal quickness carrying it out the doorway and behind the corpses that swung slowly back and forth. The figure was tall and long and scaly, and as soon as it was visible the figure disappeared into a corner of the room. *He's playing with us*, thought the Hulk.

"Emil?" Bruce said, slowly. "Emil?" The agents' headlights found their mark, each one lighting a tiny space of scaliness in the corner by the far door. In the headlights the red eyes of the Abomination burned fiery and bright. The Hulk could just barely see the whole of the figure, past the hanging handless corpses, crouching there, watching them.

Someone chambered a round and the Hulk spat. "Hold your fire!"

"Yes, yes, hold your fire, why waste bullets, eh?" came the rasping voice.

"We have more than bullets," the Hulk said, although it was almost a lie. "We have a bit of a problem, Emil."

"Do you think so?"

"Who are . . ." Why was he talking? Every instinct said, spring, or nail him with a net, *something*, but he just wanted to hear what Emil had to say before it all went to hell. "Who are these people, Emil?"

"These . . . people . . ." hissed the Abomination in the corner, "are but one thing that is an Abomination to the Lord."

"What is that thing, Emil?" the Hulk asked, slowly, moving forward a few steps.

"Hands that shed innocent blood," came the answer, and there was so much sadness in the words that the Hulk was struck instantly by the memory of the massacre.

"The sewer massacre cops."

"Give the man a prize."

"You need help, Emil. Come with me."

"You've got to be joking."

"Come with me or we'll take you by force."

"Try it," said Emil.

The Hulk stepped back, looking past the hanging corpses at the beast with the burning red eyes. Bruce threw a glance to the agent with the blinder and nodded. The agent flipped a switch.

"Now," said the Hulk, and the agent crouched to get a good shot and opened up the beam. Shots began to ring out. The light poured out of the blinder gun and struck the creature in the chest, too low. The beast moved sideways and sprang again, behind the line of corpses, shielded.

"Have to come and *get* me, Banner," hissed the Abomination, and then he turned and disappeared through the doorway.

The Hulk shoved half the bodies to one side like a curtain and moved through, and the whole chain creaked and swung in the darkness. Morgan was the next one through, followed by the rest, past the curtain of bodies and into the tunnel.

The Hulk stopped and looked ahead. There was a fork in the tunnel. He motioned to Gamma Team and said, "Morgan, take a trank gun. You, me and, ah, *these* three go right. The rest go left with Carlin. Let's try not to lose him again." *Great. I gave him away. I just let him go. Curiosity killed the cat.*

Morgan and the Hulk, followed by three agents with heavy guns, ran down the right corridor. After about ten paces the Hulk stopped to listen. The tunnel got a little steeper, running down hill. The concrete was slimy, and he was careful not to slip. *Where are you, Emil? What is your game?*

They proceeded another thirty paces, slowly. "He knew we were coming," muttered the Hulk.

"That occurred to me, too," said Morgan.

"But what—" Bruce sucked in air as something large and rock-hard lunged from an indentation in the side of the wall. Suddenly he found himself slipping on the slimy concrete with the creature wrapped around him, tumbling with the Abomination down the tunnel. Bruce heard the footsteps of Morgan and the agents in pursuit. "Don't shoot," Morgan yelled, "they're wrapped up. Banner, get him off you so we can get a clear shot!"

The Hulk grunted and reached out his feet to a rusty iron ladder as he passed it, catching it with his gigantic toes. Finding his balance, he pushed up and slammed Emil against the wall. He backed up and Morgan fired the trank gun. The dart that flew out was made of a shiny whitish metal, nearly a foot long, more a harpoon than a dart. The

Abomination ducked and lunged at the Hulk, butting his finned head against Bruce's chest. The concrete wall cracked and crumbled like plaster as Bruce's head collided with it. *God, he's strong. That actually hurt.* Bruce tried to sidestep and got a few inches before Emil brought his knee to Bruce's solar plexus. The Hulk grunted again and felt his feet slip.

"This is *my* home, Banner. How many times do I have to best you here before you figure that out?"

The Hulk went down in the muck but brought his foot up, pressing down with his hands, and felt his heel connect with Emil's scaly chin. Emil was thrown back this time, tearing away several iron pipes as he passed. The Hulk stepped back as the SAFE agents began firing. Emil caught several rounds in his chest and they slowed him down. He held up a hand and backed up. Morgan fired the trank gun again and the Hulk was clear enough to watch as Emil stood there, at a curve in the tunnel, and smiled.

And caught the dart. "Nice," said Emil, and he doubled back and threw it. The Hulk heard one of the heavy guns stop firing and clatter to the floor. The agent who had been holding it clutched the giant dart, which now stuck but a few inches out of his chest. "Man down," Morgan said over the intercom.

The Hulk looked back to see Emil had disappeared, and then caught a shadow about twenty feet farther down the tunnel, disappearing up a ladder. Suddenly Emil's head stuck out and he called out, "It's far from over, Hulk. It'll be over when I want it to be over. But I've given you everything you need to figure it out." The creature grinned. "And I do hope you figure it out. I want you to be there with me. Friends?"

"Blonsky!" shouted Morgan. "Halt! Stop where you are or I'll have every last agent under my control down here flushing you out!"

"And I'll kill every last one of them," hissed Emil.

The Abomination stopped and stared for a moment, a curious grin on his upside-down scaly face. The Cheshire Abomination. "Sean Morgan," he said again, slowly. "That is you, isn't it."

Morgan nodded. "It's me."

"It's been a long time, Morgan. How's the leg?"

And with that, the Abomination disappeared again, and by the time the Hulk reached the ladder, the creature was long gone.

The Hulk looked back and saw Sean Morgan kneeling by his wounded agent, already radioing for medical backup. Morgan clicked off his comlink and looked down the tunnel to where Emil had disappeared. His eyes were far, far away.

CHAPTER 6

Fifteen years ago . . .

S *ay what you will about the two Berlins,* Sean Morgan thought, *they're both freezing cold in October.*

Morgan winced as he stepped back onto the street. *Keep moving. Gonna hurt either way, just keep moving.* He looked down and tried to tell if his trouser leg was bulging where he had wrapped his wound or if it was just his imagination. Behind him, a small broken window in the door was the only evidence that he had broken into the clothing store. That, and the missing pair of pants, and the shirt he left on the counter with a sleeve missing. The sleeve he had used to wrap his leg when he discarded his other pants. *Keep moving.*

Thankfully, he was not leaving a blood trail. Just a grazing, really, a lucky miss when he managed to move Klaus Ganz's arm out of the way just as the gun went off. He had taken six minutes in the store. He was running late, but he had to try to appear unhurried. He pulled his coat closer around him.

Amazing, the turns life could take. The young Green Beret had been in a cute little bar in Taormina, Italy, of all places, when he had been approached by the KGB. Maybe he'd like a little extra cash. Something to pad the retirement fund, eh? Just some talk between friends, interested?

Morgan was very interested. Interested enough to set up another meeting, but not before telling a few spooks about it. So that by the time he was sitting at the amphitheater in Taormina watching a bad rendition of *Oedipus Tyrannus*, talking to the same Soviet agent, he was already on attached duty to Army Intelligence. The intel guys were pleased with his record and his ambition and wanted him to give it a shot. So Morgan entered the spook

90

side at that most dangerous of ports: the double game. That was six months ago.

Since then he had worked very hard to keep an even keel, watching his back constantly, starting small. He kept his post and passed a few tidbits along—nothing too obvious nor obviously faked. They had to trust him, to believe that Morgan was willing to sell out his country with whatever he could get his hands on. He also had to be very careful, because his game was a secret, generally, on the American side as well.

Morgan managed to develop something of a rapport with a few Soviet agents who became his KGB contacts, of sorts. He had to be extremely cautious with them. Klaus Ganz and Karl Josef were cynical enough not to give any trust much weight, and he had been allowed to give some fairly valuable submarine info to them, just to get them to settle down a bit. Blonsky, though, he liked it cold. Blonsky trusted no one.

Hence the worry about the bulge on Morgan's calf. Morgan winced and began to step more normally, feeling the pain jag through his leg. The wound was just deep enough to make walking hurt, just shallow enough that he could fake it.

East Berlin was a stretch, he had acknowledged that, and had decided to take the risk anyway. Morgan's superiors concocted some story about, cleverly enough, feeling out the East side of the Iron Curtain in hopes of recruiting a double agent for the United States. Morgan and his KGB contacts had laughed heartily at that, and all the while Morgan had sat with his Scotch and felt his stomach churning, skating close, close to the edge. There were papers leaked that confirmed that he was in East Berlin on the recruiting mission, so that the curious could see. This meant his contacts would trust him and, unfortunately, that anyone else who saw the papers would kill him. Maybe. All that trouble just so no one could catch up to the real, simple assignment, of being in East Berlin to pass along bad info.

So many ways to get killed, I just don't know which one to choose.

Morgan had almost picked one tonight. After a deliberately unsuccessful "recruiting" pitch at a strip club where a lot of officers hung out on Saturday nights, Morgan excused himself and headed immediately to meet with Klaus Ganz. He was supposed to meet Ganz at a café on Alexanderplatz and proceed west to meet Josef and Blonsky.

The moment Morgan reached the café, he knew Ganz was on to him. They sat there talking, as planned, for thirty minutes, talking in German and English and Russian, by whim, about politics and art and the intellectuals in Paris. All the while, Morgan watched Ganz, as both men flapped their mouths. And every time Ganz's hand went under the table Morgan felt near sure Ganz was going to pull a trigger. Laugh and chatter. Sound natural. At eleven o'clock, they were up and headed for the meeting with Josef and Blonsky.

They were walking down Michaelsplatz when Klaus said, very leisurely, "You know, it's funny, friend Morgan, these submarines."

Morgan made a face that indicated that this was a completely empty statement, requiring no response.

"You gave us a list of the submarines in the South Pacific last month, yes?"

Morgan nodded. "Very hard to get." This was not a complete lie. It was very hard to get, but it was simply an info dump. The army felt like risking it to gain more later.

"Handsomely paid for, as well." Klaus looked at him and smiled. A couple of young lovers passed them before he continued. "Everything there. Very helpful. Serial numbers, identification procedures, nuclear signatures."

"Mhm."

Ganz stopped under a street light. He fished out a cigarette and stuck it in his mouth, lit it, and offered one to Morgan. Morgan declined politely. "Very cold," said Ganz, looking around. "People think because I am Russian and we have cold winters that I won't mind. Nonsense! We all feel the cold."

Morgan nodded. "That's right." *Okay to be nervous here. Even if you were legitimately illegitimate, this is gonna make you nervous.*

Klaus blew out a steady stream of smoke, which mixed with the steam coming from his mouth. "What if I told you that one of those nuclear signatures were wrong?"

Morgan half-smiled and scratched the back of his neck. He wasn't afraid of this. "Well, I'd say that's entirely possible."

"Why?"

"A lot of things. Could be an error in the file when I pulled it. Could be a seed, even. Something the U.S. puts in so if they see it crop up again they know info is moving around. If there were an error, I'd tell *you* not to worry, I'll get the right info. But I'd tell myself to start watching my back at home."

Klaus chewed his lip and considered this. He threw down his cigarette. "So what if the seed were not planted by the U.S.?"

Morgan blinked. "I'm sorry?" *Kids to the left, going around the corner, out of sight again. Streets deserted.*

"What if I told you that sometimes we plant seeds ourselves?" Klaus's hand was in his coat. Morgan tried to keep his eyes off it.

"In U.S. information? In files, why would you do that?" *Not good. Not good. Danger, Will Robinson.*

"Not in files the way you mean, friend Morgan. Not in the kind you steal. In the kind of files you give to a double agent."

Morgan watched time slow to a crawl, felt the stinging

cold Berlin air and knew that the moment had come. Klaus's hand emerged, liquid and slow, and Morgan twisted and thrust the palm of his hand out and swept Klaus's arm to the side as the silenced handgun blazed, a puff of smoke and flame shooting out the end. Morgan felt the bullet tear through his calf as his stiletto dropped from his forearm to his hand. Klaus's gun hadn't even hit the ground before he had hammered the stiletto up under Klaus's ribs, putting his other arm around the agent. He held the man close, as if hugging a grieving uncle, and thrust the knife home again, and once more.

An elderly couple came around the corner and smiled at him, and he stood there, patting the dead Klaus Ganz on the back, muttering in German, "There, there."

And now Ganz was lying in an alley and Morgan was late for his meeting with the other two.

He considered not going. Chances were, Blonsky and Josef would not be there, now. The biggest mistake an agent can make is to wait too long for a contact. But if they were there, he had to show. He had to complete the mission or the whole thing was over. *Who are you kidding? It's over anyway.*

Morgan walked and thought the pain away, feeling in his coat at the microfiche to be passed. This was the big one. If the KGB took this bait, these coordinates, their whole intel would be skewered for years. The info wasn't useless or false—it was better than either of those. It was so intricately seeded that it would be impossible to notice. Like aiming a long-range gun—the slightest error could send the projectile a hundred miles off. *Gotta pull this off. Baby needs a new pair of shoes.*

Baby. Back home, David was learning to walk, he was given to understand.

Did Blonsky and Josef know the score? Had Ganz already told his suspicions to them? More than suspicions—Klaus was going to kill him. If they knew, this would be a short meeting. But they might not know. Blonsky and Josef had worked together for years, since school, apparently. Klaus was from a different section, he might have been keeping his surprise for his own reasons. Too many questions. Too many guesses. *Keep moving.*

He reached the bridge at eleven-thirty, fifteen minutes late. The Gabrielskirk Bridge was small and wooden, spanning some twenty feet at most, crossing a stream behind a church. It was surrounded by an orchard that, even in winter, looked lovely. It was a place for star-eyed couples to meet in the evenings. Star-eyed couples and cynical guys with guns.

Morgan paused by a tree about twenty yards from the bridge. By the lamppost light he could see two men, one smoking, both talking in low tones. Blonsky and Josef were waiting. Morgan began to walk again, not wanting to be seen waiting and staring. Now he was playing it by ear, no idea if he should go on or not, his legs gliding over the icy streets, pain throbbing in the back of his mind. Blonsky heard his footsteps at the foot of the bridge and tapped Josef on the shoulder, turning around.

Morgan watched their eyes as he moved up to the center of the bridge.

Blonsky was a tall man, with slick, dark hair and a strong, hawk-like nose. His black coat made him look like an undertaker. "Where is Ganz?"

Morgan felt himself shrug. "Didn't show."

"Did you wait?"

"I waited a bit. Not too long." Morgan looked at the two men. Blonsky looked at Karl Josef briefly and shrugged. *Ah, those wacky other sections, ha ha.*

"Why are you so late?" Josef took a drag on a cigarette, a Winston, Morgan noted. No one smoked Russian cigarettes.

"Recruiting," Morgan smiled. "Here I actually thought I hired a double for the U.S.!"

Blonsky chuckled. "Didn't take, then?"

"No," Morgan shook his head. "Second strike to-night. Maybe I'm not cut out for it."

"Mm," said Blonsky. "Perhaps we should arrange to have someone take your bait. Otherwise you may be re-placed with someone more successful." That was good. He had Blonsky thinking about his cover and not about Klaus Ganz.

Morgan nodded again. "If it could be arranged."

"Well," Karl Josef said, clasping his hands before him. "I take it you have something for us."

Morgan stepped forward. "I do." He felt awkward reaching into his coat for anything around these guys, but he did, found the sheet of fiche, and brought it out. "Right here."

"Excellent," said Blonsky. "You will find your pay-ment in the usual account on Tuesday morning."

Morgan blanched. *I will gladly pay you Tuesday for a microfiche today.* "Tuesday? This is Friday. Why Tues-day?"

Blonsky was turning the spool over in his hand. "Monday is a holiday. It could still be arranged, but what's an extra day?"

"Right. Of course."

"There will be a parade," said Josef. "Should be something to see."

"I just might do that," Morgan lied. With any luck he'd be on the escape line by tomorrow. With Ganz dead, there was not much point in sticking around. Then again, perhaps he should extend his stay, lest he look like he was running from the kill. *Anybody* could have knifed Klaus Ganz.

A tough game. Morgan recalled the bullet wound and felt a fresh rush of pain and stifled it.

Blonsky sniffed. Blonsky did not smoke, and his nose was legendary. He sniffed again. He said, "Someone is making bratwurst."

"Excellent," said Morgan. "Perhaps I shall go and

find it.'' They all laughed. *Someone please just end this.*

Blonsky deposited the fiche in his pocket. ''Thank you, Comrade Morgan.''

''Any time,'' the Green Beret responded. ''Good evening.''

''Good luck in finding the bratwurst.'' Blonsky sniffed again, and his eyes narrowed for a tiny moment.

The two men turned to walk in one direction and Morgan turned in the direction whence he'd come, and he felt his breath normalize. He had been holding some of it in. *Stuff like that can get you killed. Settle down.*

A wind picked up and swiped across Morgan's face. Blonsky spoke up from the bridge. ''Morgan?'' came the voice.

Morgan turned around. The two men stood near to his end of the bridge, dangerously casual looking. ''Hm?''

''Are you *bleeding*?''

Morgan stared. ''Bleeding?''

Blonsky looked down at the snow on the bridge where Morgan had been standing a few minutes earlier. The man bent down for a moment and curled a finger into the snow, and came back up. He held up his hand. In the lamplight, Morgan saw the distinct red of blood on Blonsky's fingers. Blonsky rubbed his fingers with his thumb, but his eyes were on Morgan, a drill bit grinding into Morgan's skull, and he felt the blood in his face rush out and to his extremities. He became aware of the dampness of his trouser leg, aware now that in ignoring his pain he had failed to make sure when he reached the bridge that his bandage still held.

Morgan dived for a tree as, for the second time in one night, someone pulled a gun. Two someones. Shots rang out from the bridge and he heard Josef and Blonsky moving towards the foot of the bridge. Morgan had his gun out and pressed himself against the tree, listening. He dove away from the tree, away from the walk, and rolled in the snow, firing at the two men. Puffs of snow erupted with bullets as the two agents shot at him, and he kept moving. *How lucky do you think you're going to get?* He scurried towards the bridge, saw Emil Blonsky on the bridge, looking over the side, just a few feet higher than Morgan. Where was Josef?

Morgan jumped behind another tree and prepared mentally to jump out again. *Pick out your target. Take him out. Fluid.*

The snow crunched and Morgan looked to his left and saw Josef creeping up, spun and fired twice. One caught Josef in the neck, the other in the chest, and the man crumpled into the snow. Morgan jumped out from the tree and looked for Blonsky.

Blonsky was in midair, howling. The large man landed on Morgan like a load of bricks and Morgan fell backward under him, and found himself sliding down the bank. "For that," he heard Blonsky hiss, "you will pay."

Morgan brought the butt of his gun to Blonsky's head once, but Blonsky was in a reverie, hands at Morgan's throat, beginning to press. Morgan tried to fire when he felt his head smack into a stone on the way down the bank. He instinctively threw back his hand, and felt the gun come away and land in the snow. Morgan twisted under Blonsky and used the slick snow to his advantage, and the men turned sideways and began to roll.

They splashed into the stream after punching through three inches of ice. Blonsky was the first to find his feet and immediately pressed Morgan down, and Morgan felt cold air filling his throat.

David was just beginning to walk, he was given to understand.

His hands were beginning to go numb. Find the knife. He forced his fingers to work and the stiletto came into his hand and he tore at Blonsky with it, plunging it into the agent's side. Blonsky howled in pain and Morgan stood, felt the cold water and ice flow off of him. He jammed the palm of his hand into Blonsky's nose and saw blood erupt, and Blonsky staggered back. Morgan began to scramble for the bank.

Morgan felt the blade of a knife go into his calf where his wound was. He heard himself scream and dug his fingers into the bank, and kicked with his good leg, slamming Blonsky in the nose again. Morgan scrambled up the bank and fell in the snow, looked back, and saw Blonsky emerging from the water, blood running down his face, a deadly cold look in his eyes.

Morgan saw Karl Josef's crumpled body and looked for the gun he had dropped. He dug in the snow and finally felt the icy steel, brought it up, and fired. The bullet caught Blonsky in the shoulder and Blonsky spun around with it, slipping on the ice. The agent fell back into the water.

Morgan did not wait for a second emergence. He howled in pain as he got to his feet, crawling for the sidewalk.

He crawled until he could walk. He walked for hours until he found a barn just outside of town, where he was supposed to wait if this should happen.

That is, if everything went wrong.

Present day . . .

"It's not a bomb," Smitty said.

Wulf Christopher stood in his office with his hands in the pockets of his double-breasted coat. Smitty had just brought him a package, a plain brown cardboard box addressed to Christopher at the Gaslight Club.

The Gaslight was yet another of the latest crop of "theme" restaurants opening around Manhattan. The decor was strictly Victorian, offering the patrons a chance to wander in and feel as if they had been transported to the world of Sherlock Holmes. By opting to avoid the cheesy jokes and floor show of many of his competitors, Christopher had crafted a much quieter clientele of tourists. The line stretched around the block regularly, not that Christopher cared a great deal.

The Gaslight was a front, a laundering facility that made a lot of legitimate cash in order to mask the illegitimate funds that passed through. At the top of the building that housed the Gaslight sat Wulf Christopher's office, and from there he directed his massive organization. It was no secret that he controlled multibillion dollar traffic in assorted illicit substances and items, no secret that he had a sizeable number of the police in his back pocket. Nothing stuck, if you bought the right people.

Christopher stood behind a gargantuan mahogany desk, regarding the package. The office was done up in scarlet and burgundy, tassels on the loveseat by the door, mirrors on the walls. Behind the desk and Christopher's high-backed chair sat an old-fashioned wardrobe, full of fresh clothing and shoes (Christopher liked to change often). The whole office was just garish enough that only the most cultivated might question his taste. Most of the people that worked for Christopher thought it stylish.

Christopher opened a cigar box and clipped the end, and spoke while he busied himself lighting it with a carved ivory lighter that sat by the telephone. He clicked the lighter off and puffed. "You ran it through the metal detector?"

"No metal."

"Hm." Christopher folded his arms and puffed his cigar some more. A wisp of his ash blond hair fell forward. Women often told him he resembled Julian Sands. They would have told him he looked like Oliver Hardy if he appreciated it enough. "What's in it?" A gangster has every reason in the world to regard unmarked packages with suspicion.

"I can't tell," said Smitty. The security guard wore a tan suit like the one Robert Redford wore as Gatsby, a mistake then and now. He wore a pair of Ray-Bans and had his long, blond hair, slightly darker than Christopher's ashen blond mane, pulled back in a ponytail. "Ran it through the x-ray and came up with just a blob, but no metal. There's a note on top, but I couldn't read it. There's a symbol on the envelope in there, though.''

''A symbol?''

Smitty handed Christopher a printout of the x-ray machine's findings. ''Recognize that?''

The x-ray showed a bundle, perhaps something in a sheet or blanket. Atop the bundle sat an ordinary letter envelope. In the fuzzy gray picture Christopher could just make out a stylized M with a line through the middle. He did recognize it. It was the symbol he used on any correspondence passed regarding the use of the tunnels under the city to move contraband. It was a contact.

''All right,'' said Christopher. ''Leave it. Thank you, Smitty.''

''If you're looking for a way to get killed, there could be any number of chemicals that might react when you open this up. You don't need metal to—''

''*Thank* you, Smitty.'' Christopher smirked, laying his cigar on a silver ash tray. When he was younger, he would have killed someone for giving him that kind of lip. ''I'll take care of it.'' Smitty nodded and took his leave.

When Smitty was gone, Christopher picked up a letter opener and slit the box along the taped side. Christopher sniffed, aware of a strange odor he could not quite place, and lifted the top flaps back. Inside the box was a blue bundle, tied with a string at the top, and atop that, the envelope. He picked up the envelope and opened it, extracted the piece of paper inside. It was a note, scrawled in crude, block letters:

THERE IS SOMETHING MISSING.

Christopher frowned. *What the hell?* He clasped the string at the top of the bundle and chewed his cigar as he untied the knot. Finally the blue blanket fell away, revealing a sheet of plastic lying across the top. Christopher sighed and pulled the plastic away and gasped.

(*There is something missing.*)

The box was full of hands. Human hands, stacked atop

one another, bathed in blood and cradled in the blue blanket. Christopher looked around him, feeling nauseous, and he thought about naked mole rats.

When Wulf Christopher was a child he had gone to a natural sciences museum in Des Moines. One of the exhibits was a giant network of clear plastic tubes, a small city for creatures known as hairless, or naked, mole rats. The point of the exhibit was to show how the mole rats tunneled through the hard earth and carried food to their queen. Christopher was struck as a child by the creatures, moving up and down the tiny tunnels, crawling over one another squirming hairless and pink in the corners, pushing one another out of the way, blending together, a hundred pieces of flesh biting and clawing and swimming, *swimming* in one another. His father walked up and said, ''Life is like that.''

The hands in the box reminded him of mole rats. They gestured and seemed to swim in one another, and Christopher coughed and gasped and felt the bile begin to rise in his throat. (*There is . . .*) He looked at himself in the mirror across the office and saw that he was white as a sheet. Someone would pay for this. (*. . . something missing.*)

There was a creak, a hinge moving, and Christopher watched his white face in the mirror and saw something rising behind him, behind the high-backed chair, stepping out of the great wardrobe. Now, in the light from the lamp on his desk, Christopher could see it more clearly. The creature was seven feet tall, with fins on the side of its head, and red, glowing eyes. The Abomination. Christopher reached for the red button on the underside of his desk when he heard a soft, rasping laugh and felt something grip him by the neck.

The Abomination picked Christopher up and the man hung in the air, kicking his feet up onto the desk to try to keep from hanging. The creature whipped the chair aside with a heavy claw.

"How did you get in here?" Christopher felt himself being turned over, and all at once the Abomination slammed him down on the top of the great desk and pressed him there. *Oh God oh God oh God....*

"Shh. Don't shout," growled the creature. "Don't reach for any alarms, or I'll eat you." Christopher saw the head of the Abomination, like a scaly, finned cat, come to Christopher's own face, hot, rank breath blowing against his cheek. "I'll eat you a piece at a time. Shhh."

"What do you want?"

A giant, green claw rested on Christopher's chest pressing him down. The creature put a clawed finger under the buttons of Christopher's double-breasted coat and began to pull. Christopher listened to the fabric slowly rip away. Then the claw dug into the front of his shirt, and he looked down and saw the green claw slowly tearing its way up, white cotton ripping and falling aside until his chest lay bare. The Abomination stopped, their eyes locked, a clawed forefinger tapping almost idly on Christopher's sternum.

"Ask," rasped the Abomination.

"What?"

"Aren't you curious?" The Abomination tilted his head, gargoyle teeth bared each time he opened his mouth.

"What?"

"Ask, Christopher. You're a smart fellow," rumbled the voice of the demon.

The note. (*There is something missing.*) "What is—missing?" He spoke, hopefully, ashamed to sound so small, ashamed to be so small, so weak. *Please don't kill me. If I get out of this I will hunt you down and destroy you. Please don't kill me.*

"Yeeesss," the Abomination said. "What is missing? What is *missing* is a heart." The claw tapped on his sternum a bit more forcefully, hammering away, a bruise forming. Then the claw came away and up to Christopher's Adam's apple, resting just under his silk tie, which hung to the side. The claw began to lower and Christopher felt a stabbing pain, something ripping, and then something new entirely.

"The tingling sensation you are feeling," the creature said, the hot breath still on his face, that demon face still intimately close, a new wetness on his chest, "is the skin of your chest ripping, just a tiny bit, just so much as I want."

"You want . . ."

The creature growled. "I *want* to rip your heart out, I really do."

"But . . ."

"But that would not suit you. Why illustrate the obvious?"

"I'll do anything, anything. . . ."

"You will be *silent* and you will *listen* to me," continued the Abomination. "The tightening you are feeling about your chest is not merely the weight of my hand pressing on your rib cage. The tightening is on the inside."

Christopher blinked, feeling the warm blood flow, the claw slowly moving down his sternum. "Inside?"

"A special gift from me to you," said the creature, "Tincture 6, some call it. On my claws. In your blood." The demon mouth curled up and smiled, almost singing, "Swimming in your blood, to your heart. Weakening you. Grabbing that empty heart of yours and tightening it, squeezing it. . . ."

Christopher gasped. *Please, get off of me, I feel . . .* He became aware of the swish of blood in his ears, his heartbeat, pounding, compressed. He opened his mouth and sucked in air and heard it rattle in his throat.

"Now you are going to suffer a massive cardiac arrest, Christopher. You are a very fit man," he smiled again, "so I think you might make it."

What is missing is a heart . . . What is missing is a heart . . . my heart my heart my heart . . .

"Yes. If I let you go now," continued the creature, lifting his claw away from Christopher's belly, the end of his cut, "you *might* make it to the hospital in time. If you are fast. I suspect you will."

"Oh, God," Christopher said, clasping his chest. The Abomination came around to his side and lowered down to whisper in his ear. *Please, please . . .*

"But, Christopher," rasped the Abomination, "you will live in fear. The emergency room will be a regular part of your existence. From here on out."

Missing . . . missing . . . missing a beat . . .

"This is what I have done," spoke the demon voice in his ear, "to your wicked heart, Wulf Christopher."

Christopher stared at the ceiling and heard the crash of the window as the creature leapt through it. He stared at the ceiling and tried to cry out, heard the guards running in as the world went black.

CHAPTER 7

The Hulk put the post-op photos back on Morgan's desk. "You seem to be collecting a lot of these."

Morgan nodded grimly, as did Jo Carlin. The photos showed Wulf Christopher on a hospital bed, a series of plastic tubes running to his arms and nose. "Well, he'll live."

Bruce looked out the large office window at the clouds high on the New York skyline. He had decided to come onto the Helicarrier after the message about Christopher. No sense playing shy. "I have to say it doesn't exactly grieve me to see him in that condition."

"We know that," said Carlin. "We're not torn up about Christopher, either."

"He played us all for saps," said the Hulk. "Christopher got the police to go down there and I was right in front, down there to clean out the Abomination and his followers, or whatever. I attacked Christopher myself after that. This is the only move the Abomination has made that comes as no surprise at all."

"I agree," Morgan said. "This was to be expected. Maybe we should have put guards on Christopher."

"What a shame," the Hulk nodded gravely.

"I'll say," Morgan clasped his fingers and stared over them at the Hulk and Carlin. "But I want to know what you think will happen next."

"What did the note say? Something is missing?" Bruce asked.

"Mm-hm. We managed to get out of Christopher that the 'something missing' was a heart."

"In Wulf Christopher's case," the Hulk observed, "I could have told you that."

Carlin shook her head. "So what, then? The Abomi-

108

nation is picking off personal enemies? With the cops and Christopher—''

''But he didn't hit Nadia,'' said the Hulk.

''No, but he hit around her pretty hard,'' Morgan said.

The Hulk thought back to the e-mail message. ''The message I got from Emil said that now Nadia would see only pain. So in a way, he *did* hit her. But the fact that he's aiming at others makes him a whole lot more dangerous.''

''What does he want?''

The Hulk watched the buildings and listened to the distant whooping of the great rotor blades above them. ''When I met the Abomination last, he made a threat.''

''Which was?'' Carlin asked.

''He said that by letting him get away, whatever he did, whoever he allied himself with, I brought it on myself. He said he had tried to fit into this world, even under it, and next time he returned, he wouldn't stop until he'd brought it down around us.''

Morgan tapped his desk. ''But these targets have been personal.''

''And a little too smart, sometimes.''

''Hm?''

''That thing at the theater was way too advanced for Emil. Emil kicks and bites.''

''True,'' Morgan said.

''He became the Abomination by *stepping in front of* a gamma gun I designed. Deliberately hit himself with a massive dosage, he says, under orders from the Kremlin. This is a guy who's admittedly a brilliant strategist and spy, but he was never a stickler for technical details.''

''I don't know,'' said Carlin. ''Maybe we're underestimating him. He could be on his own. There's no telling what he might familiarize himself with.''

''I see what Dr. Banner is getting at, though,'' said Morgan. ''Like the fact that he knew we were coming down below. You think there's someone working with him.''

"Maybe a lot of someones."

Carlin shook her head again. "But why would such someones want to help Emil pick off his personal enemies, harass his ex-wife, et cetera?"

"Widow," corrected the Hulk. "Nadia doesn't know Blonsky isn't dead. But in answer to your question, I don't know."

"Emil doesn't like working with teams any more than you do."

"I'm here, aren't I?" the Hulk smiled wryly.

Morgan stood up and walked over to the window to stand next to the Hulk. "Whenever I recruit someone, if we're going to have a long relationship, I like to make sure a few problems of their own get cleaned up. If you want to work with someone, the best thing in the world is to share a few objectives, make them mesh."

"What next?" the Hulk asked, hand under his chin. "What are you going to do next?"

"Well," said Morgan, "there is a pattern."

Carlin listed them as she walked over to a slate on the wall where they had been scribbling with a magnetic pen. "Eyes, with Nadia. Hands. Now Christopher's heart. Body parts."

"Not much, is it?" Morgan said tightly.

"It's a lot," said the Hulk. "I just don't see it yet."

Morgan turned around and went to the coffee maker by his desk. As he poured himself a cup, he asked, "So— all of this poetry. Has Emil ever been this cryptic before with you?"

"Not in my experience," said Bruce. "But I remember he found a great deal of peace, down below. He did always have something of a poetic soul. I have to say I think he was a bit gullible. But this is like a new Blonsky we're seeing. A new Abomination."

"It's new to me, too," said Carlin. "And I've been

studying him for a couple of years now. Maybe I haven't met him like you have, but I've been watching. I don't know. There's such rage, and yet such sentimentality."

"Hard to be sentimental while you're cutting people's hands off and stringing them up," said Morgan.

"I agree," the Hulk said. "But not impossible." The Hulk looked at Carlin. " 'Haven't met' . . . you know, that was another strange thing in the e-mail message. Emil made this weird comment about meeting six or seven times."

"So?" Morgan sipped his coffee.

"Twice he said that. Then he said, 'Who can recall these things?' "

"How many times *have* you met?" Carlin asked.

"A hell of a lot more than that."

Morgan set his cup down and looked at his watch. "Well, Dr. Banner, you may not believe this, but this isn't the only case we're working. Let's meet again later and take a fresh look. Let me know if anything occurs to you."

The door to Morgan's office slid shut behind the Hulk and Jo Carlin as they walked down the hall. The woman had a rapid stride, and she had no difficulty keeping up with the gamma giant. "When's the funeral?" Bruce said, as he reached the lift down to the hovercraft bay.

"Six o'clock this afternoon," said Carlin. "One hour."

The Hulk was pleased that she hadn't called it *eighteen-hundred hours*. "Look after him," frowned Bruce.

"I will," she said. "He's the only Morgan we have."

When Bruce got home, Betty was just sitting down to watch Rick and Marlo. "I noticed your friends dropped you off at the next block."

"Yes."

"Kind of them."

"What's on?"

Betty had a quart of Häagen-Dazs in front of her and gestured with a scooper. "Rick's got Senator Hill today. A real hoot-and-holler. Want some?" She indicated a second bowl, which already was lined with slices of peach.

"Absolutely," the Hulk said. "How was school?" He sat down on the reinforced couch and it gave out the same whine every other piece of steel-reinforced furniture they had did.

"Carla the Brain showed up for the second time and we worked on her paper," Betty said, scooping ice cream into Bruce's bowl. She licked the scooper and continued. "I've seen this kid's writing. Excellent methodology, good diction. I think she can publish it if I can guide her correctly."

Bruce smiled broadly.

"What?"

"I just—I just like hearing you so content."

"Well, it's a change for the better," she said, although her voice dropped a bit. "How goes the hunt?"

Rick was on TV now, next to Marlo, his wife, seated in their chairs. Rick was introducing Terence Hill, saying he was going to run a campaign clip. The thin, gray form of Senator Hill came on after that, giving his usual speech.

"Eyes," said Bruce, poking at his ice cream with a spoon. "Hands. Heart. Body parts. What do you think?"

"Huh." Betty laid down her spoon and popped a slice of peach in her mouth, turning to him on the couch. "Well, there's other extremities to go for. Feet, for instance."

"Yeah. And every connection so far is personal. Nadia, Emil's wife. The cops who killed his people down below. The billionaire who sent them."

"Who else does he hate?" Betty asked.

"He hates me," Bruce said, staring through the TV.

She nodded, gravely. "Yes. He does. But he hasn't come after you yet."

"I don't think he knows where I am. He sent me his message on the Internet."

"Yeah," she said. Betty pulled a printout of the e-mail from under her bowl of ice cream. "I've been thinking about that. 'I will be what I am. What are you?' "

Bruce nodded. "Underground, he listed Abominations. Things that are Abominations to the Lord."

"Emil is an Abomination."

"Duh."

"No, I mean, look. 'I will be what I am.' Let's not overlook the simple parts. What is Emil?"

"Like you said," Bruce hit the mute button and Senator Hill shut up. "An Abomination."

Betty the Religious Studies instructor looked back at him. "A thing reprehensible to God or to men. A spiritual mistake, or a spiritual accident. A hole where there should be something good."

The Hulk stood up and got behind the couch to read the message over Betty's shoulder. " 'Nadia had haughty eyes, now she sees only pain.' 'I will be what I am, what are you? What will I make you see?' " He was whispering, trying to wring it out. "Hands that shed innocent blood are an Abomination. A wicked heart is an Abomination."

Betty looked up. "Can't figure this guy out. Where is Emil from?"

"Former Soviet Union."

"No, what state?"

The Hulk thought for a moment, the wheels turning, pages flipping back in his head. "Georgia."

The instructor chewed her thumbnail. "You know, the Georgians managed to maintain their Christianity even after the October Revolution."

"I thought all that was, ah, stamped out."

She shrugged. "That's what people say, but it's a hard thing in practice. It was a sticking point, but Georgia continued to observe religious holidays fairly regularly. If

Emil was born at the height of Soviet Communism, he would have grown up serving two masters."

"The Church and the State."

"And probably constantly balancing between the two."

The Hulk tapped his chin and began to pace. " 'What are you?' That's an identity question. Struggling with your identity," he whispered, the words tripping over themselves. " 'What are you?' "

"A spy."

"Yes," Bruce said, "before that, a child; after being a spy, a monster. A monster people call the Abomination."

"What happened to Emil after the change?"

"The KGB hung him out to dry," Bruce said. "He's been on his own, rejected even by his own people."

" 'O God, my God, why have you forsaken me?' That state was like a religion in itself, or tried to be."

"Yes," said the Hulk. "Yes! And he's been cast out of both of those, but now he's talking about *what he is*, affirmatively. Not searching. 'I will be *what I am*.' It's for the rest of us to realize ourselves, he knows what he is."

"And he's going to show us."

The Hulk paced back and looked at the sheet again. "Yes, he's going to show us. He said in the tunnel he'd given me everything."

"I think he has," Betty said. "Numbers are very important to someone with a spiritual bent. Names, too. Numbers and names are magical, they have reasons for being. Numbers and names are never an accident." She stood up and disappeared into the study. Bruce pounded after her as she continued, "You just have to know where to look! Lordy, what kind of morons are we?"

"Hey, gimme a break, a few years ago I didn't use articles and spoke about myself in the third person."

She was sitting down at Bruce's computer and

smirked at him as he came in the study. "I remember. 'Hulk hate stupid purple corduroys. Hulk need fresh pair.' "

"Don't remind me."

"Hey, you put 'em on. Thank God we got married or you'd never have discovered Dockers."

Bruce grinned as Betty moved the mouse and the modem began to dial.

"Six or seven times," Betty said. "That's too obviously a clue. Emil's not trying to be secret here, he just wants you to work for it. He wants you to notice him while you get to the answers."

"Okay," said Bruce. She had connected to their online service and she clicked a few more times to bring up a search engine, then typed a series of words. "What are you getting?"

"The Bible," she said, shaking her head as one of the many on-line translations came up. "Amazing, when you think about it. Used to be there was a skill called recall that made professors rich and famous for their ability to recognize patterns and find them in a stack of books."

"Don't you have a concordance?" Bruce asked.

"Oh, sure. And I can look up a word like Abomination and get every verse with the word in it. But that's as intelligent a search as you could do. That recall skill was still the lifesaver. Now, look at this, I can do a search smarter than I am." She brought up a search screen and typed +SIX +SEVEN +ABOMINATION.

Something came up. "I could have done this on paper," Betty said. "But not in ten seconds."

Floating on the screen, lighting the faces of Bruce and Betty, read the following words:

PROVERBS 6:16
THERE ARE SIX THINGS WHICH THE LORD HATETH;
YEA, SEVEN WHICH ARE AN ABOMINATION UNTO HIM:

HAUGHTY EYES, A LYING TONGUE,

AND HANDS THAT SHED INNOCENT BLOOD;

A HEART THAT DEVISETH WICKED PURPOSES,

FEET THAT ARE SWIFT IN RUNNING TO MISCHIEF,

A FALSE WITNESS THAT UTTERETH LIES,

AND HE THAT SOWETH DISCORD AMONG BRETHREN.

"I knew it," she said. "I knew I'd seen that before."

The Hulk grinned. "We should all join a convent from time to time."

"It's a hard habit to break." She raised an eyebrow as the verse printed out. "You better call Morgan."

The Hulk looked at the clock and shook his head, "Later."

She looked up. "You think you should wait?"

"His kid's funeral," Bruce sighed. "I'll give him a couple hours. Meantime," he picked up the printout, "let's have a look."

"Coffee?"

"Right."

They reconvened in the kitchen, Betty sitting on the counter next to where the Hulk stood, shoulder to shoulder. "He's acting out, as Leonard would say," said Bruce, referring to his gamma-enhanced psychiatrist friend Doc Samson.

"Yeah," she said, "but it's not that simple. He's acting out and getting everybody else involved. He's not just an Abomination, he's the king of Abominations and the punisher of them all."

"The haughty eyes of Nadia and her audience," said Bruce. "That's really scary. Every one of those people, he injured just to make a point. The hands that shed innocent blood, just like he told me. Betty, I could kiss you."

"Oh, you owe me bigger than that," she said. "The

heart that deviseth wickedness, that's Wulf Christopher.''

"But you forgot lying," said Bruce. "The order is eyes, lying tongue, *then* hands, then heart.''

"So he skipped lying," she said. "So he doesn't mind breaking the order.''

"Why make it easy?" Bruce mused, tilting his head. "Funny thing is lying is here twice—the lying tongue and then the false witness that uttereth lies.''

"Right," said Betty. "If I had to guess I'd say that's why you have the odd 'six or seven' confusion at the beginning. Lying is two-in-one. Maybe a private lie, versus a witness, a public lie.''

"Hm. Then what?" Bruce mused. "Feet that are swift in running to mischief. Just like you guessed, feet.''

"Feet." They stared at one another, waiting for lightening to strike.

"Not a thing," said Bruce.

"Search me," Betty shrugged.

"Great," Bruce chewed his lip. "And there's no guarantee it'll be just one person. People get hurt around his targets. Think. Feet that are swift in running to mischief.''

"Someone Emil has a reason to hate.''

"Connected to him personally, in some way. Like the cops, and Christopher by extension.''

"Who else? What next?''

My eyes on the stars . . .

Bruce turned around and looked past Betty. The kitchen in the condo had a bar over the counter, and above the bar was a space in the wall so one could serve guests in the living room. And in the living room, he could see the television. "My eyes on the stars," muttered Bruce. "Feet . . . running . . . to mischief . . .''

Betty looked at him. "Hey, partner. Whatcha got?''

My eyes on the stars . . .

"Up a . . . Hill . . ." The Hulk bounded into the living room and hit the mute button, busting the remote in the process. "Like a politician, running, like a crooked—''

"What?"

"Something I read about Christopher, God, I forgot his connections with—"

Senator Hill was still talking to Marlo, and they were running another clip, and there it was, and Hulk turned the volume up high. "Look!"

"My eyes on the stars, my feet on the ground!" And the flag was waving and people were cheering. *Emil, you're a bad, bad poet.*

"The senator," said Betty.

"Terence Hill made his fortune, before becoming a senator, as a secret partner with Wulf Christopher. Rick wanted to talk about that on his show but they wouldn't let him. Is this show live?"

Betty stared. "Usually. Oh, no, Rick and Marlo!"

The Hulk grabbed the phone, clicked it on, and punched eleven digits. After a moment somebody answered. "Rick Jones, please, it's an emergency."

"I'm sorry," came the female voice on the other end. "But he's already left."

The Hulk stared at the television. "But the show's on the air."

"Yeah!" came the chirping answer. "We all get off early today because we filmed it on delay. The senator had to make a flight."

Bruce felt his chest tighten. "Delay by how long?"

"One hour. Can I get you anyone else?"

"What airport?"

"What?"

The Hulk yelled. "What airport, Kennedy, LaGuardia, or Newark?"

"Did you say emergency?"

"Yes. Please."

There was a pause and a smack of gum. "Limo went to Kennedy. Plane takes off at seven."

The Hulk clicked off the phone.

There was a sound, an electronic chirp from the study.

The Hulk walked into the study with the handset, already dialing another eleven-digit number.

A familiar, female voice answered. "Jo Carlin."

"Jo?" Bruce looked at his computer screen. He had e-mail. Anonymous e-mail. "Jo, I'm headed for the airport. Senator Hill is gonna have trouble." He clicked on the message beacon and the message opened up. He stared:

TOO LATE.

"Jo?" Bruce called. "Jo, are you there?"

The line was dead. Bruce clicked the phone off and dropped it. Within seconds he was out the door and in the air.

CHAPTER 8

I am not resigned, Sean Morgan thought, *to the shutting away of loving hearts in the cold, cold ground.*

The fair-haired colonel stood still next to Margaret Morgan, his coat flapping in the chill wind. The priest was reading from his Bible, speaking softly. A large black box that held his only son was being lowered into a hole. Morgan heard nothing, and stared ahead into the distance.

Give me this, God. Give me this. Take this away from him and give it to me. Replace us. Please. It was a crazy thought, a stupid prayer, answered by only the wind and the soft murmuring of the priest. The Edna St. Vincent Millay poem continued in the back of his head: *So it is, so it shall be, so it has been, time out of mind.*

Morgan glanced at Margaret. She seemed to sense it and looked back with what could only be received as an icy stare. They had not been this close in years. Margaret's hair had begun to go a bit gray at the temples, he noticed, but she was still lovely, her red hair pulled back and set off by the black hat and veil. She whispered, and as she did her face softened into a sullen frown.

"I'm glad you could make it, Sean."

He could not tell if that sounded bitter or not. He tried not to care. "Thank you." He could think of nothing else to say.

"I want this to be over," she said flatly, and then he saw tears well up, and she sniffed. He blinked several times.

"Me, too." Morgan felt awkward, his limbs heavy and stupid, as he reached out his hand and took hers. He was shaking. For a brief second it felt as if she was going to swat him away but then her hand clasped his in return. "Me, too."

122

"I want it to be over and gone," she whispered. "Over and not even real."

"I know," he said. "I didn't, uh," the words were coming on their own, meaningless, "I didn't see him at Christmas, I was—" Why did he say that? Why was he starting her side of an old argument?

"Please, Sean," she sniffed. "Not now." And she could have said, *You didn't see him a lot of Christmases. You didn't see him a lot, period.*

His voice cracked and he whispered, "I'm sorry, Margaret," and now she was in his arms, crying into his chest, and it was the first time he had held her in ten years, easily. "I'm so sorry." *He looked . . . so much like you. So much like both of us. So much is gone, Margaret.*

And she was crying into his coat and he was holding her, smelling her hair, that smell he hadn't smelled in years, and he was holding back tears for some reason, some awful, evil reason. The world was gone around them, and they floated in cold space, alone, terribly alone. Even in one another's arms, alone.

There was a strange sifting sound, dirt falling off the edges of the grave and onto the metal coffin. And over the end of the priest's speech, a humming sound, alien to the cold cemetery.

But not alien to Morgan. The Green Beret looked up from Margaret's shoulder and saw a hovercraft topping the hill, moving slowly over the graveyard. *Oh, no, say it isn't so . . .*

Margaret looked up. "Sean?"

He let go of her and stepped back, and for a brief moment wanted to say something, anything that could possibly explain. But he saw her eyes, that cold stare again, that stare he remembered now and that burned into him like a hot brand. Sean Morgan looked away, at the hovercraft that now hung a few yards off the interment site, and hung his head in shame.

"I have to—"

"Go," she mouthed. She wasn't crying anymore. Morgan bit his lip and turned and began to walk towards the hovercraft, certain that he had just seen something gone for years come to life, and die forever.

"Talk to me," Morgan said, once the hovercraft was in the air. He felt the cool veneer of professionalism slide over him like a garment.

An agent named Russel Banks sat across from Morgan. "Terribly sorry for the timing, sir."

"Just tell me what the problem is," Morgan held up a hand. They wouldn't do this to him if it wasn't necessary. He hoped.

"We have a situation at JFK, Colonel."

"What?"

"Jo Carlin radioed Gamma Team that the Hulk suddenly went crazy. He said he's headed for the airport, and he's going to attack a plane carrying a United States senator."

"*What?*" The hovercraft had already made it to the docking bay of the helicarrier.

"You can listen to the traffic if you—"

"Right." Morgan grabbed the headset off of one of the other agents. He fastened the mike and spoke as he rode the lift. "This is Morgan, what the hell is going on out there?" He turned to Banks, who was following, but barely able to keep up: "Where's Carlin?"

"Like I said, she and Gamma Team headed for the airport."

What seemed to be a thousand voices were speaking at once in Morgan's ear.

". . . got right past me, Jo, Jesus, he's fast . . ."

". . . police and media choppers, please disperse . . ."

". . . nearly knocked that reporter out of the sky, I'm surprised that . . ."

". . . get those choppers out of here before they hit one another?"

Police? Media?

"I can't leave you people alone for a second," Morgan hissed. The two men burst into Morgan's office and switched on a television screen on the wall across from his desk. Sure enough, there was a news report. All hell was breaking loose.

On the screen he could see reporters and police cars swarming the field. A cheery woman was announcing how exciting it was that the Hulk had announced his intention to down a plane.

"How'd the media get this?" Morgan turned and looked at Tom Hampton, who ran in the room. He waited a half-second for a response, then signed the question.

"Something went wrong," Tom signed back. "Someone below was monitoring Jo's call, and it was tapped by the media."

"What are you saying, they heard what Jo heard?"

Tom kept signing but switched on his voice modulator as he brought up a second screen and pulled up the GammaTrac. "They heard what Jo heard, and heard her call out Gamma Team." The screen zoomed down to the airfield, and there was the blob of green labelled HULK, moving towards a white unit that seemed to be taxiiing.

The phone rang on Morgan's desk and Banks snapped it up. "Betty Banner on line one."

"Intercom," snapped Morgan. "Mrs. Banner, we—"

"Mr. Morgan this is a mistake. Bruce is trying to save him! The Abomination is out to—"

Morgan looked at the GammaTrac and at Tom. "Is Blonsky anywhere near the field?"

Tom shook his head.

"Wonderful." Morgan spoke into the mike: "Jo, this is Morgan, talk to me!"

The mike crackled and Jo came in. He could hear the hum of the hovercraft she was riding. Shots were being fired behind her. "Colonel! God, it's a mess out here."

"What's happening?"

Jo, the woman on the television, and Tom Hampton's voice modulator all answered at once: "He's going for the plane."

When the Hulk sprang from his condo towards John F. Kennedy Airport he was still trying to figure out how he was going to guess which plane would be Senator Hill's. *Beyond that, who cut my phone line?* There was someone in SAFE who didn't belong there. There was someone pulling a few too many strings.

The gamma giant rocketed through the air and landed on a freeway, and leapt into the air again. Cold wind whipped through his green hair and stung his eyes. He could cover at least a mile with each leap, more if he really put his legs into it. The Hulk used to drive the army crazy leaping all over the Arizona desert, and more recently did the same thing to his SAFE tails. Before everyone found out where he lived.

Land. Smash. Another leap. Hopefully, he would spot Emil on the field before he had to find the plane. *Seven o'clock. It should be almost seven now.* He berated himself with each leap that he might be going off half-cocked, that the field might not be the answer. Emil might decide to crush the limo, instead, or attack the senator at the airport. But something told him the drama of a downed plane would be just too attractive. Too attractive not to check, at least. (*Too late.*)

After a few more leaps he saw the sprawling airport, and past the buildings, the field itself, barriered by tall fences and topped by barbed wire. As he leapt into the air again he looked around for Emil. *Where are you?*

Only then did he notice the vans. At least twenty of them: cable, radio, broadcast television station vans, all corralled around the fence like a wagon train waiting for an attack.

Waiting for an attack . . .

Police lights caught his eye and he saw the squad cars

swarming onto the field, headed for the east-most runway. *What the hell are they doing?*

There were three planes taxiing, all runways lined up. Two of the taxiing planes he dismissed; those were jumbo jets. The third was private.

Bingo.

Something leaden and heavy struck the Hulk in the back. He was being shot at. His trajectory was finished; he dropped to the ground and prepared to leap again. The small plane was just beginning to take off.

"Hulk!" A hovercraft zipped from behind. "Turn around and go back!" On the hovercraft, a female agent held a megaphone and the agents behind her held several large guns.

Bruce tried to yell. "Jo! Look for Emil! He's got to be here!" He leapt into the air and barely held his direction as several large-calibre bullets slammed him in the side. He growled in pain but kept himself aimed in the direction of the jet, which now had lifted about thirty feet off the ground and was still climbing. "Radio them!" he yelled to Gamma Team. "Warn them!"

They couldn't hear him, because they were shooting at him. The Hulk twisted and flipped, heading downward, when he nearly collided with a media chopper.

The Hulk looked up and saw the plane in the air, heading out, and two more hovercrafts zipped around him and opened fire. Bruce took to the air, flying past Jo's hovercraft. He aimed straight for the cockpit of the jet.

Within seconds he was alongside it, flying fast, and the pilot looked out and saw him and was shouting something into his headset. Bruce pointed at the ground. He pointed at the ground again. "Put *down*!" he shouted, pointing. "*Down!*"

The pilot looked at the Hulk and was still yelling into his headset when Bruce felt himself propelled violently backwards, as the plane exploded in one great, fiery blast.

· · ·

Not far away, exposed for all the world to see if they bothered to look, under a tiny tree by the fence on the other side of the field from the circus of vans and helicopters and hovercraft, the Abomination put away the detonator and listened to the radio. And as he listened to the reports (''Oh my God he blew up the plane . . .''), he laughed. The feet were through running, the false witness had begun. Two down in one fell swoop.

He couldn't stop laughing.

After a moment the Hulk hit the ground, digging a fifteen-foot trench. When he crawled out he heard the laughter, not a hundred yards off.

CHAPTER 9

Let's talk power.

Power is a steam train seen for the first time when all you've ever witnessed is a horse and carriage. Power is a lever when all you've ever used is your knees. Power is an arrow flying through the air at someone who has, up to that point, thought you had to stand before a creature to strike it down.

Power is anger, real anger, when up to then you haven't really had the angry man's full attention.

Power was the Hulk, a green rage flying through the air at the beast.

And the Abomination was thrilled, absolutely thrilled, to have finally gotten the Hulk's attention. The Hulk could tell, because the demon was laughing at him.

All right, Emil. You've pretty much ruined it for me now. The Hulk saw the Abomination smiling at him, that long, alligator mouth curling like a Greek mask as Emil put something away in his coat and got up, almost casually. Emil moved casually and fluidly, shaking his finned, red-eyed, demon head. He held his hat and his coat was flapping. He was beginning to laugh, and as the Hulk rocketed towards Emil, Emil almost imperceptibly began to speed up. He stepped into the satellite parking area, moving between a pair of matching Lincolns.

All those people back there. A plane equipped with one senator and a host of staffers, down, and the whole world thinks I did it. You must really be proud of yourself.

The Hulk was a missile, arms outstretched, hands locked like claws, ready to grab onto whatever ended up in his grasp, and as he zeroed in he saw Emil leap into the air.

The Hulk hit the ground on the other side of the fence that surrounded the field. The Abomination was leaping and removing the long, brown coat he wore, the hat falling to the side. In the distance Bruce could hear the helicopters and sirens. He looked over his shoulder and saw the hovercars zipping across the field, intent on catching up to him.

Something slammed into a car with the ripping force of an ICBM and the Hulk looked back to see a Mercedes explode. He saw the roof of the vehicle pulled downward, windows busting out, the entire vehicle collapsing like a tent into the hole in the asphalt left by the Abomination as he dove through it. The Hulk bound into the air, flipping, pointing his feet downward, and followed. The crumpled Mercedes disappeared from around him and he fell in darkness, underground once more.

The hole burrowed by the plummeting Abomination ended and Bruce landed, sinking his feet into the wet concrete of another sewer tunnel. He looked ahead of him, then in the opposite direction. In the distant gloom, he saw the Abomination standing, shrouded in shadow and half-hidden by the corner, waiting for him. "Emil!"

The figure disappeared, and something like laughter, gurgling and raspy, echoed through the tunnel.

The Hulk stood still and breathed. Overhead, in the distance, helicopters and hovercars circled. He closed his eyes for a tenth of a second and let the vehicle sounds disappear from his mind. Deep within his breast a savage beast was growling. This entire fiasco with Emil was too complex for the savage to understand. The savage never would have been in this situation.

Not complex. Simple. Get him.

Bruce felt a wave pass over him, a tingling arc charging through gamma-irradiated muscles, and he heard the laugh of the Abomination. The beast told him to move. But it was Bruce who did so.

It would be so much simpler if I were still that mindless, savage Hulk. Hulk would smash, and smash, until nothing was left. Hulk would not be fooled by ploys or

*computer messages or idiotic poetry or attacks on his
sense of guilt and honor.*

The giant began to move again; less than a second
gone, and his legs and arms began to sweep in long green
arcs.

But it is not simple. It will never be simple again.

Long, green arcs, hands reaching out to clutch pipes
as the Hulk burst down the tunnel. Slithery creatures stood
up on hind legs and swiveled their heads, watching the
green blur moving through the dimness, feet slamming
against wet slimy concrete, cymbal crashes in the sym-
phony of drips and drops in the murky shadows.

Around a corner, the Hulk sped, spinning as he turned,
realigning himself, and now in the distance he saw Emil
again, stopped momentarily. About fifty yards away stood
the demon, feet balanced on a ledge, and the tunnel
seemed to open out. The Hulk saw the shimmer of arti-
ficial light coming into the tunnel from the space beyond.
Emil looked back and saw the Hulk, and both men leapt
at once.

The Hulk sailed into the air, past the mouth of the
tunnel through which Emil had just flown, falling. Emil
had gone farther out and now sailed downward. The Hulk
saw the creature's legs and grabbed on in the flickering
red light. The two gamma giants travelled twenty feet,
falling, the Hulk wrapped around the legs of the Abomination.

Emil looked down at his feet and kicked. "Finally we
have it out."

The Hulk cursed as the scaly foot collided with his
jaw. He looked down just in time to see a network of
metal platforms and walkways, before the tumbling pair
collided with the first one.

Metal shrieked and gave way, the gamma giants tearing through girders and steel tubes. The Hulk felt the railing of a walkway below flatten out on either side as he
came to a slamming stop crosswise on the metal, and he

winced again as Emil's weight came down on top of him.

Bruce looked around quickly at the red-lit room. They seemed to be inside a great, concrete barrel, lit here and there by a shimmering light, metal walkways travelling from tunnel opening to tunnel opening, here and there the monotonous rust and slime interrupted by a metal wheel or meter. They were in some part of the water treatment system, a gateway of sorts.

Emil stood up on the walkway and picked up Bruce by the hair. Bruce felt the Abomination's kick in his ribs and he shot out his fist, felt it connect with razor teeth. He fell backwards with the force of Emil's kick, taking out more metal as he went, grabbing onto another walkway. Bruce slammed into a walkway and the air rushed out of his lungs as the metal pressed into his chest, but it did not break. Now he looked down for a brief moment, saw the pool, thirty or so feet below, swirling and murky. *This is treatment?* The Hulk heard the metal groan as he flipped over, throwing himself back up, finding the railway next to Emil and flipping again, landing both feet in Emil's chest. Emil tumbled backwards, but managed to get a spring off the metal girder as he passed, and he shot out to the concrete edge of the barrel. Emil caught onto the lip of another tunnel and looked back, hanging there, and shouted across the chasm.

"Dr. Banner, this is so much *fun.*"

The Hulk sprang, landing on the wall, hands digging into the concrete and catching metal underneath, and he held himself in place, pounding his fist into Emil's solar plexus. "You killed them back there, Emil. You killed them to make a *point.* You're insane!"

Emil grunted with Bruce's blow and laughed, let go of the edge of the tunnel and let himself slip beneath the Hulk on the wall. Bruce looked down and saw the Abomination slide along the dirty concrete, grab a ladder, twist, and spring, and the demon was sailing again. A clawed fist caught him in the jaw as the figure passed, and Bruce twisted around. He brought his free hand up to his mouth and felt the flow of blood, so rare. Emil landed with a crunch at the lip of another sewer tunnel, on the other side of the barrel.

"Heh," growled the demon. Bruce hung there, bleeding, watching Emil clinging to the twisted metal, the red lights bouncing off deep green, scaly skin, and he saw the insanity. It was evident even in the curious twisted way Emil hung there, like a gargoyle, or a gamma-irradiated ape, enjoying the show Bruce was putting on. "You idiot," said Emil, hanging there, breath rasping. "More fun than a barrel of gamma giants, no? You and I could keep this up for hours."

Bruce shook his head. "Emil—"

"We can be gods, in our own way, bashing one another's head into walls and feeling almost nothing. Doesn't it get you going, Hulk? Doesn't it make you thirst for more? To know that only someone like myself can give you this kind of workout?"

"You're wrong," said the Hulk. "There's always the Thing."

"Cheesecake," said the Abomination, and the Hulk was in the air again, fists outstretched, a green missile. Emil threw up a hand and deflected Bruce's fists upwards. Bruce's body rolled, but before Emil could deliver a blow the Hulk brought his knees square into Emil's chin. The concrete barrel shook as Emil's head busted the concrete behind him and he lost his grip on the wall. They began to fall again.

Twisting and spinning in the air, this time the metal girders they hit barely squealed as the gamma twins tore through them. The Hulk saw his sparring partner smiling and laughing, and suddenly the air turned to liquid as they hit the pool below.

Two tons of dense green flesh hit the murky water and plunged, and the Hulk opened his eyes under the water and saw only blackness, the slightest hint of red light shimmering through, as he and Emil sank another fifteen feet.

The Hulk's feet hit concrete and he slipped and settled onto the slimy ground, limbs flailing through the stagnant morass. He saw the shadow of Emil, settling to the bottom with him.

Emil scuttled backwards for a moment, like a crab, and the Hulk looked around him. *Why Emil, you take me to the nicest places.*

They were at the bottom of the barrel, a twenty-foot circle surrounded by curving concrete walls, laced with a hundred pipes of unknown origin or use. Something slick and primitive brushed by Bruce's leg. He looked down, then back at the shadow where Emil had been. In the water swam shimmering silver things, snapping and slithering, as if someone had created a dark reflection of a dime-store snow globe and shaken it.

The shadow had moved. Bruce cursed and looked around, and then Emil had him, coming from above, claws grabbing his throat, clawing at his eyes. The Hulk clamped his eyes closed and grabbed onto Emil's arms, trying to slam the demon back against the rusted metal wall, but he was moving through molasses, and the two merely floated back.

The Hulk had run into this problem before. There were benefits to weighing a ton and having extremely dense, thick, quickly-regenerating skin. He could count those benefits on a hand, and Doc Samson advised him to do so just about every session. Buoyancy was not among them.

Bruce began to use his elbows, slamming back against the Abomination, one side after another. The slithering thing below moved past his feet as he danced, causing the thick water to shimmer, the slithering silver creatures flying in all directions. Suddenly Emil was slipping, and had to use his arms to right himself. The Hulk pushed away, let his tremendous weight settle to the bottom, and spread his legs, spreading his toes out to cover as much area as possible. He felt mud, alive with tubular, squirming life, squish between his toes, as he forced his toes down and ground them into the concrete. He lowered himself slowly, thick water flowing around him, and then let go. The dense body began to move, the Hulk's leg muscles springing up, stretching out, and he let go of the concrete and felt the water sailing past him.

Sure would hate to end up on the bottom of the ocean, thought Bruce. *I'd end up having to walk to shore.*

The Hulk burst through the black surface and the red light filled his eyes. He breast-stroked to the edge and grabbed a large pipe where it was fused to the wall and began to pull himself up, then yanked hard, lifting himself fully out of the water. In the end, he was nimble. Big and dense, but nimble. The Hulk found his place at the mouth of a lower tunnel and looked back down at the pool of sludge.

The black water was trembling in the red light, betraying movement below. Bruce stared, waiting for the Abomination to resurface. Briefly, Bruce considered jumping back down there, but decided scuffling in that goo was not worth it. He would wait.

Black water burbled and waved and something burst from the surface, a dark green set of head and shoulders. Emil held back his head and roared, holding up his arm, and in the red light Bruce saw that he was not alone. Something bone white and thick, a snake of some sort, ten inches wide easily, had wrapped around Emil's chest and Emil had it by the throat, a long, fanged mouth hissing and snapping at him. The albino snake snapped again at Emil's face and Emil began to pull. Bruce saw the thing slowly stretching with Emil's arm, uncoiling from around the Abomination's scaly chest. Then the Hulk heard another sound, as the snake uncoiled completely, held below the jaw by one green claw.

Emil was laughing. The Abomination's red eyes stared

into the pink eyes of the albino serpent and his laughter howled, profane and deadly. The creature writhed in the red light, the white, scaly body dancing on the water like a pressurized hose, black water dancing all around the two, and Emil looked up at Bruce.

"I am as one gone down to the pit," said Emil. "You can never catch me here."

Suddenly black water flew and the Hulk saw a white-scaled body flying towards him, a fanged mouth spitting and tumbling as Emil flung the creature up at Bruce's face. Bruce held up a hand and felt the creature clamp down on his wrist, causing just enough of an indentation to hold on and begin to wrap itself about him. Bruce cried out in surprise and blinked at the black water in his eyes. The creature was *huge*, and now it wrapped around his ankles. The slime on the bottom of the tunnel's mouth gave below his feet and he fell backwards.

The Abomination was still laughing. The Hulk looked across the barrel and saw Emil at another tunnel mouth. "You never cease to amuse me, Hulk! I play the tune and you dance. That is what you are, Hulk! A house slave, a performer. You were better off stupid, because now you amuse the world and you have to *know* how useless you are."

Stop wasting time, Bruce thought, and he squeezed the serpent and slammed it against the wall. The thing snapped at him and he felt bones snap and saw the pink eyes roll. "Emil, I'm tired of—"

Emil's laughter echoed from the tunnel entry and Bruce shook his head, sliding the serpent off of his body. His cotton pants were practically black with muck. *Enough.* The Hulk sprang across the barrel and into the tunnel. He saw the shadow of the Abomination, moving faster now, laughing all the way. Bruce began to run.

Rats and snakes running for their lives, spider webs tangling in his hair. The tunnel proceeded nearly a mile before a turn, no possible exits, and Bruce doggedly pursued, hearing the cement thunder as he passed by. *Putting me through paces, amusing himself with my performance. What is this, Emil? What is your game?*

The tunnel ended a few hundred yards ahead. Bruce saw a ladder lit by a red light. He slowed as he got closer, looking around. A trench of muck, an indentation in the tunnel, began a few yards before the end, and Bruce hopped over to one side and continued running along the seven inches of semidry floor. He reached the ladder and looked up.

There was a portal, shut and cobwebbed. Bruce reached up and touched it and realized that no one had gone through there for years.

The water in the trench moved, and Bruce looked down. A scaly, demonic giant began to sit up, black water and silver worms flowing off his scales. He sat there at Bruce's feet, and the water ran away from his glowing red eyes.

"Hm," he said. "Dead end."

"What is this, Emil?" *You could have escaped at any time.* "What are you doing?"

"Bruce," Emil said, a serpent in the pool. The red eyes blinked away the water and he sniffed. "I'm really going to miss you."

"Let's go, Emil," Bruce sneered. "That's enough." He moved towards the trench where Emil sat and the Abomination looked up.

"Go? Oh, absolutely. The only difference between us," he said, "is you have no idea of the extent to which I'm willing to go."

Emil sprang again, catching Bruce in the chin as he smashed into the roof and sailed. The Hulk staggered back and looked up past the falling chunks of concrete and rusted metal and saw light and air, heard running water. Emil had led him to the surface. Bruce sprang quickly through the hole Emil had left. *I'm not losing you this time.*

Bruce went twenty feet in the air and began to fall back and saw Emil on the—*tiles*? The Hulk set down on slick tile and shuddered. There was white tile and metal furniture everywhere. Someone began to scream. *Not the surface. Not quite. Just a much more inhabited part of the underground.* They were in a large, circular room about an eighth of a mile in diameter. Scattered throughout the area were people, young, old, families, all admiring one another and various brightly-colored purchases. All around the perimeter were the familiar corporate logos of a dozen different fast-food eateries. He heard high heels clacking on stone and saw a man and a woman scrambling up a wide stone staircase. Above the staircase was a sign: WELCOME TO THE MOLE COURT.

Great. There had to be a hundred people here, scarfing food in a safe, air-conditioned underground environment. And the Abomination had just burst among them.

Something rumbled and ripped. Emil roared and the Hulk looked back in time to see a table flying at him, a massive, white, formica-topped table, chunks of concrete and mesh dangling from the legs where Emil had torn it free. The table smashed into the Hulk and he batted it aside with his hand, sending it flying, then he gasped, followed it with his eye.

The table sailed, spinning toward the far corner. Bruce yelled in terror as a sandy-haired kid looked up from a plate of kung pao chicken and a comic book and opened his mouth. The kid hit the deck as the table sailed past him, the dangling mesh swiping a piece of white concrete lined with torn linoleum across the tabletop, sending chicken flying. The table slammed into the granite wall on the other side with a massive harangue, right next to the Insta-Wok, and the neon sign identifying that particular establishment sputtered in electronic torment. The Hulk watched the kid scramble towards the staircase, turn back, grab the comic, then hightail it out of there, fanboy dedication at its best.

Got to get him out of here, the Hulk thought. He saw the Abomination tearing across the food court. People were beginning to run, some for the exits, some in the wrong direction. Madness in pinstripe.

The Hulk bounded towards the Abomination, looking down. God, so many people to be avoided. Someone howled in pain and Bruce saw the claws on Emil's feet dig into a man's leg as Emil trampled him and the man rolled out of the way.

"*Never,*" cried the Abomination, grabbing onto another table. "You will *never* know the extent to which I am willing to go!" People got out of the way and scrambled as Emil grunted and began to tear another table out of the floor.

The Hulk snarled as he hit the Abomination with both fists, flying into him, both of them toppling and slamming against a counter. "To do *what?*" he cried. "You want to have it out, you want to destroy me, let's do it, but *not here.*" He had Emil pinned beneath his legs and was pounding his fists into Emil's face, and Emil was swiping his claws at him. A couple connected and Bruce felt green blood fly from his cheek.

"Here is *perfect!*" Emil growled. "I don't want *you.*" Emil rolled to the left, bringing the Hulk with him, then rolled to the right forcefully, and they tumbled over. Emil was on top, clawing at the Hulk. "I have no intention of *killing* you. We could run across the city duking it out, and I might have to hurl you into a volcano before we actually die. Don't you understand, you fool? I want to crush you by crushing everything around you." A claw swiped Bruce's lip and tore slivers of green flesh away. "I want you to know how useless you are, how meaningless."

"And *what,*" Bruce growled, bringing up his knees, "pray tell, are *you*?" He kicked, hard, and Emil sailed backwards across the court, slamming into one of the reinforced, tiled columns that littered the place.

Emil was on the ground, chunks of tile and plaster falling on his head. The column buckled a bit and then something in the roof began to sag. Emil stood up slowly as Bruce moved toward him, and all of the sudden he was a performer, wiping plaster off himself in a dramatic gesture. He curtsied and spoke slowly. "Haven't you learned yet?" The Abomination stepped to the side, looking around. "I am an *Abomination.*"

The Hulk saw what Emil was about to do and shouted, "No!" at the same time that Emil reared his arm, stepping back further, and howled. Bruce watched the dark green arm drive through the column, taking out a four-foot chunk of girded concrete and tile. He threw the chunk at the Hulk and Bruce felt it collide with his face as he flipped backwards with the force, flying through one of the fast-food counters. He blinked and found himself buried in the ruins of a shiny metal kitchen, steel counters and trays and grills wrapped around him.

The Hulk heard a new sound, a terrible whine, and he looked up and saw plaster falling. *Oh no.* He roared and threw the stove to the other side, desperately hoping the proprietors were nowhere near, much less healthily insured. He felt something like rain, concrete and plaster rain, and he stood up and saw pieces of the roof falling, playing the tabletops like a xylophone.

Bruce looked over the ruined counter and saw Emil at another column. He was tearing it loose, and already the roof was sagging. "No!" Bruce jumped over the counter and felt the wind of the next meter-long piece of column fly past him. "Please, it won't hold, these people . . ." They were falling all over themselves at the staircase, a bunch of them pushing into a doorway next to the restrooms where a sign blazed FIRE EXIT. Too many. They were jammed in. The lights began to fail, blinking like an oddly-timed strobe.

Emil brushed his hands, wiping off the plaster. He went over to one of the tables and looked under it to see a man in a suit cowering there. The man had brown hair and was wearing the remnants of his salad. The Hulk stopped moving when Emil grabbed the man by the arm and hauled him out, picking him up and holding him aloft by the collar.

"Emil!" Bruce looked around, running to one of the columns. The space where the chunk had been torn out was getting smaller. There had to be a lobby, an entire office building above them. This place was going to flatten. "Please!"

Emil held the man aloft and took the man's arm, and the man howled in desperation. "Hush," Emil spat. Then, he looked at the man's watch. And dropped him. Emil looked at the Hulk. "I have to go."

"The roof!" *All the people. The people above.*

"Handle it," said Emil. "You can do that, can't you?" The suited man surveyed his arm presumably to assure himself it was still attached, and joined the pack at the exit. The group was moving, but slowly.

Emil leapt into the air, a green streak, and he tore through the ceiling and was gone. Chunks of plaster and more concrete flew as he passed through.

The Hulk grunted, holding the column, staring at the other one Emil had destroyed. "People! This roof won't hold!" The lights blinked off and on again, more rapidly, and some of them gave, sparks flying. "Take the main exit! Go!" In the distance he heard the sound of sirens. He waited, holding the column. Tons of material pressed down on the incredible Hulk as he wrapped his hands underneath the column and stood, watching the people scrambling out.

The lights went black and a system of red lights sparkled and whined into prominence. The roof groaned again, and the Hulk saw with horror that the two parts of the other broken column were just beginning to touch now under the weight. *Go ahead and admit it, this one's coming down, too.*

No more screams. The people were gone. Sirens howled far out of the tunnel and the court was empty and, he hoped, so was the lobby above. He looked around, preparing to let go, to burst out, try to find the way that would do the least damage. He breathed once, plaster fog filling his lungs, and began to relax his fingers. Then he heard the cry.

The Hulk felt his neck muscles straining, felt as if green blood vessels were about to burst through his skin. He blinked the sweat and plaster from his eyes and looked in the direction of the human sound.

There was a child, a boy, about nine. He was lying at the bottom of the stairs, one blue-jeaned leg horridly twisted and swelled. He was grasping at the stairs, trying to haul himself to the next step.

Something above Bruce cracked and howled. The boy yelped as a piece of plaster smacked him on the shoulder and he shook his head, determined, fighting, and crying all at once.

You and me, then, the Hulk realized. *You and me.*

He leapt. The column gave. The Hulk landed over the boy, a human tent, and curled, his back stiff and high like a cat. He brought his head and knees close and felt the boy curled within him, felt the small heart beating against his knee. He opened his eyes and saw the child, silent, staring into his eyes.

And in one cacophonous howl, the roof collapsed.

CHAPTER 10

organ leaned against his desk and sighed. This was turning into the worst week of his life. "What the hell went on out there, Jo?"

"He downed a plane," said Jo. She shook her head as if she couldn't believe it.

"Mhm," he nodded. He looked up at the screen across from the desk, which showed the Hulk jumping into the air. "He gets past Gamma Team, without, I might add, too much difficulty. He jumps for the plane. It's fuzzy there," Morgan noted. The video was grainy, but Morgan could see Banner leaping up, arm outstretched. The angle of the shot was such that he disappeared behind the nose of the plane. Then the explosion.

"That's not right," said Morgan, shaking his head.

"Sir . . ."

"I can't tell if he even *touched* it," Morgan snapped. "What else can we believe?"

Morgan turned around and circled his desk, and sat down. He picked up his coffee cup and studied it. "Jo, you've been trained to follow gamma threats and study them and catch them. If the Hulk were going to down a plane, is this what it would look like?"

She stared at him, then back at the video. Jo picked up a remote and ran the video back and froze it at the blast. The plane sat in midair, the nose flying apart. "An explosive?"

"That's what I'm asking, shouldn't we be seeing the Hulk tearing through the fuselage or an engine or something?"

"Maybe he's not that predictable."

Morgan stared at his desk. "No, he's not. Because an hour later he crawls out of an evacuated building with a nine-year-old in his arms and hands him over to the po-

146

lice. And the Abomination was there. Witnesses say Blonsky tore the place down and the Hulk was there to help stop him.''

''Others are saying it was the other way around.''

''And how much sense does *that* make?'' Morgan snarled. ''He's supposed to be working with us. This is a mess.''

Jo cleared her throat. ''What are you going to tell the President?''

''Don't even ask.'' He studied her for a moment, running through the events in his mind. She was watching him. She looked wary, afraid he was going to demote her, most likely. He just might. SAFE hadn't been around very long, but they'd accomplished the few missions they'd had so far. They couldn't afford this kind of screwup this early in their operational life. ''I think Gamma Team needs an overhaul.''

Jo shriveled a bit. ''I understand,'' she said. ''I can move to—''

''Not you,'' he said. ''I want your people to go over everything we know and go over it again. Learn to use those weapons. Friend or foe, the Hulk should have been stopped.''

''With all due respect, sir, that's a tall order.''

He nodded. After a moment he said, ''What happened with the call, Jo?''

''The call?''

''Banner called you,'' Morgan said. ''And Tom said half the world heard the conversation. Tell me about that.''

She shrugged. ''I received a phone call from Dr. Banner. He made a reference to Senator Hill's plane and then clicked off.''

''Clicked off.'' He glared at her.

''Yes, sir.''

''And you perceived that as a threat?'' He stood up,

came around beside her in a fluid motion, hovering over her shoulder.

"Sir," she said, "if you get a call from a one-ton gamma-augmented creature who's a known security threat and he tells you to go to the airport because a plane is about to have trouble, you go."

He folded his arms. "All right. But what about the media, monitoring the call?"

She looked at him, her dark eyes searching for an answer that would satisfy him. "A security breach of enormous proportions."

He rubbed his eyes and breathed into his hands. He felt as bad as he was sure he looked. "I want the communications system gone over with a fine-tooth comb. I want every log-in checked. Someone's taking us for a ride, and I want that ride to end. Now."

"I was thinking the same thing," she said.

The screen behind the desk crackled and Morgan turned around. It fizzed white for a few moments before coming alive. There, over the desk, in a nice mahogany frame where Morgan alternated a series of favorite works of art, was the face of the President of the United States.

And the saints come marching in. "Mr. President."

"Sean." The man in the screen was sitting behind his desk. He was wearing a polo shirt and appeared just this side of livid. "So we're working with assassins, now, is that it?"

"I don't have a confirm on that yet, sir."

"Looks pretty confirmed on the ten o'clock news," said the President, scowling. "Do I need to remind you that SAFE is still a fairly unwelcome pet project in some circles? Your budget is as expendable as it is limited, and this Hulk thing . . ." The man paused, swiping his hand across his desk. "This really looks bad."

"Mr. President," said Sean, "I'm not sure he did it."

"Come again?" The chief executive officer looked

bewildered. "I've seen the films myself. He jumped up there and—"

"And it blew up." Morgan closed his eyes. "And I myself have been aware of similar public occurrences that were complete ruses." *Planned a few, too.*

"Yeah, I'll bet."

"Sir—"

"I want the Hulk and SAFE as far apart as possible."

Morgan was ready for that. Jo had her arms folded, head straight, but she was watching Morgan as if she had been personally wounded. "We need him for this one."

"The Abomination thing?"

"Yes, sir, the Abomination thing." *Blonsky is slaughtering people and the President calls it a "thing."* Everything always came down to perspective.

"I just got off the horn with S.H.I.E.L.D., and they think—"

"This is a SAFE operation, sir. Domestic. It's off S.H.I.E.L.D.'s turf."

The President went on as if Morgan hadn't spoken. "They don't trust the Hulk, for obvious reasons."

"Sir, the public hardly knows SAFE exists."

"And this is a terrible way to introduce yourselves."

"I think something big is happening. And I think the Hulk is important to us in solving it. He tore through us like papier-maché, sir. The Abomination can do the same. But I think Banner is still on our side, the same way he was during that mess with Spider-Man, Hydra, and A.I.M., and I want his help."

The President nodded, but not in agreement. "Sean, the public perception at this hour is that the Hulk just killed a national figure for no reason."

"And I think it's wrong."

"And I'm telling you," said the man behind the desk, "that on my side of the fence perception is not just reality, it's *everything.*"

Morgan looked at Jo. Amazing. All those stiletto-wielding years and his true talents were being tested in a game of politics. "Mr. President." Morgan waited a second. "The Abomination is our main concern right now. I've got weird things happening and the Abomination doing increasingly dangerous things. I think, somehow, he may have been involved in the assassination. And if I need the Hulk—"

"Use him," the President interrupted.

"Sorry?"

"I said use him. But it's your head." The man looked down at his desk and looked at his watch. He reached toward an intercom and said, "This conversation never happened."

The screen blinked off abruptly. Morgan shook his head.

He turned to Jo, stabbing at her with a finger. "Let's get on the ball," said Morgan. "I want all systems go."

"He's completely insane," Betty said. She ran a towel through Bruce's hair, and he leaned his head back against her chest as she did so. Bruce's study was dark, lit only by the constant glow from the screen. Betty brought the white towel away and inspected it. "Finally," she said. "I think the third wash finally got all the gunk out."

"Sorry," he mumbled. He scratched his chin and jerked his head sideways while she knuckled at his ear with the towel. Bruce sat facing the computer, like Betty, still dripping wet, wearing only a towel. (Actually, it was a terrycloth blanket, formerly a robe. Life with the Banners was a constant juryrig.)

Betty had been shocked when Bruce had finally made it home in the dead of night. She had seen him on television, the death of the senator so near. Some reports said that he appeared to meet with or pursue another green-skinned creature off the field. She saw the film of her husband emerging from the rubble of the building, the front falling and spewing dense clouds of particles and building materials and glass. And there was Bruce, up from the rubble, his arms wrapped as if in prayer around a child so small he nestled in the groove between Bruce's arms. She saw the people back away. She saw her husband set the child down as the people flinched back, and he flinched himself. And then the police started to move and Bruce leapt. Two hours later he was home.

"I saw a mention on the eleven o'clock report about the kid in the cave-in," Betty said helpfully. He just looked up at her. It was not enough. The plane was bigger news, the strange incident with the collapsing building more like an aberration, hard to reconcile with conventional wisdom and thus bound to be publicly ignored. "I guess we're lucky we haven't been raided yet, huh?"

He nodded, looking back at the computer. "I think so," he said. He looked at her again. "I think we have a guardian angel. Someone is protecting us."

"Morgan?" Betty asked. When Bruce nodded she said, "Then I guess we gotta catch Emil, huh? Earn our keep."

The Hulk nodded, taking her by the arm, gently and bringing her around before him. Bruce scrolled down the Proverb as Betty climbed into place on Bruce's massive right leg, nestled against his torso. "That's true," he said. "But more than that, you're right. Emil is completely insane." Bruce studied her eyes, then the verse. "He's just so—so disparate. At one minute he's sitting in the dark reciting poetry, then he's blowing up planes by remote control. He'll be sensitive and even seem almost—" Bruce struggled for a word "—sorrowful, and then he's throwing columns at me, deliberately endangering the lives of the people in the area."

"Is this still revenge?" Betty asked.

"I'm not sure," Bruce mused. "Morgan suggested that maybe Emil is working with someone, someone who could provide him with technology to get a few of his own grudges out of the way. But what next?"

Betty leaned back against him, folding her arms over her chest, above the edge of her towel. The fold slipped and she busied herself loosely refolding it. "So where are we on the list?"

"He made some progress," said Bruce. "Eyes, hands, heart, and feet are down."

"All the body parts," she mused. "Hm. Except the lying tongue."

"That's different, though. That's interior, the others are all extremities. He took care of extremities first. Personal," Bruce whispered. "Personal! Body parts!"

"I think I understand," she said, "but go ahead and enlighten me anyway."

"I think Emil's played all the personal cards," said Bruce. "And if this is the formula he's working from, then it's possible the next moves might not involve him personally at all. Whatever his deal is, it might fit into the next dominoes to fall."

"Maybe not, though," said Betty. "Too early to say. He got another one, too. The false witness that uttereth lies. He created that 'Abomination' himself."

"By setting me up," Bruce sighed angrily.

"Concentrate on what it means, hon," she said. "It means he's not above making an Abomination if there's not one around to punish."

"Maybe," he said. "Or maybe the press was already an Abomination and he just gave them a part to play. And he punished *me*, not them."

"So what's left?"

"Only two. The tongue—"

"And the person," she said. The last Abomination is a whole person: 'He that soweth discord among brethren.'"

"God, I wish he'd be consistent," Bruce sighed. "We can't know if that's a sower of discord he'll punish, or if—"

"Or if Emil will be the sower of discord himself. But

remember what he said. 'I will be what I am.' "

"And what he is, is an Abomination." Bruce pulled her back against him, gently, and whispered into her hair. "And what *I* am is a fool. That's what he's helping me see."

"No."

"Yes," he whispered. "Emil has played me like a violin. You can't deny that."

"You do what you have to," she said, turning around slightly in his lap to look in his eyes, the towels sliding around on damp skin. "Bruce, listen: you're doing the best you can with Emil. He lures you into situations and he ties your hands behind your back because he *knows*. He knows that the biggest difference between you two is that he doesn't care who gets hurt. Emil has divorced himself from the whole world, he may not even consider himself human anymore."

Bruce turned his head away, looking at the black curtains, the giant green jaw clenched. "And what should I consider myself?"

"You," she said, turning his chin back and kissing it, "are Bruce. A giant green Bruce, but a human Bruce nevertheless."

"I know," he nodded, "I know. But there are times when I'm down there underground and Emil is waiting in the darkness and I realize something. Something frightening."

"What?"

"The savage Hulk would never get in these situations. In the back of my head there's a creature that wants to lash out, that doesn't follow clues and has no interest in science, that would know exactly how to stop this monster. *Exactly* how. And the horrible truth is, it's not by stopping to hold roofs up." He looked into her eyes. "Do you understand? That's the fool he's shown me to be— or that he's trying to show me. That I'm the only one who can stop him and I won't because I'm a fool, because—

because I refuse to be shown what I really am.''

Betty trembled a bit. ''And what is that?''

''A savage,'' he said. ''A beast. An avenger for him.''

Betty's mind filled with images from years of her life she tried to forget. All those years that Bruce had no control, when he lashed out in rage and anger and had no desire to control his strength. And deep inside she knew that she had been in danger so many times, that it was only the last vestiges of the human within the savage Hulk that had recognized her, time and time again, when he could just as easily have exploded, have taken her and squashed her like a bug.

''But that's not what you are,'' she said, sitting up a little, clamping her fingers around his giant jaw, looking Bruce in the eye. ''Even when you were the savage Hulk you were never. . . . Bruce, you never hurt me. And you could have. I've seen violent men. And you had physical, brute strength like no one had ever seen, the same strength you now have. But even then, there was something good in you.''

''But I did hurt people,'' he said, far away.

''You just—'' she started, closing her eyes, breathing on his cheek. She could play the stories he had told her in her head like home movies: Bruce's father the monster, the tyrant, the destroyer; Bruce the child, the victim, the anger boiling inside him and finally unleashed, after all those years of control, in one blinding flash in the sandy desert. She thought about that child, the fists pounding into tiny shoulder blades and ears, the screams of hatred from the father, and she reached out in her mind, grasping at the image. So much could have been avoided. ''You just wanted to be left alone. I know there are demons inside you, Bruce. I know you sit in the dark and brood because you worry that you're going to lose control. But I know in my very bones that you won't.''

''How?'' the Hulk whispered.

''Because you beat those demons, day after day. And

I know that if they were held in check while you really were the savage, then you will always hold them in check now that you aren't.''

"Betty," the Hulk said, half smiling, his giant hands wrapped around either side of her slender waist. "How did you ever get to have so much faith in me?"

She bent forward, wrapping her arms around his neck, the towel falling away. "You have to ask?"

Sarah Josef of URSA, late of the KGB, walked quickly up the stairs to her Greenwich Village apartment. The exercise did her good, legs pumping steadily up the ten flights, her breath barely registering the exertion. Besides, it fit the part she played here, that of an art student at CUNY with a penchant for the hardbody thing. The doorman and she exchanged pleasantries, but he would be one of the few people who would see her—taking the stairs rather than the elevator kept her from spending too much time in small rooms with strangers who might want to talk with an attractive young student, might memorize too many features. Soon, she would be gone.

Sarah reached her door and silently extracted her key as she ran a finger softly down the edge of the door. Her fingertip brushed the tiny hair she had deftly wedged between the door and the frame—a ridiculously outdated trick, but generally effective. She twisted her lip, reasonably satisfied, then placed the key in the lock, turned it, and let the door fall open with a slight shove. The hair fell, black and ghostly, disappearing into the old carpet.

The URSA operative stepped into the entry hall. The television was still playing as she had left it, displaying one of a thousand talk shows that infested American daytime television, she was given to understand, since the programmers had discovered that such nonsense was far cheaper than reruns of old programs. In fact, she was somewhat nostalgic about that, she observed as she set her handbag down on the table in the drab kitchenette.

Sarah had been raised most of her life in what she had
been told was a perfect model of an American town, save
its placement in the outskirts of Moscow. Television was
a major part of their training—she had to learn how
Americans watched it, deferred to it, prayed to it.

In fact, Sarah was speaking English with her fellow
trainees, her "cousins," and watching *The Andy Griffith
Show* when she had been called out of the living room,
all those years ago. Told her father had been killed by an
American operative. Told to mourn.

Sarah stared at the table and saw her reflection in the
glass tabletop, haloed by a chintzy chandelier behind her
head, in what was optimistically referred to as a den. The
chandelier was a tasteless ode to extravagance such as
might be found throughout the United States, from its
ugly glass clumps and bulbs to the ugly rusted gold base
from which it hung.

Her eyes travelled back to her own reflection. She had
received the news of her father's death with a dull, aching
tranquility. She had wandered back to the living room and
sat down beside her cousins, the ache ripping through her,
tearing apart every cell and rebuilding it as she stared
intently at the pixellated images of Andy and Barney. At
the feet of the laughing pair lay the body of her father, a
big man who loved her and provided for her and served
his country honestly and loyally. Who held her on his
knee every third Wednesday when she could have visitors,
who was proud of her intelligence and her placement in
the home of the cousins.

She had wished she were out on the obstacle course,
tearing the throat out of a dummy with a straight razor,
but one had a schedule, and there she sat, the razor in her
mind only, her eyes on Andy. And Andy didn't trust Barney and he only let him have one bullet, ha ha. And there
was a man out there like Andy who had met her father
on a foot bridge and shot him to death and disappeared.
She watched the American lawman on television, sitting

on the porch with a freckle-faced boy, eating the pie offered by the corpulent aunt he kept as a servant. And in his pleasant smiles and laughs she saw a burn of evil and a sound of malevolence, in her dreams the sheriff patted Opie on the head and walked down the street with his gun to the footbridge and shot her father. For years, as Sarah trained, fists pounding into straw men and razors slicing through latex necks and real necks alike, every face was Andy.

Until one day, at the same time the Berlin Wall was falling and the cousins were seeing less and less of one another and some were wondering if there could ever be a place for them, Sarah was given a dossier that finally busted Andy's face, sent the shards of apple-pie warmth and Aunt-Bea slavery spinning into the abyss. And as Mayberry shattered into shards of glass and apple pie, Sean Morgan's face settled onto the wiry frame of the sheriff. And that was the day she grew up.

Sarah stared into the glass tabletop at the reflection of her own head and the ridiculous chandelier halo, the shards clumping back together here, in New York, where it would finally happen. She saw Sean Morgan, her razor finding its mark, blood flying like liquid shards, and she thought she saw the blood blend into the spots of rust on the gold-painted metal base of the chandelier, the whole mess reflected in the tabletop, the room warped and reflected in the gold, a reflection in a reflection. There was a shape on the couch. She heard a metallic creak.

There was a shape in the gold base. *A reflection— someone on the couch, how did I not see—*

Sarah spun around, dropping, gun appearing from her sleeve. Then she sighed.

Emil Blonsky, in all his scaly glory, sat still, one long, clawed hand stretched over the back of the couch, mouth curled in what might have been, save for the monstrous gamma disfigurement, a smile. "Sarah."

Sarah holstered her sidearm and brightened. "You slipped through my defenses, Uncle."

"A hair across the window sill? You read too many Fleming novels," said Emil. "I trust using your apartment is acceptable."

She nodded. "Absolutely. Your underground lair is being crawled over by SAFE agents far too often for you to stay there. And you needn't worry, you won't be found here."

"What about the satellite?"

"The GammaTrac?" Sarah cocked an eyebrow and smiled. "Our person on the inside has taken care of that. The Abomination has been quietly and reliably deselected. You won't even show up onscreen."

"Not until I am there," said Emil.

"Until we are both there," Sarah replied. She looked at his claw where it lay on the couch and saw that Emil held a small box, wrapped in gold paper. Sarah went to the couch and sat next to Emil. He was hideous, it was true. And dangerous. But somewhere in there was the man she had called uncle, who came to visit with her father, all those years ago, before Father's death and Emil's disappearance. Emil had not recognized her when she had first come to visit, but she had certainly recognized him, the tall, strong man underneath, the one who sniffed the air and could find the chewing gum hidden in the secret compartment underneath her desk. Who could do magic. Utterly different, but there underneath the scaly skin of this Abominable thing. She sat on the couch looking at the Abomination and seeing Uncle, and indicated the package. "What's this?"

"Ah," said Emil. He lifted the small box. "Today is the eighth of March, of course."

She shook her head. "The eighth of March?"

The red eyes glimmered. "You know nothing of this—International Women's Day?"

Her cheeks flushed. "The truth is, Uncle, the cousins

didn't observe the holidays everyone else did.''

"Hm," Emil said, looking at the floor. "It is a pity you missed them. When I was a child we lived for the state holidays—all of them in celebration of the citizens and the people. Well." He handed the package to her, and she took it in both hands. "International Women's Day is the day when all the boys bring small gifts for the girls with whom they share desks in school."

Underneath the gold paper was a thin cardboard box, and this she opened. Poking though a layer of styrofoam packing kernels she saw a porcelain head, painted yellow. Sarah extracted the statuette and set it on the coffee table.

"Who is it?"

"Why," said Emil, "this is Princess Vasilissa and the Horse of Power."

Sitting on a small black base was a mound of porcelain painted to resemble a grassy field. Standing upon the mound were two figures—one a golden-haired woman, undoubtedly a princess by the crown and robe. Next to her was a horse, gray and strong, nuzzling the princess's cheek. "The Horse of Power."

"Do you know the tale?"

She felt embarrassed again. Her childhood was filled with training and reruns. "No, Uncle."

"The Horse of Power was a magical creature, wise and powerful. He led his master the archer to the Princess Vasilissa. Vasilissa won the kingdom for the archer, and helped vanquish the evil Tzar. Even the fairy tale said that there were no such horses today—but that they sleep."

Sarah stared at the figures, running a slender hand along the back of the horse. She looked back at Emil. "They sleep?"

"The horses of old sleep underground with the bogatirs who rode them," Emil rasped, red eyes sparkling. "And someday the horn will sound, and the bogatirs will rise with the horses of power, the snow will crack and steam and the hooves will break through, and the bogatirs and the horses of power will reclaim the land, and vanquish the foes of God and the Tzar.'' Emil looked at her, eyes narrowing, and Sarah held her breath. His voice was hypnotic, when he wanted it to be, when he cared about the subject. ''That is the legend, anyway.''

She shook her head. ''Thank you.''

''It is a small thing, a child's gift,'' Emil chuckled. ''It saddens me that you know so little of the culture. Especially when you work for an organization that holds the restoration of Soviet culture as one of its primary goals.''

''My reasons for belonging to, for working for URSA, are my own,'' she said.

''And do *all* of them center on revenge for the death of your father?'' Emil asked.

''My father believed in something that Russia does not. He served the Soviet Union. I was raised for that same purpose,'' she said. ''The country doesn't even know itself anymore.''

''That may be,'' Emil scratched his scaled chin. ''But the country you knew, the Soviet Union I knew as a child, were far different from the Russia of Nicky and Alexandra's Russia. Identities of states change. I may be terribly romantic about the past, but all states evolve.''

''Do you think the move away from Communism was an evolution?''

He sighed. ''I don't know. Sometimes I think perhaps the move away from old-fashioned feudalism was a mistake. But it's hard to be fair. I miss the Soviet Union because I knew it as a child. Do I think about bread lines? No. Wretched food? No. I think about *Sputnik* and parades and public performances of Prokofiev's *Alexander Nevsky*. I miss the pseudohistory that tied Kruschev's Russia to the Horse of Power. So many falsehoods and truths, and what do I miss most? International Women's Day.''

Sarah looked down at the statuette and somehow saw

Andy Griffith shooting it to smithereens. "Tell me about my father."

"Karl Josef," Emil nodded. "Karl was a good man, and I mean that sincerely. I met Karl in grade school. He was an excellent marksman, and when he was twelve your grandfather gave him a competition-style rifle, a beautiful piece. I remember he used it forever. There was a time in Istanbul when I wasn't sure he was alive, and we had another three days before our intended next meeting. I was afraid I'd have to go home without him, tell your mother the awful news. And I heard that rifle of his, across the city, while I sat in a café. It was a good rifle—distinctive."

"Yes," she said. "I know."

"Ah. Of course." He sighed. "As it happened, your mother passed on before Karl did. And I was not the one to break the news to you, because I was sent almost immediately to the United States again. By that time I dare say I would not have recognized you anyway. Those were heady times. I don't think Karl and I had had the chance to see *you* for five years. When you showed up underground, I had almost forgotten that there *was* a Sarah Josef."

"You're a hero, Uncle, do you know that?"

"A hero," Emil replied, setting the glass down. "They have a fine way of showing it."

"What do you mean?"

"Sarah, the government you are trying to revive hung me out to dry the moment I became *this*," Emil spat, holding out his claws. "They wanted nothing more to do with me. All lines were closed. I couldn't even get in touch with my *wife*. Would you believe they told Nadia I was *dead*?"

"I know," Sarah said. "But there are those who talk about you, Emil. Who know that there was an operative called Blonsky who came to the U.S. and fought their champion—however a misunderstanding that might be—

the Hulk, and was turned into a monster. URSA knows about that. You're a model of dedication. It's not the foul bureaucrats who betrayed you that URSA wants to restore to power. They want to give it a better try, to do Communism *right*. No backstabbing, no interdepartmental intrigue. You are a model for that kind of dedication.'' She heard herself talking and saw him watching her and she stopped. She sounded like a fool, but she continued. ''Our plan is the perfect end to the standing government. So much will be accomplished when the Russian Embassy is destroyed by the United States government before the eyes of the nation. The Cold War will be dug up and reheated within hours. The new government at home will be in place, guaranteed, by the time you get there, Uncle. And I'm sure you can find a pl—''

''No,'' Emil said. ''When this is over, do what you will. The Abomination will be no more. You can make the world over in whatever image you like. I have my own plans.''

''And I mine,'' said Sarah. ''And they start with the death of Sean Morgan.''

''Oh, yes,'' said Emil, and he smiled. ''No safety net for him, I'm afraid.''

CHAPTER 11

S he hasn't taken a lot of visitors," said the ambassador's assistant, whose name was Krupke.

"I'm very pleased that she agreed to see me." Betty walked with her hands on her handbag, pressed against her belly, as if in supplication. They were walking along a brightly lit hallway that shone of gold and marble. At the end of the hall was a large, glass, double-door, exit which looked out onto a sun deck and a lovely garden, perfect for entertaining. As daughter to General Thaddeus "Thunderbolt" Ross she had spent time in consulates before, at Christmas parties and the like. As a girl, places like this had made her nervous—all the crystal and china, the prefect rugs. As an adult, she felt the paranoia coming back, the sense that at any moment she would stumble and knock something priceless onto the floor and into a thousand pieces.

"She didn't agree," came a voice. A tall, athletic-looking man in a dark suit appeared from an office and joined Betty and Krupke.

Betty looked up. The man was perfectly framed by the office door behind him, a large rectangle of dark wood behind a perfectly triangular torso. "I'm sorry?"

"Greg Vranjesevic," the man said, extending a firm hand, which Betty grasped and shook.

"Oh! Mr. Ambassador," she said. "I'm Betty Gaynor, Richards College."

"I know," he said, smiling. He had a disarming smile. Betty bit her lip. "Should I call you Mr. Vran—"

"Vranjesevic?" He grinned, saying the name quickly. Betty processed the sound for about the fortieth time and still couldn't decide if it sounded like Fran-chez-eh-vick or Vrahn-yez-eeh-veesh. Greg saw her trying to mouth it and said, "The problem is that you're trying to imagine

164

it written in Arabic letters. Call me Greg, everyone does.''

"Thank you," she said, staring at the tall man. "You said that Nadia didn't want to see me?"

"It's not that," said Greg. His English was almost perfect, with the slightest accent, a hint of Bela Lugosi to drive the locals wild. "It's just that she hasn't much felt like seeing anyone since the incident at the Langley. But I thought perhaps it's time she came out of her shell a little bit."

Betty nodded. Bruce had wanted to talk to Nadia Dornova, to see what else might be learned from her. And since Bruce was big, green, and a fugitive, Betty was the only choice for the job.

Betty nodded. "She's something of an idol of mine," she lied cheerfully. "And my class has been studying *Antigone*, and the relation of religion and piety to the state. I thought perhaps I could talk to her. But perhaps—"

"That's fine," said Greg, nodding equally cheerfully. He seemed to come just short of winking at her. Betty looked past him into Greg's office. There was a man by the window muttering into a cellular phone, in an equally severe suit. She heard a Midwestern accent and saw the man look away from the lovely curtains and throw her a glance, nodding. A SAFE agent.

Greg tapped her on the arm and led her down the hall to the door onto the deck. "At any rate," he said, "if she won't come out of her shell—perhaps you should go in?"

Betty opened the door and stepped onto the deck which buttressed the garden and heard the door click shut behind her.

Greg entered his office again and said, "Who is she?"

Julius Timm clicked his phone shut and stuck it in his pocket. He shrugged. "Upstairs said let her in. She's safe, that's all I can say."

"Really? Safe or SAFE?" Greg frowned, sitting at his desk. "That's all you can say? I have an American agent in my office and another one waltzing down the hall and even the KGB tells me to be nice to her, and even they aren't sure why."

"Cooperation," smiled Timm, "is a wonderful thing."

"All *I* can say," Greg mused, putting his hands behind his head, "is that I hate being out of the loop. So the KGB is cooperating with SAFE, is it? And Nadia knows something?"

Timm shrugged. "Can't hurt to have a visitor."

"Is she really a professor?" he said.

"Oh, yes."

Greg frowned again. "Fine. But remember—you assured me that this woman had been checked out by both governments, and that at the very least she's not an assassin."

"She's not an assassin."

"So who is she?"

"Betty Gaynor."

Greg resisted an urge to pummel Timm into the ground. "Who is she really?"

"A very helpful angle, hopefully."

Sunlight dappled the garden and lit the water in the fountain. Betty looked around her, stepping out on the stone deck. Here and there statues danced and played instruments, moss grew out of stone navels and mouths. Betty held up a hand to shield her eyes and looked back, to the stone wall on the other end of the garden. Ivy covered the wall, and she caught the blue glint of a peacock wandering by. Then she saw the garden chair and the blonde woman on it. She wore a silk kimono, a cup of coffee by her side.

"Ms. Dornova?" Betty stepped off the deck and onto the beautifully manicured lawn. Nadia was staring at the peacock and looked up.

"Yes?" Nadia frowned, but it was an almost sweet frown, as if she didn't want to be rude.

"Hello, I'm terribly sorry to bother you."

"Are you a reporter?" Nadia threw a quick glance up and down Betty's blazer and skirt.

"No, I'm a teacher."

Nadia sat up a bit as Betty stood by another lawn chair, fingering the iron lip of the chair back. "What can I do for you, Ms.—?"

"Gaynor," Betty said. "Betty Gaynor." She held out a hand and Nadia took it. Her grasp was timid, as if she were floating and afraid to touch anything lest she gain weight and fall. Nadia had been here, at the consulate, ever since the incident at the Langley. She was not giving interviews. The show did not go on. Betty continued, "I read about what happened, what happened to you—"

"Not to me," Nadia shook her head. "Everyone but me."

"If I may," said Betty, gently, "everyone *and* you. You were the target. He did this to hurt you. And it worked."

"Ah, you're a psychiatrist."

"No," Betty said, smiling. "I was almost a nun, once. And I've been a counselor, but, as the saying goes, I'm not a licensed therapist."

"I don't know why that comforts me."

"I teach a religion class at Richards College. Ostensibly I'm here to ask you your thoughts about *Antigone*. Since you play her every night, perhaps you had some insight."

Nadia leaned forward and picked up her glass of tea. She lowered her sunglasses, smiling. "Please," she said, "sit down. I can't believe how rude I can be. Would you like some iced tea?"

Betty thought about that as she sat down on the ornate iron lawn chair. "Iced tea? Where does a Russian girl develop an affinity for iced tea?"

"On tour in Texas, that's where," laughed Nadia. "I know what you mean, though." Nadia pushed a buzzer on the small table and shortly thereafter, a servant appeared in the garden. Nadia spoke a quick Russian word and the servant disappeared again.

Nadia leaned back. "Ostensibly."

"Hm?" Betty's tea appeared and she thanked the waiter graciously as he dissolved through the stone and moss and back into the consulate.

"You said that *Antigone* was what you were here about, 'ostensibly.' "

Betty smiled. "Very good. Very good." She sipped her tea.

"I don't know why I feel like talking to you, Ms. Gaynor. Perhaps it's your disdain for a straight answer. Or maybe it's just the hint of fallen nun about you."

"Betty," the fallen nun said. "Call me Betty."

"Not easy to get into the consulate. They let me in because I'm the ambassador's girlfriend."

Betty looked at the peacock. "Do you ever want to go home, Ms. Dornova?"

"Nadia. Sometimes."

"Why don't you?" Betty asked, and then she felt the harshness of the question.

Nadia didn't seem to consider it harsh, or ignored that. "Things change. People are gone. It's a cliché to say you can't go home, but it's not any less true."

Betty shifted her weight and sipped her iced tea. "You were married once."

"Yes," Nadia nodded. "For about six years."

"What was his name?"

"Emil," she said. "Emil Blonsky. My—what's that other cliché?—my high school sweetheart? We shared desks when we were young."

"Really?" Betty laughed. She wasn't sure why that was funny, except that she was trying to picture the Abomination behind a child's desk. The moment she caught the image the green monster shrank in her mind, and all the lost mass became a wave of sadness that washed over her and killed the laughter.

"Yes," Nadia said. "And on March 8th, Women's Day, at the end of our last class together, he gave me an engagement ring." Nadia rested her chin on her palm, a dainty pose, elbow on the arm or her chair. "He was going in the Army, he said, and had bought the ring with his savings. Hard to save money, then."

"Is that what your husband did?"

"You know," Nadia Dornova looked at the peacock, bobbing along, blue and green feathers glinting, eyes watching. "There are cultures in this world where a man is not known for what he does. You meet people at a party and you ask what books they read, what films they watch—even what they like to eat. Where they like to go in the summer. And what they 'do' never even enters the conversation. America, I have found, is not one of those cultures." She arched an eyebrow. "And neither was the Soviet Union. Yes. He was in the Army. And I think it's common enough information that he was with the KGB."

"My father was a general in the United States Army," said Betty.

"Still alive?"

"No," she said, "but he died recently."

"I'm sorry," said Nadia. She had such a sweet face. Such a sad, sweet face. "My husband died several years ago."

"How did he die?"

Nadia's eyes grew wide, but not in an insulted or intruded-upon way. She simply seemed to be sizing Betty up. She thought for a second and cleared her throat. "He was away. He went away a lot in those days. All I can tell you is that he didn't come back." She shrugged. " 'Terribly sorry, Mrs. Blonsky, here's your widow's pension.' Twenty-six and a widow already, where does one go from there?"

"Where did you go?"

"I went to work just like always," Nadia sighed. "I was a dancer, but never the angel of the stage that I wanted to be. Slowly they let me move into acting, and I turned out to be fairly good at it. And then, a few years ago, I defected."

"Why?"

"Too much," she shook her head, "too much past at home. Too many memories. And let's be frank, Betty. For years the only thing my government saw fit to spend money on was weaponry. We had *you* to race against, after all. Lines for everything. *Everything!* Finally I just, I guess I just thought, what am I doing here? Am I waiting for Emil to come back to life, spirit me off to some hidden castle? I decided to take my life into my own hands. So the first thing I did was leave the country."

Betty looked down at the table, fingering the rivulets of condensation on her glass of tea. "Do you ever think about Emil?"

Nadia chewed her lip. "What kind of question is that?"

"I don't mean to be rude—"

"No," Nadia smiled. "You ask a lot of questions, but you're anything but rude. I mean, what do you want to know? Do I think about him every day?"

"I guess," said Betty.

"Let me tell you," Nadia tapped the armchair. She tilted her head and her blonde hair swayed magically, betraying a hint of gray at the sun-dappled temples. "Emil had a grave. No body, but a grave. Decorated beautifully, with fine chiselling and a picture of him, that mountainous man with a perfect nose and a beautiful smile—the one picture I could get him to smile for. I sent him back to the photographer after the first batch with orders to *smile* this time. And when first he died, I went there every day." She shook her head, stretching out the words. "Every day. I felt as if I could talk to that stone and that piece of earth, even without a body in it, and he could hear me. You know, we're clay, that's what they say, ashes to ashes, dust to dust, and all that. So I thought, he's in the earth, somewhere, all of us will be. And in my mind I saw the earth passing my words along to him, like an operator, you know?"

Nadia gave a short laugh, through her nose, more a sniff. "And every day I talked to him, sitting on this little stone bench, about what happened that day. How long the lines were, how nasty the people at the commissary could be. And I cried each day when I left. And at night I cried, alone in that big bed. And after about a year, I skipped a day."

Betty leaned forward. "How did you feel?"

"Horrible," Nadia shook her head emphatically, her eyes wide. "I felt like a monster. Like I had betrayed him by not visiting his earth."

Betty thought. She was supposed to learn about Emil. "Was your husband a religious man?"

Nadia thought. "In his way. Emil was a quiet man. He worked very hard. He very much believed in the purpose he served in the State. But to be honest, he kept to himself a lot of his feelings about things."

"Did you keep visiting the grave?"

"Hah! After skipping it once, I went back the next day. The next month, I skipped another day. And another. And after a time, I was visiting him once a week. Once a week, and we would talk, I would catch him up and the earth would pass Emil my message."

"And when you left?"

"When I left I was still visiting him once a week. And—this is silly, Betty, but—" Nadia looked around and said, "I'll tell you a secret!"

Betty leaned forward expectantly.

Nadia reached into her pocket and fished around, finally drawing out a small glass vial. She held it up, showing it to Betty. Inside of it was about two inches of packed earth. "I took this with me."

"What is it?" Betty asked, but she knew.

"It's earth from Emil's grave." She clasped it in her hands and said, chuckling. "I know, it's a stupid, girlish thing to do. But I thought, the earth is still magical. I wanted some of it to carry here, to talk to."

"You talk to the vial?"

"Well . . ." Nadia tilted her head. "Sort of. I carry it around. I pray with my hand upon it, sometimes. And soon—I haven't found the right place for it yet, but I'm going to plant this, mix this earth in, perhaps under a new tree. I have a new house upstate, if I stay, if I feel at home there, I think I'll mix this in, and the tree will be Emil's new grave for me."

Betty nodded, smiling. "You carry him around with you."

"In my own way. We all do that, don't we?"

Betty said, "Of course we do."

"But of course," Nadia shook her finger, "I know this isn't what you wanted to talk about."

"Hm. I'm not sure." Betty sipped her iced tea again and said. "I have a confession to make."

"Please. It's all the rage these days."

"My husband worked for the Army as well," said Betty. "A long time ago."

Nadia saw the distant look in Betty's eyes and said, "I'm sorry. You're a widow, as well?"

"No," Betty said. "Not a widow. He was in—an accident. A horrible accident. He, ah, hasn't been the same since."

Nadia closed her eyes and bowed her head slightly. "I could say a thousand things you've heard before. Is he still with you?"

"Yes," Betty said. "Actually, I knew him, but the accident was before we were married. God, we were both so young. And I—'' She shook her head, not finding the words.

''What?'' Nadia asked softly.

''I always wonder, what our life might have been like, if things had been different. If we could go back, and make it go away, everything we didn't want, and keep what we did. Does that make sense?''

''Yes, of course,'' Nadia sighed. ''Absolutely it makes sense. What is it like?''

''He keeps to himself,'' Betty murmured. ''He sits in the dark. He opens up sometimes, when I pry at him.''

''And does he ever let you in?''

Betty had to smile. ''Yes. Thank God, yes. But it's so hard. So much to get through. The fact that his life has gone on now for so long like this.''

Nadia pushed back her hair. ''And your life?''

''My life is— My life became wrapped up in his so long ago that I can barely separate them.''

''Are you going to stay?''

''I can't imagine not staying.''

''So here we are,'' said Nadia. ''Widow to the dead and widow to the half-living.'' Betty looked up at her, startled by the irony of the statement.

''Maybe we're both.''

''What do you mean?''

''I mean—'' Betty wanted to tell her everything. *He's alive! He's alive and he's a maniac!* But she was thinking about Bruce and about the need to keep secrets. Nadia knew nothing of Emil, she felt certain, nothing of today's Emil. There was nothing to tell her. Finally she said, ''I mean, maybe my husband is dead, in a way. Maybe the man I knew is dead. Sometimes I think that. In the same way that the girl I was is dead. And I *grieve*, God, I grieve for what we were. And then I look at you and your vial of earth and I say, whatever happened to Emil, he's alive. The Emil you knew will always be alive.''

Nadia whispered, ''And maybe the husband you

knew, somewhere, will always be alive." She looked at Betty, and the blue eyes locked in. "The past is alive in us, Betty. We carry it and we grieve like widows and orphans, but it's there, and it's real. Thomas Hobbes said that memory and imagination amounted to the same thing, called different names for different purposes."

Betty sniffed, wiped her eyes. "My God, an educated actress."

Nadia smiled, a bit proudly, "But of course. And never underestimate the power of a good book of quotations for lively conversation." Nadia took Betty by the hand. "You must promise me something."

"Yes."

"I don't know you or your husband or his problem. But stay with him. Or don't. But be true to yourself, the living, walking Betty Gaynor that you are today. Explore what he is *today*. And if the present sends you apart, then go. And if you stay together, stay. But don't let the past run your life. Don't let what he was color your life with him as he is."

Betty wiped her eyes again and looked at her watch. "Oh!" She frowned. "I have a class. I have to—"

"We'll talk about *Antigone* another time."

"I have to be honest," said Betty, leaning forward. "I wanted to help, you know? But I think you've helped me more than you can imagine. And we haven't even gotten to—"

"To my problems?" Nadia laughed, waving a hand. "Not to worry. I'll be back on stage soon," said Nadia. "Just a little exhausted. I couldn't understand why I would be the target of this thing, but I have to go on."

"We really do, don't we?"

Sean Morgan swiveled around in his chair and regarded the split screen on the wall. There were two men staring at him. He sighed and ran his fingers through his sandy hair, then with his right hand grasped the space between his thumb and forefinger of the left, squeezing the nerve, and felt his fresh headache slowly ebb away. "I wish I had more to tell you two."

"Be straight, Colonel Morgan," spoke an American voice belonging to the man on the left. He was a balding man, in shirtsleeves, a pair of reading glasses tucked into his breast pocket. "The Company wants to know what you're up to on our turf."

"I would hardly call the Russian Consulate," spoke the next man, in a Russian accent, "the 'turf' of the CIA."

Morgan cleared his throat and folded his fingers together. "General. Director. Listen. We're just exploring a lead or two in an operation. The source happened to be at the consulate, so we sent our man there."

The CIA man leaned forward. "Report says there's a visitor there now, but it's a woman. Is she one of yours?"

Morgan looked at the director. "We're using her in this Abomination business. She's a professor."

"Does she have any connection with the Hulk?"

"I'm sorry?"

"You're also using the Hulk, does she have any connection with the Hulk?"

"None at all," Morgan lied. "Betty Gaynor is a religious studies professor at Richards. She has no connection with the Hulk whatsoever." He paused. Back up. "Except, of course, that both she and the Hulk are now trying to help us find Emil Blonsky before he does anything dangerous. Anything else, that is."

The general spoke up. "I trust you have not forgotten that Blonsky is to be delivered to us."

"Not at all," Morgan said to the Russian. He turned to the American. "You don't have a problem with that, do you, Jim?"

"We're making our own arrangements with General Voyskunsky."

"Good," said Morgan. "You two told me I could run

my operation and get Blonsky, and I think it should come as no surprise that that means SAFE is going to wander into your yards a little bit. Back off, guys. Cut me a little slack here.''

The CIA man grinned. "Right, right. Just don't take too many liberties.''

"Wouldn't think of it.''

After a few more words the screen went blank. Morgan rubbed his eyes and felt the headache coming back. Betty had better get her little interview over with. Someone was liable to take a picture.

He drummed his fingertips. Who was he kidding? Sending Betty into the consulate was dangerously close to blowing her cover. But Banner had agreed with the idea. Nadia had looked like a good source of information, and all had agreed that Betty, with her fine possibilities for commiseration, was the prime candidate. Should it matter that chances were that this would ruin Betty Gaynor, professor? Maybe and maybe not. He had to think.

Morgan looked at the clock on his desk as the printer next to the telephone began to hum. It was a transcript of the meeting with Nadia, which seemed to have concluded. He read it quickly and shook his head, looked at the clock again. He had a lunch date with the Hulk.

CHAPTER 12

Y ou want to set down somewhere," Morgan asked, "or just circle?"

Bruce looked the SAFE director up and down and smiled. "Where are we gonna go?"

"Go ahead and circle, Bernie," Morgan shouted over his shoulder to the pilot at the front of the hovercraft. The Hulk saw the pilot nod once and flip a few switches on the display in from of him. Morgan tossed the Hulk a soft cellophane tube as they passed under the raised arm of Lady Liberty.

The Hulk snatched the tube out of the air and unwrapped his sandwich as Morgan did the same. He raised a green eyebrow. "Turkey."

Morgan leaned on the rail, surveying Ellis Island. "Hope you're not a vegetarian."

"Betty tells me to stay clear of red meat. She'd approve of this." The Hulk chewed and leaned on the rail. "We have to stop meeting like this. What's happening?"

"Your wife just finished with Nadia."

"Okay," said the Hulk. "And?"

"I want to use her."

"Don't you have employees of your own, Colonel? I think Betty's done enough."

"No," said Morgan, wiping his mouth with a paper napkin. "I mean Nadia. I think she could be of use."

Bruce looked down at the water as they began to follow the edge of the island. He tapped the rail a few times, absently. "No."

"Blonsky's got a soft spot for her. He wouldn't harm her. I think maybe she should be brought in."

"Look," the Hulk shook his massive head. "Obviously I'm not in charge of Nadia. But I advise against it. Do you realize she doesn't even know Emil is still alive?"

"I realize that."

"No, see . . . Emil even kidnapped her once, tried to tell her himself. But he backed off. I think he knows that would crush her. She thinks the Abomination is a monster."

"He is a monster."

"Morgan, *I* convinced Emil not to tell. I convinced him to let her go." He looked out at the clouds. It was cold; even Morgan was shivering a bit beneath his topcoat. "It would be—"

Morgan came closer, stood next to the giant. "What?"

"It would be a betrayal. I can't help but feel that. Emil has this idea about my sense of honor; it's a sore spot he keeps hitting. Putting his wife in the line of fire—"

"Ex-wife," Morgan said. "*Widow.* Have you forgotten who we're talking about here? I'm not interested in sparing Blonsky's feelings. He's put too many people in danger. My God, you were there underground, you were there on the field. What does it take with you?"

"What do you want?" Bruce snapped. "We'll stop him."

"We haven't stopped him yet."

"Don't you think Nadia's been through enough? That woman has been the focus of one of his attacks, you want to turn around and tell her that her husband is *alive,* and it's *him*? How many old wounds do you want to reopen?" The Hulk looked down at the SAFE director, watching his face. Morgan's eyes were sunken; the man looked like he hadn't been sleeping. "All I see coming from that is failure and misery."

Morgan's head trembled a bit and he moved his lips, then closed them. Then, abruptly, he threw down his sandwich. "All *I* see, Dr. Banner, is a man who refuses to do what it takes to get the job done."

"What?"

"You heard me," Morgan snapped. "I've gone to bat for you, Banner. I've kept the heat off you even though you're believed to have blown up a senator on national television. I have the executive office and S.H.I.E.L.D. breathing down my neck, and so far you've delivered zilch. And when we think we have an angle on Blonsky you *back down*. You *react*, but you refuse to *act*."

"That's not true," Bruce said.

"Isn't it?" Morgan was a couple heads shorter than the Hulk but stood next to him, dressing Bruce down like a cadet. "This guy is a killer. He's not to be coddled."

"Morgan," said the Hulk, "I don't know if you remember, but this is *my* operation. You put me in charge, and if I think we don't use Nadia, then we don't use her. What on Earth do you want to do, use her as some sort of negotiator? A hostage?"

Morgan shook his head, exasperated. "I have no intention of putting an innocent life in danger."

"That's what it would mean," Bruce countered. "Emil sees we've got Nadia, he'll either feel betrayed or angered, and he'll lash out."

"People are going to die if we don't stop him."

"And this isn't the way, Morgan."

"Oh yeah, I forgot," Morgan said coolly, lips curled, a husky, extremely uncharacteristic anger rumbling through the colonel's voice. "You're *used* to letting people die."

Bruce looked down at the man and felt himself recoil as if struck. He bit his lip, breathed slowly, a long, sighing breath. "So that's it. Morgan, there was nothing—"

"Nothing you could do? You're out with your head hung low, hands in your pockets, walking after midnight. Do you ever wonder, could I have looked up, could I have been watching around me, could I ever prevent instead of just reacting, too little, too late? Do you lie awake at night wondering if you heard the brakes squealing, if you could have leapt a bit faster, could you have stopped the accident? Could you have done it, Banner?" Morgan was searching Bruce's eyes, anger and desperation warbling over one another. "All this power, and for what? Why don't you ever use it right? Could you have done it differently? Could David still be alive?"

It was the longest number of words Banner had ever heard Sean Morgan string together in their short acquaintance. He could hardly credit that this was the same man who didn't flinch when, during their first meeting, the Hulk lifted him up by his neck and almost strangled him. Then, his gray eyes were unblinking, almost uncaring. Now, they pleaded—the eyes of a man long past the end of his rope.

The Hulk closed his eyes. He saw Galactus and the Beyonder and trucks on fire, jelly, glass, and a lake of flame. "Do you really want to know?"

"Yeah. I want to know."

"No," he shook his head. "I *moved* as fast as I could. I *did* everything I could. I tried everything I knew. I lie awake at night and I ask myself, was there anything more I could do? And the answer is no." The Hulk chewed his lip and said, "And that's the truth."

Morgan turned around, leaned on the rail again, his collar flapping in the cold wind. "It just— I needed to hear that. I guess the truth is, I was hoping you were wrong. I wish there was something you could have done. It's easier to believe that his death could have been prevented. Because the truth is I don't want to own up to my own fault."

"Your fault? You weren't anywhere near there."

"That's right," said Morgan. "And even if I were, like you said, there was nothing I could do. My fault is that I forgot that that happens. That any of us can go at any time, for any reason, for no reason at all. And the only thing we can do about that is be prepared." He thrust his hands in his pockets. "You want to know what I could have done? I could have seen my son more."

Bruce nodded slowly. "How much did you see him?"

"Not much," Morgan said, his voice expertly controlled, yet timorous, choked in the back. "Margaret and I didn't last long, and David kind of knew better than to forgive me for being as—absent as I was. The truth is I don't think he hated me. Frankly, I don't think he gave me much thought. I guess hate would have been an investment. And he knew better than to make an investment when he wasn't sure he could expect a return."

"That's very clinical, Morgan."

"It is, isn't it?" The colonel sighed. "Now is the time to be clinical. The time to involve oneself, the time to feel, to live, not to analyze—that time is gone. The time has come to analyze, and grieve. Except I don't know what to grieve about." He shook his head. "I barely knew him."

"I understand."

"Do you? There's a hole in me the size of my son and I don't know how to fix it because I don't have any idea what I'm missing. All there is is ache and loss, like I lost a limb I never used and now that it's gone I don't know how to repair myself."

Bruce shook his head again. He remembered standing in an underground cavern in an alternate future, trying desperately to connect with a son who had grown up without him. He remembered that boy's twin, lying dead only hours after he was born. And he found, bizarrely, that he envied Sean Morgan, because at least he had *some* time with his offspring.

"You say you didn't know him. At all?"

Morgan thought for a second. "I visited him a few times a year. There was more back when he was a lot younger."

"What kinds of things did he like to do?"

"Apparently he liked driving with his buddy to a monster movie marathon at a community college out near Margaret." Morgan smiled a bit. "I don't really know anything about that," he said. "There are fragments in my brain of him, pieces of him that I can string together to try to fill the hole. But the fragments don't add up to much."

"What is grief?" the Hulk whispered.

"Hm?"

"Betty was teaching a class on Genesis and one of the questions she kept asking as she prepared was, 'What is grief?' The most common kind of grief is *this* thing, when we lose someone. But I think that's not really accurate, not an accurate way to think about it. We think of grief as the pain we feel over something being gone from our lives. But I think grief is something else—it's the pain we feel about what we didn't do to make the most of what we had. The pain we feel about not making things happen differently. Sometimes I think grief is how people wish that they had the powers of a god. Our hatred of being human, not being able to stop time from passing, people from dying, from getting angry when you should be making up."

Morgan scratched his chin, then splayed his fingers out and in, exercising them. He put on a pair of gloves and held the rail in front of him. "What is it like, then to be as close as you are?"

The Hulk looked down to the street far below, the tiny people scurrying in and out of stores and taxis. "You know, it's funny. There's a joke, a tellingly unfunny joke that goes around the super hero community. The joke goes, 'Why did the chicken cross the road?' "

"I take it the answer isn't the usual."

Bruce smiled and threw him a sideways glance. "The answer is 'unstable molecules.' "

Morgan said, "I don't get it."

"That's the point. It's not funny. Besides the obvious point that Reed Richards's discovery of unstable molecules has been the answer to a lot of questions, it's not funny. Hell, Reed doesn't get it. I asked him once what he thought it meant and he assured me he'd look into it. His sense of humor is not legend."

"So I've heard," said Morgan.

"I mean, you pick a joke apart and you ruin it, but I've thought about this," Bruce said, scratching his head. "And maybe my sense of humor isn't the best, either. But I think it sums a lot of things up in one tiny little piece of nonsense. Here we are, all us 'paranormals,' or whatever they're calling us. We know we scare people. There's religious coalitions that wish all of us would go away; we challenge a lot of long-held beliefs about power and autonomy. They wonder if humanity can actually have any uniqueness if there is a new race of beings, so many of them, who fly and lift tons. They think *we're* Abominations. Years ago, the Avengers set up an office of volunteers who deal strictly with sending pamphlets to people, *Why Thor is Not Allied with the Antichrist,* or some such nonsense. But the fact is a lot of us, we don't know what to do with these powers, either: do we work for the government? Do we work alone, as vigilantes? Why do we have to do *anything,* just because we're this powerful? But I think that joke spells out a real, terrible fear that moves through this community like a virus."

"What's that?"

"That we're *powerless,*" said the Hulk. "That it really doesn't matter. That I can have the strength of a thousand men and Reed Richards can open a window in the living room while he's standing in the kitchen, and it makes *no difference at all.* That we still can't answer the basic questions. We have very different, but still very wrong, answers. We still guess. The Avengers can travel to other planets, but we can't stop war, really. And we sure can't make time move backwards. And even if some of us can come awful close, we never know quite what to do. We can't change human nature. We can't figure out why some people live until they're ninety and die in their beds and other people die in car accidents."

"Infinity is meaningless," said Morgan.

"What?"

"Aristotle and the classical philosophers were deeply troubled by the concept of infinity," Morgan said. "The reason they were troubled was because, they said, if things just went on forever, if there was no limit to how high you could count, for instance, then really, nothing made any difference."

"Right," said the Hulk, "I know the argument. If the end never really comes then progress never amounts to anything. I see what you're relating this to. We keep doing grander and grander things, but it's just more of the same. Nothing changes. It all just goes on. And the worst part is, we still feel pain."

"Yes. Every new loss is fresh, even if it's happened a thousand times. The police handle small-time thugs and you guys get in between the Kree and the Skrulls. And on and on, until the world ends."

"Sometimes it's like there's not supposed to be a finish at all," said the Hulk. "Like infinity, dangerous as it is, is a part of our lives. Nothing stays solved. No one stays happy. No one stays dead. The story never ends. Continuous upheaval. Another damsel in distress, another world threat."

"Until you're dead, for good," said Morgan. "I have news for you; it's the same for us."

"And still I ask, why can't we change? Why do we still grieve our mistakes? Why *can't* I be there a minute earlier, stop the accident, or change the past? Or why do I care? Why does it keep us up at night?"

"Unstable molecules," said Morgan, chuckling softly.

The Hulk muttered. "Yeah, right. Unstable molecules."

Sarah Josef of URSA rolled down the window and leaned out, touching the green button. A striped wooden arm raised itself before her and she drove into the parking lot. A sign overhead said, YOU'LL FIND IT AT ZITHERS. She brought the subcompact three levels down, parking near the elevator on the second lowest level. Sarah took the stairs one level further down and let the door to the stairwell slam behind her as she moved quickly across the parking garage. She turned a corner and heard a whirring, mechanical sound, accompanied by a muffled sound like a chainsaw under heavy shielding. The work on the tunnel was progressing.

Up ahead was a gigantic plastic curtain which swayed with the air-conditioning. A few sawhorses ostentatiously warned anyone who might wander by: CAUTION—MEN AT WORK. Indeed. Sarah nodded at one of the workers who sat on a stool by the black curtain, wearing a Dickeys overall and a hard hat. The man looked up from his magazine and nodded at Sarah. She returned the nod as he held back the plastic curtain for her and she stepped into the guarded, curtained off section.

The work section was about twelve feet across, taking up a corner of the Zithers parking garage. Naturally, all the right people had been bribed. All the right people at Zithers were looking the other way for just so long as URSA needed.

"Comrade Josef!" An agent poked his head out of a hole in the concrete wall and deftly shimmied out. He removed his hard hat to reveal a head of red hair and a Trotskyesque beard of the type many of the URSA boys were affecting these days.

"Andre," said Sarah. Bending her knees, she dropped down next to the hole in the wall. "How are we progressing?"

"Right on schedule," replied the URSA agent. "I should say *exactly* on schedule. We just broke through the wall into the tunnels under the consulate."

Sarah looked back at him, then peered again up the dark tunnel. "You haven't gone through, have you?"

"No. Waiting on your orders."

"All right," she said, looking once at her watch. "Get everyone together."

• • •

Far above them and a half-block away from the land on which Zithers's parking garage sat, a new guard sat down at the security desk in the Russian Consulate, relieving the prior shift. The first thing David Selznick did, after saying good-bye to the leaving security guard, was to bring up all remote cameras and survey each of them, as per usual. Camera Thirty-Five showed a corner of one of the access tunnels on the east side. Something metallic was poking through the wall. Selznick took a couple of minutes resetting the cameras so that numbers Thirty through Forty, the east side, duplicated Twenty through Thirty, the west side. Satisfied that the east side underground was now safely dark, Selznick got up and went to get some coffee.

Sarah surveyed her team, consulting her watch once more. "Now, gentlemen," she said, as Andre and Stefan struggled to remove the gopher from the tunnel. The machine that had chewed its way through nearly a quarter mile of concrete finally emerged, and the two men handled it, especially the jewel-embedded teeth, with great respect. Once the gopher was on the ground Sarah said, "Our man upstairs should have killed the cameras on the delivery/ maintenance tunnels. Andre, let's see it."

Andre nodded to her and wiped the sweat off his brow, then turned around to regard a unit that stood next to the wall, covered in a blanket. It seemed to be shaped like a large globe, of the type one would find in a museum store. Andre pulled the blanket away and Sarah practically gasped at the beauty of the green glow beneath.

It was a gamma device of a kind the world had never seen. The circular, shiny top glowed green and opaque, the metal frame shiny and dark and tractor-mounted for easy transportation. It was a stunning piece of work. "The gamma bomb developed by Bruce Banner for the American government was the beginning of an era," she whispered. "But only the beginning. This device is the culmination of that work. It's beautiful, isn't it?"

Andre regarded the bomb with a shrug. "It's dangerous, I'll give you that."

Sarah grinned. "I'm not a cartoon character, Andre. I'm not writhing in ecstasy over a bomb and failing to respect its awesome destructive power, I assure you. Oh, you're absolutely right. This device is dangerous. But it's perfect poetry, chiseled down and refined, so different from that fifteen-foot-tall monstrosity that Banner built in the desert." She ran her hands over the opaque green metal that topped the device. "And if I were to take it apart, and lay the pieces out, every piece would proclaim it to be an American creation." She gestured to two agents, who lifted the bomb up and shoved it into the crawlspace. The two men began to clamber in, followed by Andre and Sarah.

"What do you mean?" Andre said.

Sarah chuckled, crawling by the light of the lamps on her head. "Andre, it wouldn't do any good to just blow up the consulate, now would it? This bomb is a calling card. Our person inside SAFE has provided me with everything the designers needed to riddle every part of that device with identifying serial numbers—SAFE serial numbers. To all intents and purposes, the materials are SAFE. And whatever is removed after it goes off will reveal that."

"Commander, we're about there," a voice crackled in Sarah's ear.

"Fine," she said, "let me handle the entrance to the tunnel."

The two men pressed against the sides of the crawlspace as Sarah pushed through and between them, finally moving in front of them, passing the gamma device as she did. It smiled green and softly humming as she passed it. Sarah blew a few strands of hair out of her face and reached the end of the crawlspace.

There was a hole made of Sheetrock in the end of the crawlspace, through which poured a steady stream of white light. She could make out white-painted concrete walls on the other side. She breathed a few times and closed her eyes, holding up a hand behind her, telling everyone to wait. Sarah did everything on her own time.

Pebbles chewed at her elbows. She blinked and that pain went away. She had scuffed the top of her head while crawling past her two agents. That pain too went away. She was lying on her belly in a hole, a bomb at her ankles and a silencer coming out of her vest and into her hand. Sarah breathed again, felt her body become like a wave of energy, moving as one thing instead of a pile of inter-connected bone and muscles and flesh. She was one thing, a fluid, corded wave of energy. She flipped over on her back and brought her knees up to her chest, and let her boots fly back, then forward.

A chunk of sheetrock burst out into the tunnel. Sarah did not hesitate in following through; she shimmied through the hole in the wall. The hole was about three feet off the ground, and she dropped out and crouched in the bits of sheetrock, looking around. Sarah wound her arm several times at the entrance of the tunnel and heard her team coming out, just as the sound of running foot-steps in the delivery tunnel echoed around the corner.

Sarah slowly walked towards the corner. Around the corner, there would be two guards next to the delivery elevator, spending most of their time signing invoices and allowing brie and vodka to go up to the consulate. They would be out of practice. *Right now*, she thought as she stopped next to the corner, *they have heard a strange crashing noise from where I have just kicked through the wall of the tunnel, and now they are running this way. They have their guns in front of them, their arms pumping in sync with their feet. They are scared.*

Sarah looked back at her man Andre and Andre nod-ded. As the footsteps got closer to the corner, Sarah dove.

She hit the ground as the two men turned the corner. The first one gasped loudly, looking down, dancing awkwardly to keep from getting his legs caught up in Sarah's limbs.

Sarah's silenced gun flared once and bore a hole through the underside of one guard's chin, and she rose and slunk to the side as his body struck the ground and she fired again, taking out the second man. Sarah holstered her sidearm and stepped over them, motioning to her team, moving on to the elevator.

Two plastic chairs sat by the elevator entrance, the forty-hour-per-week home of the dead sentries. Sarah bent down by one of the plastic chairs, lifting a styrofoam cup. She raised an eyebrow. "Coffee." Within moments the maintenance elevator was opened. "Andre," she asked, "how long until you can have the timer set?"

"No time at all," he said, as the agents rolled the device onto the elevator.

Sarah drank down the dead man's coffee and winced. It was bitter. "It's your show, Andre," she said. "But I trust you." Sarah looked at her watch. "Stick to the schedule, you guys get out of here, get Andre on the roof across the street, and make URSA proud."

Sarah patted the Trotsky-bearded man on the shoulder and slunk away, back to the crawlspace. She had an appointment to keep. "Hell," she said as she turned back briefly, "make *me* proud and everything will be fine."

Betty stepped out of the ladies' room and into the hallway. Behind her, the glass doors out to the garden patio shrank. The hallway took on the curious yellow hue that indoor lights have just as the sun begins to go down and the eye becomes aware of the dueling light sources. She trusted that SAFE had heard her conversation with Nadia. Of course, not much would come of it, she suspected. Nadia was too far removed from Emil now for any involvement on her part to be of much use, short of ruining the woman's life.

Don't kid yourself. They're not above that. This is the government we're talking about. Betty shrugged inwardly as she approached the security desk at the entrance. Part of her wanted to believe that SAFE was on the side of the angels. They were, after all, instrumental in rescuing Betty from a rogue secret agent who had kidnapped her to keep Bruce in line. But most of her, the Army brat in her, knew all too well that government agencies were not above using people for what they jokingly thought of as "the greater good." Right now, she wanted nothing more than to go home and peel the white tape and microphone off of her chest.

The security guard sitting behind the large, semicircular desk was a different one from the man who had let her pass on the way in. Of course. The shifts had changed. She'd better hurry if she were going to make her six-thirty class. She nodded at the dark-haired Russian behind the desk and stepped towards the exit, which stood adjacent to the metal-detector entrance.

"Excuse me," came the voice of the guard. "Ma'am?"

Betty looked back. "Yes?"

"I'm afraid I can't let you leave just yet."

CHAPTER 13

Sean Morgan walked along the carpeted halls of the Helicarrier to Tom Hampton's GammaTrac station and stuck his head in the door. "Tom?"

The back of Tom's head was silhouetted against the green GammaTrac screen. Tom typed away as another screen next to him lit up with the increased noise level in the room from Morgan's call. Tom looked over his shoulder and Morgan entered, signing. "What's the story with the Abomination?"

Tom indicated a swiveling stool next to his and Morgan lowered his nattily attired self onto it, crossing his arms. "I think he's under again," Tom signed.

The technician went to plug in his voice modulator but Morgan waved at him, saying, "No, that's fine, I prefer your real voice. Under, you said?"

Tom nodded. "The Abomination is lying low. His marker hasn't shown since the thing at the airport."

Morgan frowned. "Great." He looked at a stapled sheet of papers on Tom's console. "What's that?"

Tom picked up the report and handed it to him. "Jo dropped this off earlier. I think you have a copy on your desk as we speak," Tom shrugged, signing. "It's Gamma Team's analysis based on what Banner told us about the last part of the proverb—the sower of discord among brethren."

"Blonsky's next move. What did they decide?"

Tom grimaced. His long fingers flew, speaking. "You ought to ask Jo. But between you and me, I don't think they've discovered a great deal. I mean, the funny thing is, Blonsky keeps switching between being and punishing Abominations. So the next Abomination is sowing discord among brethren. So what?"

"Right," nodded Morgan, signing. "Is he the sower,

or the punisher of the sower? Or both? And who are the brethren to suffer the discord?''

"There's a lot of ideas in there," Tom signed, tilting his head toward the report. "Could be anything. Congress. The UN. Even the Soviet Union, that's *Blonsky's* brethren. But it's all guesswork."

Morgan sighed, stood up. "I'll read my own. Let me know if anything happens. And Tom, run a diagnostic on the equipment. I don't want the Abomination suddenly appearing where we couldn't see him, okay?''

"Right, Colonel," Tom said. The screen next to him danced with light, reporting Sean Morgan's fast-falling footsteps as the SAFE director exited the officelike station.

Tom shrugged and sat back, regarding the monitor. The green hand swept around the screen, the green blip of the Hulk wavering in Westchester, no other gamma readings inside. He pursed his lips and whistled idly, or thought he did. Whatever sound he produced, he had no idea. He reached out and tapped on the screen. Magic words, why not? *Hello? Blonsky? Appear, please. Open sezzme.*

The green arm moved over the screen. Tom focused on the sweep, slowed down the vision in his brain, watched the tiny pixels of green. Westchester, the Hulk blipped. The island, nothing. The Hudson River, nothing.

The arm jumped. Nothing. The arm swept around again and Tom raised an eyebrow as he saw it again, a tiny nonblip, a variation, a *blankout* when the arm passed over the Hudson. A ghost-blip. *What the—?*

Tom turned to the darkened monitor to his left and brought it to life, a sinking feeling coming over him. *Someone inside, someone* ... He logged onto the screen and entered his password. Another second and lines of green code swept up from the bottom of the screen, flying past him. *Let's say you come to rely on a machine to tell you where the monsters are*, he thought to himself. *And*

let's say you're an idiot. It took another minute to find
the subroutine that allowed for identification of large concentrations of gamma radiation, a minute past that to find
the sets of received "names" for those concentrations. It
was impossible, though, to see if anything had been
changed. Tom looked back at the sweeping hand. It was
clearer, now, now that he was looking for it. Each time
the arm swept around, there was a shadow of a blip, a
bare fade of the green, like a deliberate cloak.

Tom called up the modification dates for the various
routines. *Let's see, March 2nd, we were putting the last
touches, I typed in the names the other day, that was
March 4th. . . .* So far, so good. The dates on the labelling
subroutine read March 4th, as expected. Tom frowned.
Not there. He brought up the main routine.

March 8th. Tom felt a buzzing in his brain, alarms
going off. He could spend forever picking through this to
see what was added or changed or he could simply switch
to primary backup. Tom waited another two minutes as
the GammaTrac screen went offline and dark. Then, after
a moment, it came up again. And read exactly the same.

Tom sat back and brought up the modification dates
on the left screen, already knowing what he was going to
see. The changes of March 8th were there, too. Whoever
had done their work had not been stupid. *And something
tells me checking the secondary backup will yield the
same results.*

Tom pushed away from his console and stepped
quickly to the door, moving fast down the hall. He
thought about calling Morgan as he got on the lift down
to his locker, but he wanted to have another look at this
before blowing the whistle. This was his project, how stupid did he want to look? No. He would fix it first.

Tom keyed the combination into his locker, swaying
a bit. He blinked. He was feeling a bit woozy. As usual,
the world swayed in silence, steam rising out of the showers adjacent to the lockers. He saw a few agents with

boxing gloves over their shoulders coming into the locker room as his locker door swung open and he rummaged in his duffel bag. He drew out a rolled-up sweat sock, turned it inside out. The magnetic tape inside fell into his hand and he slammed the locker shut, turning to race back to the lift. The fact was he wasn't sure why he kept a back-up of the routines in his locker, for his own purposes. Perhaps because it was, ultimately, his own neck on the line.

The buzzing in Tom's brain continued. He rubbed his eyes with the back of his hand as the lift opened up and he stepped back into the corridor, headed for his station. The walls blurred past him as he moved, only making his headache worse. Tom turned into the doorway and sat down at the station, flipping a switch and causing the whole station to go dark, slamming the tape into a shiny black maw underneath the screen.

Another two minutes and the screen was dancing again. The green arm swept majestically across the screen. Westchester: the Hulk. The Hudson River: the Abomination. *There you are. Someone's been hiding you.* Tom shook his head and flipped on his voice modulator and then the intercom, keying in Morgan's extension. "Colonel Morgan, you should. . . ."

He looked back at the screen, his head pounding as the room swum like putty and he focused on the green blip. It was growing. It was moving fast, towards the center of the screen. The blip was getting larger. "You better . . . have a . . ."

He choked, feeling the bile in his throat, his eyelids heavy. The blotch of green grew larger, closing in, moving straight up, very fast. He felt a tug and looked over to see a pair of wire cutters, severing the wires of his voice modulator.

He's coming . . . he's coming . . .

Tom spun around in his chair, his head swimming. He

saw the silencer on the gun as it spat once, flaring in the phosphorescent light.

Sean Morgan shot out of his office, jogging down the hall. Tom had started to say something and had been cut off. He stopped jogging and threw a hand to his forehead as the first wave of nausea hit. He shook his head, looking up at the vents. He had been in the business long enough to know when he was being gassed. *Hell.* He kept moving, taking short breaths. He slapped a panic button as he turned the corner and got on the lift to Tom's level. As the lift doors closed, he heard the alarm bells begin to ring.

Morgan spat into the mike on his throat. "Bridge? What's going on?" No answer. The lift whined to a stop, opened up, and Morgan felt himself spilling into the hall. Morgan thought about racing up the bridge immediately but had to check on Tom first. He turned a corner and stepped over a uniformed SAFE agent slumped against the wall. Morgan continued his short bursts of breath and dropped, running a pair of fingers over the agent's neck. He felt a pulse. In Morgan's mind, an animal growled in the distance, the animal sleep, waiting to devour him, a fog lowering for a moment over his brain. He shook it off. *Keep moving.*

Morgan slammed against the wall as the whole of the Helicarrier rocked with an impact like a missile hitting the underbelly. He felt one of the lights along the edge of the wall bust, sparks flying, as the toe of his right shoe crushed it. He pushed off. "Bridge," he growled, the red carpet moving fast under his jogging feet, "anyone . . . masks . . . something hit us; we're under attack . . ." Tom's GammaTrac station was up ahead on the left. He reached the door and propped himself against it, head swimming as he turned into the room and saw that the lights were out.

Morgan's eyes adjusted, his head pounding with the

sound of the alarm, the animal sleep beckoning. The dark
room was aglow with the green of the GammaTrac, and
the first thing Morgan saw was the sweeping green arm
on the GammaTrac screen, moving at a turgid clip, keeping time with the blaring alarms that now reverberated
throughout the Helicarrier. Tom was staring at him,
twisted backward, shoulders against the console, a hole in
his head where his right eye should be, and each time the
green arm swept it lit up, from underneath, the red glop
on the screen.

Not good. Not good. Danger, Will Robinson.

Morgan moved forward, feeling the nausea hit him,
the fog filling his mind, curtains lowering over his eyes.
"Tom . . ."

He bent forward, leaning on the dark console, and
turned around when he heard someone move behind him
in the dark. A figure in a jumpsuit and a gas mask moved
into the green-glimmering light.

Morgan coughed, losing the battle against the animal.
"Jo . . ."

Something metal flashed and he felt a bony hand grab
him by the collar and throw him to the ground. "Don't
fall asleep, Morgan, I want you to know."

"Jo . . ."

"Allow me to reintroduce myself," she said, strad-
dling his chest, a razor in her hand, flashing like a *geisha*
fan next to her eyes and the grille-covered mouth. Her
voice burst through the mask, muffled and harsh. "My
real name is Sarah Josef. I believe you knew my father."

"What do you mean, I can't leave yet?" Betty looked at
the guard. The tag on his chest said David Selznick.

"Well," Selznick said, "we got this message about
you being some sort of . . ." he chuckled, as if a bit embarrassed.

"What?"

"Professor Gaynor, you wouldn't happen to have any identification on you, would you?"

Betty eyed the security guard warily. "I have a class to get to, Mr. Selznick."

"I understand. If you please." He indicated Betty's handbag.

Betty groused, opening her handbag. "I got in without any problem, sir," she said, rummaging through her bag.

She found her wallet as she heard a tinny voice on a headset next to Selznick: "Selznick, we're in place here . . ."

"You know," said Betty, looking up, "I left my wallet outside with Nadia. I was showing her pictures. I'll go back for it."

She turned and began walking fast toward the patio. She heard the security guard call after her. "Ah, that won't be necessary, Mrs. Banner."

Betty stopped and turned around. The man was smiling, genuinely smiling. In his hand was a gun.

The patio doors burst open down the hall and Nadia came in, a pair of men on either arm, dragging her as the woman cursed loudly, "Let me *go!* Of all the nerve." Nadia saw Betty standing there, backing up, and called out, "Greg! Greg!"

Greg Vranjesevic's office door opened and his assistant, Krupke, looked out. He stood there in the doorway, in silence, a strange look on his face.

Nadia stopped before him, fighting off the two men who held firmly to her elbows. "Krupke, what in hell is going on?"

Krupke stared at her, blinking. Then, in one long, fluid motion, the man fell forward on his face.

Nadia screamed, dropping to the suited man. There was something metallic and bloody sticking out of his back.

"There, there, Nadia," came the voice of the man she

knew as Timm. "Don't mind our friend. Mr. Krupke is just dead."

Timm emerged from the ambassador's office, one arm around Greg Vranjesevic, a gun to the man's ribs. The athletic ambassador looked with an ashen face at Nadia and nodded to her as the two men swept out in front of Nadia and began walking down the hallway. "David?" Timm called out to the security guard. "You can play it, now."

The two URSA agents who had Nadia moved into the lobby near the security desk behind Greg and Timm as Selznick hit a button on the security desk in front of him and a tape began to play.

"Greetings, comrades," came the voice of a woman. "This is Sarah Josef of URSA. This tape is being played to inform you of the part you are going to play in URSA's plans, and, frankly, to pass the time for you as you sit out your last hours. We have taken control of the consulate."

Greg howled in outrage and broke free from Timm, diving for a panic button on Selznick's console. The consulate erupted in the blaring sound of security alarms, red lights on the walls beginning to whip around. Selznick brought his gun down on Greg's hand and the man yelped as two more security guards came running up from the east wing. The men reached the lobby, guns drawn, and stopped to regard the security guard.

As Timm and Selznick wasted no time pumping two shots each into the security guards, Betty moved. "Please," Selznick said to the two corpses, "if you don't mind, we have a message to listen to."

Betty heard the ladies' room door shut behind her and Selznick calling out, almost amused, "All right, shut that alarm off. And someone find the Banner woman. She seems to have run off."

And blaring across the PA system, the URSA woman droned on.

CHAPTER 14

Ten years ago . . .

Sean Morgan dropped off of the fire escape and ran down the street in the rain. He turned a corner and found a coffee shop, entered, bought coffee in a plastic cup and a newspaper from the vendor next to the door. He wandered a few yards down the street and took his place on the stoop, shielded from the rain by the awning of an apartment building.

Paris had just gotten hot again, and it was time to get out. Morgan did not look at his watch, did not wish to appear hurried. He waited for Mickey. The dead courier in the apartment building a stone's throw away would be discovered within the quarter hour. He had some time, though not much.

Six minutes later, at half past two in the afternoon, a taxicab turned the corner and pulled up in front of the stoop, splashing water onto Morgan's shoes. Morgan gulped down the remainder of his coffee as a woman got out, walked up the stoop, and rang the bell. Morgan crossed her path as he got into the cab. Morgan slid in, and Darla moved over a bit in the back seat, giving him room.

"My God, you're soaking," she said.

"Let's go."

"Really?" Mickey's eyes met his in the rearview mirror. "You don't think I should just drive around the block a few times?"

"Fine with me," Morgan said. "It was clean. Smoothest operation I've ever seen," he lied, as the cab pulled out into traffic and was lost in a sea of nondescript cars.

"You get him?"

"I got him." Morgan smiled. "I'm tellin' ya, Mick.

I need a challenge. These guys think running a double game is easy, but man, they've never been hustled by the best."

"Ooh," Mickey winked at Darla, who was now nuzzling up against Morgan. She was wearing a dashing beret, very underground-chic, presumably on the notion that no one would suspect a person who dressed like a spy of being a spy. "Listen to the man," said Mickey. "Thinks he's the Muhammad Ali of mole hunting."

"Bite your tongue," Darla laughed, opening her purse. "Jack Dempsey," she said, "or no one at all." She pulled out a manila envelope and tore it open, removing a rubber-banded bundle of papers. Mickey reached back as Darla handed him his papers, and she gave Morgan his. "All right, gentlemen, this is the drill. Sean and I are married and Mickey's the little brother."

"Sorry, Mick," Morgan said.

"I'm used to it by now," Mickey said, zipping through a wet intersection, leaning on the horn as he did. "May as well just call me the chauffeur."

"I promise, next time, you get the girl," Morgan said.

"Oh, Captain Morgan," Darla clicked her tongue, "trying to get rid of me?"

"Not at all," Morgan said. "Just trying to spread the wealth around. I figure we can dig up a companion to play Mickey's wife. How about it, Mick?" Morgan sat up, leaning over the front seat. "That new girl, Cecilia. Helluva driver, I hear."

"No good," Mickey shook his head. "She's a driver, what am I gonna do?"

"I was kinda thinkin' you'd get promoted," Morgan said, throwing a glance back at Darla, who winked at him.

Mickey shot around a corner and barely missed a Fiat, the horn of which sang out and disappeared behind them. The driver waited a long time, making eye contact with Morgan, before he said, "You pullin' my leg, here, Morgan?"

"Hell, no, buddy." Morgan watched his friend beam. "Or should I say, Captain."

"What, you . . ."

"Oh, I guess you hadn't heard," Darla said, leaning over the front seat as Morgan did. "The brass is pretty impressed with our fearless leader here; they seem to think it rubs off."

"All right then," Mickey said. "All right then! Let's celebrate!"

"Fine with me," Morgan said. "Just get us to the other car. After the switch I figure we can kill a few hours before we make the train."

Darla smiled again, but a hint of concern showed. "Sean, now, don't be cocky. We're not home free yet."

"Might as well be," Morgan said.

"It's not in the orders."

"Come on," Morgan said. "A few hours downtime, they want us to sit in an airport all that time? Doesn't sound safe to me." He smiled. "Someone might make us."

"That's the spirit," Mickey said. "Hey, Darla, listen to the master!"

"Yeah, well, they could make us in the local tavern, too. The master could get us killed because he suddenly thinks he's bulletproof."

Morgan grinned sheepishly, but he knew some of the hurt reflected in his eyes. "What, you don't trust me?"

"It's not that," she said. "But you've been cutting it a little close. I mean, that thing with Mansfield in London, you took a few extra risks there, Sean." Darla's brown eyes locked onto Morgan's, and he failed to hold his grin.

Mansfield had been a CIA man, a loose cannon who had started hiring out to all the wrong people. Morgan had spent four days hunting him through the streets of London. Frankly, it had been fun, even if Mansfield had nearly killed him two or three times. It had become a game, for real. Mansfield was a clown, really, a joker in a baseball cap who killed without remorse and bragged openly about his ability to disappear. *See how I can disappear, even in this silly Yankees cap?* And he could. Plainest face you ever saw. Just sucked the light from around him and he disappeared. Morgan had finally settled on foiling Mansfield's London hit and taking out a couple of the double's contacts. And it had been fun.

Only Darla had frowned at the report. The brass had answered his cockiness with a commendation. *Okay,* he wanted to say. *Okay, tell me the rest. Tell me how I'm taking too many risks because it's all I have now.* Margaret had been gone for, what, a year and a half? Her and David, off to Chicago or someplace, so Margaret could work on a doctorate. At first she had come home on weekends, but when was he ever home on weekends? The work took its toll; who wouldn't play the game a little closer when the game was all you had? But let's face it, it was true what Mickey said. He was the best. The best in a long time, anyway. Yeah, that Berlin thing went bad five years ago, but since then? Smooth. Clockwork. Why not have a little fun?

"Yeah, well," Morgan recovered, moving his hand through his blond hair. "Yeah, okay." He looked at Mickey. "Tell ya what, Mick. We'll get a drink at the airport, celebrate there."

Mickey grinned, but there was a twist on the end, as if he felt uncomfortable seeing his buddy lose a minor battle. The taxi turned another corner and suddenly the world was a dark wasteland of warehouses.

"Car's at loading dock seventy-three," Morgan said. Darla's hand was on his lap and he took it, looking at her. There was a coldness in the air. She had dressed him down as much as anyone dared, and she wasn't sure how to proceed. He wasn't either.

The rain poured down on the taxicab in waves, dumping gray and dirty against the windshield, and Mickey slowed down noticeably as he maneuvered between parked trucks and dumpsters and the occasional truck backing out of the loading docks. The light was low, the sun blocked by heavy black clouds, what little daylight there was sinking into the gray stone and concrete and disappearing.

Morgan held Darla's hand, feeling stupid. This was silly. He was acting like a kid. It wasn't him. Darla and him acting like teenagers hunting moles and zipping around with Mickey at the wheel. What the hell was he doing? Something in the back of his head told him Margaret might still take him back. *She might, you know. She might. No offense, Darla, but there's a place I'm supposed to be.* He reached out his empty left hand and swatted the idea aside. That was the danger in getting serious, you think crazy, idle thoughts. *Stay loose.*

Darla nuzzled against him as the taxi whipped around a dumpster and entered the seventy block. "Hey, Sean."

"Hm."

"How about a little vacation? You know, a little fun in the sun?" she whispered. "Cancun? You've got some time saved up, surely."

"Surely," he said idly. On the left a Mercedes flatbed truck was approaching, signalling to pass in the narrow lane between the loading docks. The truck roared up close, flashing, blaring it's horn. "But I like the rain," Morgan said.

Mickey swore. "All right, all right," he muttered, bearing to the right as the truck passed.

"I'm sure they have rain in Cancun."

Morgan smiled. "Yeah." He watched the waves of gray rain pound against the window as the flatbed passed. Through the drizzle he saw four or five men on the back, workmen getting soaked in the Paris rain. Each of them had a parcel. One of them wore a baseball cap.

"Maybe you're right," Morgan yawned. "I'm sorry, maybe you're right. I have been pushing a little hard."

A baseball cap. "Mickey . . ." Through the tidal wave

on the windshield Morgan saw the brake lights on the flatbed flare and loom towards the taxi.

Mickey cursed, hit the brakes, and swerved to the right.

Slow motion, now, as Morgan looked at Darla and saw the inch-wide perforations pushing through the roof of the taxicab. Morgan felt himself looking around, dumbstruck, paralyzed, head swivelling to look at the gang of four on the back of the flatbed, pumping bullets into the top of the car. Something in the front seat burst, and Morgan felt himself doubling over in the back seat, warm sticky wetness pouring red over his hands, something that may have been one of Darla's teeth grazing his cheek.

Bullets hailing in, Morgan reaching for his gun, less than a second having passed since the first shots, and his arm sluggish, moving through quicksand, his shoulder a mess. Something collided dully with his shoulder and Morgan gasped in shock.

Cutting it a little close. Thinking of yourself. Not paying attention. Nothing left, who the hell cares, Margaret gone, David gone, what do I care?

Darla's teeth and Mickey's blood were in Morgan's hair and his own blood oozed out of him like a beer tap, running and soaking and bringing the cold and sluggish sleep to him.

Squiggles of red and black swarmed over Morgan's eyes and blotted out what was left of the sun.

Morgan opened his eyes and the first thing he saw was the glint of steel, a razor high in Jo Carlin's right hand, a muscular, thin arm pulled back, ready to swipe down, fingernails and cold steel glinting in the glimmering green light.

Morgan blinked, fighting the paralyzing gas that still crept through his system, giving sleep free reign. *Move! Respond!*

And sometimes response was not possible, just as the

Hulk could not respond in time to save David and he could not respond in time to save Darla and Mickey and he stood there and looked stupid. *But even if you had moved, you would have failed.*

Not this time. *Move!*

Jo Carlin's hand was dropping, now, in slow motion, sweeping down in a glistening arc, Jo's eyes aflame with triumph.

Jo was Sarah Josef. Sarah Josef was KGB. He'd read the dossier, but she'd managed to escape being photographed. Jo Carlin had been a very deep cover. Very well done.

That was no excuse at all. Morgan watched the hand come down and felt the blood flow back into his limbs and felt his brain start talking to his muscles again and he moved his arm.

And caught Jo's wrist.

Jo's whole body fell forward an inch as Morgan interrupted the force of her slicing blow. As Jo lost her balance he looked in her eyes, which came close to his, their faces nearly touching, his hand around her razor-wielding wrist, off to the side, her knees pressing his ribs, and now that the feeling was coming back his ribs were starting to hurt . . .

Her eyes were on fire and he saw the hatred there. *It's true, Jo. I did kill him.*

Right arm thrusting up against Jo's sternum lifting her up, now bringing his forehead up against her nose. Blood flew down over Morgan's eyes as she moved back, her left hand tearing at his face, his left hand still on her right wrist, bending her wrist back as Morgan rolled to the right, their outstretched arms coming up and around, Jo rolling under him, and as her right hand hit the deck Morgan felt the fingers loosen, and the razor bounce away.

It's what I do.

"So you're Sarah Josef," Morgan grunted. "I've heard about you."

"You're a fool."

"And you're also my mole. So what just hit us like a ton of bricks, I take it that was Blonsky? You two have it in for me?"

She laughed. "Emil Blonsky and I have business with URSA. *I* have it in for you." Morgan let go of the agent's wrist as Jo Carlin brought in her legs and kicked him, hard and rapid, in the face and then the chest, sending him back against the wall.

The Hulk looked up from his keyboard. He had not heard from Betty. She was supposed to call after the visit with Nadia.

Hold on, there. She has a class. Hell, the other night you didn't call and didn't come home until the morning, buddy.

But still.

Bruce stood up and stretched, scraping flecks of ceiling into the air with his knuckles as he did so. He turned around and picked up the telephone, dialing Sean Morgan's number.

The phone rang seven times before he got voicemail, of all things. Funny that SAFE would have voicemail. *Press one if you want to send a box of hands. Press two if there is an exploding airplane involved.*

Bruce clicked off the phone and looked at the clock, then recalled the headset Morgan had given him on the trip underground. He sat down in his gigantic chair and swivelled around, facing the window. The extra-large headset fit snugly against his head and Banner felt the mike rubbing between his lower lip and chin. He bent it outward a little bit, wondering what to say.

Bruce keyed the mike and said, "Hulk to Morgan. Pick up, Morgan."

Nothing. The Hulk tapped his desk a few times. "Ahem. Open Channel D."

Static.

Come on, don't these guys have secretaries?

"Hulk calling Orson. Come in, Orson," Bruce smiled, but this was beginning not to be funny. "Hey, SAFE crackers, anyone there?"

There was a crackle and hiss, then a sound sliding through, wet and guttural. "Hello, Hulk."

Bruce spun around, sitting bolt upright. He was silent for a long moment, then he whispered, "Emil?"

"Hello, Doctor," the voice slithered. The study was dark, and the Hulk felt himself floating in space, just him and the voice in his ear, somewhere out there, disembodied, making a connection.

"Where are you, Emil?"

"I've been thinking, Dr. Banner," the voice rasped. The voice sounded like it oozed green, gamma-irradiated and boiling. "When this is over, I just might keep the 'carrier. If there's anything left."

Bruce spoke slowly, rising. "Emil, where's Morgan?" *Morgan? Where the hell is all of SAFE?*

"Better yet," whispered the voice on the other end. "I don't expect to come through. So I think you can have it. What better home for a man all alone than in the sky?"

On the bridge of the Helicarrier, the Abomination pushed a technician aside and sat down at his console, keying into the late Tom Hampton's GammaTrac station, bringing it up on screen. He watched the green arm sweep around, and sighed almost lovingly as a blip in Westchester jumped, moving fast south and, suddenly, gaining altitude.

Emil Blonsky looked over his shoulder at the bridge crew, all of whom had been felled by the same sleeping gas Sarah had set up to knock out the entire populace of the Helicarrier. Having no one to speak to in particular, the massive, garish monster shrugged. "Hulk approaching."

CHAPTER 15

Anyone seen leaving," came the voice on the loud-speaker, "will only cause more destruction and loss of life."

Betty whipped off her heels and stuffed them in the garbage. *What would Daddy do?*

General "Thunderbolt" Ross would storm and threaten and bluster and boil. He would insult and insinuate. And he would probably get himself shot. *What would Daddy do? Screw that, what will I do?*

A teacher, yes, and a fine one. Nearly a nun, once. Also a pilot with survivalist training, although no one brought it up very much. Betty scanned the ceiling of the ladies room as footsteps echoed in the hall, the woman on the PA system continuing her tirade.

"All of you are being filmed for the better of the recipients of our message."

There was a panel above the third stall, a maintenance shaft entry.

"I urge you all to be brave and face your fate with the stoicism of those who are now in control. Just as they are expected to sacrifice, so are you. This consulate is but a growth of our mother country."

Betty entered a stall, climbed up on top of the toilet, reaching up to the panel. She pushed once, heaving. It did not budge. Calm down. Footsteps. Calm down. She ran her hands around the edge of the panel.

"And sometimes growths must be severed, boils must be lanced, for the betterment of the whole."

On one edge was a sort of handle, a flat circular impression like a screw. Underneath would be a bar that would slide out of the way and allow the panel to push upward.

"All will soon become clear. Please be patient."

The ladies' room door slammed open and three URSA
agents entered, fanning out. They did not see the panel
slide softly back into place in the ceiling.

"This message has been prerecorded."

God, she does go on, doesn't she? Betty began to
crawl, gingerly placing her weight on the metal frames on
either side of the shaft, trying to keep from sending a
ceiling lamp crashing down to the floor—or worse, from
crashing through herself.

She heard an agent below her say, as the three ran out
of the ladies' room, "Find the runaway."

Bruce leapt from the ground outside his condo and landed
just north of Central Park. He scanned the air, spotting
the Helicarrier hovering above the World Trade Center,
brushing past the twin towers at a stunningly close prox-
imity. He leapt, wind sailing past him, and fell towards
the earth again, landing on a crowded street in midtown.

When you're seven feet tall and weigh twelve hundred
pounds and you land next to a newsstand, people get out
of the way. Bruce barely noted the pulverized concrete
beneath his feet as he crouched and leapt again, landing
this time on a street closer to the World Trade Center. He
leapt again, now aiming for the mammoth 'carrier that
crossed the avenue, casting its shadow the length of a city
block.

As he soared, he noted electrical sparks spraying out
from the underbelly of the helicarrier. It looked like someone had punched through the underside. Someone heavy,
with claws. The jagged metal rim of Emil's entryway
came flying towards the Hulk so fast he barely had time
to reach out his hands and catch it. Giant green fingers
wrapped around toothy metal and sparking, jumping
wires, as the Hulk whipped his body around to plant his
feet on the other edge of the hole, toes and fingers digging
into the steel. The SAFE Helicarrier rocked in the air as,
for the second time within half an hour, a twelve-hundred-

pound gamma giant collided with its underbelly.

There were jets in the air, small ones zipping around, circling wide. The Hulk hung and stared at them, far off. Fighter planes. What was going on?

Bruce could hear alarms ringing on the inside, blaring away, and there was a pulsating red light emanating from the hole in the 'carrier's hull. The Hulk let go his feet, swung down, hanging from the rim, feet pointing towards the earth, swung again, and let go his hands as he flipped up and through the hole and onto the slick floor of what appeared to be a full-sized basketball court. The entry hole had ripped right through the center, neatly between the two goals, each back-board proudly bearing the emblem of SAFE. The backboards glared beautifully in the red emergency lights cast by the wall alarms, the reflective, sparkly fiberglass covers flashing. The Hulk surveyed the SAFE basketball court with an approving nod.

Nice place to work.

Bruce began to jog, exiting the gym and passing into the locker room. As he entered, he was accosted by a wave of steam rising from showers that still ran and spattered water. The steam swirled in the pulsating red light, and Bruce had difficulty making sense of the different images. The regular lights didn't seem to be working so well. He was about to start jogging again when he noticed a shape on the floor and bent down, brushing his hand. There was a naked man on the floor, a towel clutched in his hand, next to Bruce's right foot. The Hulk crouched for a moment, feeling for a pulse. He sniffed. Gas? If so, it had dissipated, especially with all this steam moving around.

Mr. Morgan, we have some security problems.

Bruce moved steadily through the locker room, avoiding stepping on any of the fallen SAFE agents who lay scattered about like rag dolls. It was difficult, weighing what he did, being as large as he was. There was a recurring dream Bruce used to have, in the days when he had no control over his Hulk persona. The dream was not that he would kill a sizeable number of soldiers, or even that he would bring entire planes full of innocents out of the sky.

The dream had been one in which he lived out again and again a very basic fear that he would step on someone. Just take a step and crush a body. He would wake up in the middle of the night drenched in sweat. He did not need violence to do harm. The Hulk was a danger merely by virtue of his size and strength.

Bruce stepped gingerly over a woman who leaned, towel-wrapped, against a locker. She wore small eyeglasses that glinted red in the swirling steam. Bruce stopped for a moment, disoriented. Every drop in the air was lit up red, and he had no idea how many people were under his feet. He had reached the end of a line of lockers. He looked around, red-bursting steam flowing like fog. *Where in hell is the exit?* He walked along another line of lockers and turned, to find another line of green metal doors and benches.

The Hulk put his hand on the wall and slid his feet along a slick, tiled floor he could barely see, and felt sleeping flesh push aside as his foot moved through. Surely he could get more light in here. *This is great. Attack the Helicarrier and get lost in a locker room roughly the size of Kansas.*

The Hulk looked to his left and saw the communal shower, a large circular room with a spewing post of showerheads in the center. There was another door on the other side. Which probably led to more lockers. Or might lead to a lift.

Bruce winced. The alarm siren was beginning to echo in his head, blood washing through his ears with every burst of sound. He decided to cut through the shower and stepped through the white door, steam whipping around him.

Something moved out of the corner, a garish shape in

pulsing red and green, barely registering out of the corner of Bruce's left eye. Something butted a scaly head against the Hulk's lower back. Bruce saw the fog splitting, pulsing brilliant red light, as the force sent him colliding with the far wall.

The Hulk slid to the ground, kicking a SAFE agent as gingerly as one can kick a naked man out of the way. "There you are."

"If I waited for you to find your way up the bridge," said the Abomination, "it could take *years*."

"Unhand me," Greg Vranjesevic said.

Selznick leaned against the security desk and nodded at the two agents who held the ambassador. "Fine," Selznick said, as he leaned against the desk. "Mr. Vranjesevic, I don't mean to make you suffer. Really. And if you promise to behave I'm happy to let you stand there like a dignified man. All right?"

Vranjesevic nodded as the agents on either side let go of his arms. He stepped over to Nadia, who sat on a chair, staring at Selznick and Timm. "What are you people? Selznick and Timm? You sound American, what's your connection with an outfit like URSA?"

Selznick threw a glance at Timm, who up until a few minutes ago had been safely ensconced in his role as an agent of SAFE. Selznick smiled, then laughed a bit, reaching in his breast pocket for something. He frowned, patted his pockets, then looked at Timm and said, in perfect Russian, "I can't find my cigarettes, you have any?"

Timm fished out a pack of Morleys and tossed a cigarette to Selznick, looking at Greg. He, too, spoke now in perfect Russian. "Just because you can't get rid of your accent doesn't mean we can't. That's child's play, Gregor. At least," he looked at Selznick, who was lighting his cigarette, "it was for us."

Greg folded his arms. After a moment he nodded. "Ah. Cousins. Yes, I've heard of you brats. Get to spend your mornings watching *Captain Kangaroo* and your afternoons blowing up libraries, or something like that?''

''It was a very different time,'' Timm said wistfully.

Selznick looked at his watch and said, ''You know what? I think we should watch some television.'' He tipped his head in the direction of a large television in the lobby—which was actually more of a den, decorated as it was in serene yellow and brown—and Timm strode to the television and flipped on the switch.

Greg heard Selznick engage in a quick conversation by radio with the two agents who were looking for Betty Gaynor. Or was it Banner? Whoever she was. So with Selznick and Timm, and those two—what were their names? His mind zipped back to quickly-seen chest badges. Spacey and Kimball. So there were four of these URSA people here. Four of them waiting for some kind of sacrifice.

''Should be about now,'' Selznick said idly, flipping to a news broadcast. There was a man reading a report, and now Greg heard sirens again. For an instant he thought the alarms in the consulate had been turned back on, but no—this was outside the window. He looked at the front window, a large, reinforced, bay-style affair, then looked at Selznick.

''Go ahead, Ambassador, have a look.''

Greg was already there, and he lifted back the heavy red curtain. There were fire trucks, two of them, pulling up in front of the iron gate in front of the embassy. He counted at least three police cars. ''We are not alone,'' Greg said.

''Just watch the television, Mr. Vranjesevic,'' Timm said.

On the screen, a man with wind-blown hair held a microphone to his face and stood in front of a line of police cars. Greg realized that those were the same cars he was seeing out the window.

''. . . New York police received a frightened phone

call just under an hour ago from a woman who identified herself only as Jo. We have procured a copy of that call for you.''

The screen went blue and a small rectangle with a ridiculously dramatic question mark and the name ''Jo'' covered the screen, white words transcribing the voice Greg and the rest of the city now heard:

''Please!'' the woman whispered. ''Please, you've got to hurry. This is Jo, security verify Tanqueray nine-oh-seven. You've got to stop them; I can't do anything else. SAFE is going to bomb the consulate, the Russian consulate, they—they're acting under orders from the President himself, I swear . . . The Helicarrier is going to bomb it. It's too late for a rescue mission, all the loyals inside are under guard, they said if someone tries to rescue them they'll blow it up . . . No! Wait!'' There were shots, then, two of them, and the tape went blank.

Greg looked at Selznick, twisting his lips. ''That's the woman we just heard, that Sarah Josef.''

Selznick nodded, a gleam in his eye.

''Are you telling me,'' Greg said, regarding the trucks outside, ''seriously telling me, that you are on a suicide mission?''

Selznick looked at Timm, sliding onto the couch. ''And not even drooling, is that your point? That we don't seem crazy, we're not robots, even though we expect to die? It does happen that something can be important enough to die for with a clear head.''

Greg banged several times on the window when he saw a man in a fireman's outfit look over the iron fence, the light outside dimming. ''Hey!''

''Greg,'' said Timm, ''forget it. They don't know what to do. So they're not going to do anything. They're here to make sure whatever happens keeps itself contained.''

The reporter on the television continued: ''Ladies and gentlemen, this has been a lot of information to try to organize in such a short time. But inside sources in the government say that, indeed, there is a covert organization called SAFE, which *apparently* is a loose arm of the executive branch. Neither the President nor his press secretary could be reached for comment at this time.''

''Dick, is SAFE another S.H.I.E.L.D.?'' the anchorman came on, calling out to the man on the ground.

''Uh, no, Jerry, S.H.I.E.L.D. we've known about, of course, they're a UN arm. But SAFE apparently has a Helicarrier, just like S.H.I.E.L.D., and in fact we've seen the 'carrier wandering around. Most of us assumed that was S.H.I.E.L.D.'s.''

''So where is the helicarrier now?'' the anchorman asked.

Dick, on the ground, who looked as though he would rather be covering a hurricane, looked up. ''Ah—Jerry, it looks like it's here.''

Greg looked away from the television and out the window, into the sky. There was a massive shape moving over the embassy, like a steel blimp, only about five times larger.

''This is crazy,'' Greg said. ''This is insane. Why would the United States government blow up a consulate? That doesn't make sense.''

Selznick stood up, taking a drag on his cigarette. ''Greg, Greg.'' He walked over to the window and stood at the window, peering out the curtain. He pulled in close, breathing on Greg's shoulder, the gun still in his hand. ''It doesn't have to make sense. Perception is reality. That's a cliché, but the funny thing about clichés is that they often turn out to be true.'' Selznick looked back at the people sitting in the den. Nadia, and two servants, both of whom appeared to be wishing they had gotten off early today.

''Let's say something horrible happens, anywhere. One thing you notice is that everybody begins to make up *theories*. The one thing we can't handle is the idea that something could happen for a reason that doesn't make sense. We'll make it make sense. So what do you know? A woman calls the police and says the government is going to do a horrible thing. She gives a security code that the FBI can run and verify that she is, in fact, connected. So everyone runs to the consulate to watch. And maybe it doesn't blow up, and everyone goes home, and wonders, what the hell was that about?'' He crushed out his cigarette in a standing ashtray and continued. ''But there's the Helicarrier. And let's say the consulate does blow up. Whose version of events will win? I'll tell you: the one they were already looking for.''

Greg looked at him, a mass of bile sliding down his throat. ''And all you really need is an explosion.''

Nadia spoke up, staring at Timm. ''Why? Why would you do such a thing?''

Timm said, ''My partner talks too much. All will become clear, ma'am.''

There was a chime in the lobby, behind the security desk.

''That's the elevator,'' Greg said.

''Yes,'' said Timm.

Nadia asked, ''Where does it come from?''

''Below,'' said Greg. ''The delivery tunnels.''

The elevator doors chimed, and began to open. Greg approached it. There sat a device the size of a vacuum cleaner, a shimmering green globe on top. And it was humming.

The Hulk and the Abomination spilled through the doorway on the other side of the shower and fell back against the tiles, sliding across the red-pulsing, steaming floor. The 'carrier pitched, and it felt like a whole building tipping over, and Bruce grabbed at the wall as he began to slide across this new room. ''What in hell?''

Emil tumbled across the Hulk, tearing at Bruce's throat. ''Helicarrier is driving itself. It's not very smart.

It wants to avoid hitting buildings,'' he said, as Bruce kicked at him viciously. Emil's claw hooked the Hulk's foot and drew blood as Bruce flipped over, his chin slamming into the tiles, cracking them. "But it doesn't care how sloppy it is at driving."

Bruce looked around. They were in a spa, but there were no agents around. No one to crush as Emil and he threw one another around. "Where's Morgan?" he said, jumping. "Where's Betty?"

"Morgan's being taken care of," Emil said, as the palm of Bruce's hand collided with the Abomination's throat. "Soon I'll have his lying tongue on a *keychain*."

"I thought you said you didn't expect to come out of this."

"You can always dream," Emil said. The scaly demon fell backwards, and the Abomination gasped for air as his back struck the tiles, the long ridge of scales down his back cutting a wide gash into the floor. His red eyes flared in the steamy fog.

"Where's Betty?" Bruce had Emil by the throat. He pushed with his feet and they slid another meter or two, and now Emil's head was hanging over the edge of a hot tub, the bubbling water swirling and pulsating with the red emergency lights.

"No idea."

"Wrong answer," said Bruce. He raised his back and plunged his hands forward with Emil's head, and saw the red eyes plunge down under the water.

There was a noise, the scaly, finned head moving under the water, and when the head came back up, Emil spat water and twisted, rising, Bruce's arms bending as Emil moved in one vicious arc, his body whipping up. Bruce felt razor-sharp teeth dig into his shoulder and he winced. Bruce rolled back and sent Emil flying, and felt tiny pieces of dense flesh from his shoulder go with him.

"You want to see Betty?" Emil spat. "I have something to show you." The Abomination sprang up and ran through the doorway, moving like a green, scaly panther, gone in a red-pulsing flash.

The Hulk wasted no time running after him. He turned the corner, following the deep impressions of Emil's feet. Another corner and he felt and saw red carpeting as he spilled into one of the business corridors of the Helicarrier. The steam dissipated; now there was only the glaring red emergency pulses of light and the loud alarms, which still blared, deafening, in his ears. And now there were people.

The Hulk reached the end of the hallway. *How does he move so fast?*

Bruce stopped. There was a fork. Now, he had to decide which way to go, and as if the heavy indentions of Emil's feet didn't point the way enough, Emil had left him a sign: there was a SAFE agent tossed against the wall, one knee up, as if he were resting, one arm on the knee, pointing the way, the head rolling back. Except he wasn't pointing the way. Because Emil had taken to hand stealing again.

The Hulk ran left as the hand that wasn't there told him, moving down the corridor. He reached the lift bay at the end of the hall.

The SAFE Helicarrier, like most good places to work, had so many stories that the elevator bays held nine elevators, three for the first eleven floors, three for 12–24, and three for 25–37. The Hulk surveyed each wall until he found the one with drops of blood running down the button panel. He pressed the *up* button, and in a moment a door to his left shot open with a pneumatic hiss. The Hulk got in. There was blood on number 26, a sign next to it labeled BRIDGE.

Inside the lift, the sound of the alarms was distant, a pulsing bass cry in the bowels of the ship, and Bruce realized his ears had been slightly deafened by the sound, because now the comparative quiet of the lift felt like the curiously loud silence you hear when you leave a concert.

Blood on the walls. WANT TO WATCH A MOVIE?

The doors opened and the Hulk saw a splotch of blood on a panel on the wall, and followed the smudges to the notation that said A/V ROOM, ROOM 2698.

All this and an A/V geek, too.

Bruce ran a quarter mile, green feet padding along Morgan's expensive carpets, before he found the large double-doors labeled 2698. He looked down in disgust to see the dead man's hand, tossed aside. Bruce pushed the doors open and saw John Wayne.

The room was dark except for the red emergency lights which lit up the dark backs of the audience seats. Twelve large screens attached to one another so that they could make one big picture played, light and color mixing with the pulsing red. And John Wayne was on screen, in a helmet.

"*The Green Berets,*" the Hulk said, turning around. Near a control panel in the back sat a figure in the dark, a pair of red eyes on a great, scaly form, the whole person lit up every half-second by the red lamps.

"Yes," said Emil. "One of the worst war movies ever made about any war, fittingly about Vietnam. Also one of the few where the sun sets in the east—but no one stayed that long."

"Where's Betty?" The Hulk started to step toward Emil and the Abomination spoke.

"More violence, Dr. Banner? Don't move and I'll tell you. Actually, I think she's still at the embassy." The Abomination sat there in the chair, idly watching John Wayne being brave and wooden. Emil flipped a switch and a news report came up on one of the lower screens. The Hulk listened for a moment, over the blaring sirens. After a moment he said, "What do you plan to do? Fire a missile? They'll never let that happen. I saw fighters out there; they'll blow this 'carrier out of the sky if—"

"Really?" The scaly claws flipped more switches and now the screen lit up with twelve different images, alternating, changing, and Bruce's mind tumbled across all of them as the Abomination spoke. There was Nikita Kruschev, shoe slamming against the table, there was Ike, there was Kennedy. Reagan in an old submarine movie. James Bond. "I doubt they'll do that. They can't blow up a vessel this size this low," the slithery voice said. "It'll scatter across twenty city blocks. Untold thousands could die. Is one consulate worth that?"

"They might shoot a missile out of the air," the Hulk said.

"Yes," said Emil. "They could do that." Khrushchev ballooned to fill six screens, Kennedy exploding to the other six, both men waving their arms, Nikita's shoe pounding, foaming at the mouth. "If there were a missile." The shoe, falling, slamming against the table, Kennedy verbally signing a blank check, *pay any price, bear any burden* . . . "Those were the glory days, there," Emil said, his red eyes glowing. "We never felt more alive than when we hated one another the most."

"What do you mean, 'If there were a missile'?"

"I was in the United States when Kent State happened. Do you remember that?" Emil smiled, the face lighting up with the pulsing red and plunging back into darkness, the red eyes burning throughout. "An interesting lesson. Do you know what that lesson was?"

Bruce swallowed. There were jets circling out there. *Where is Morgan?* "I don't have time for this."

"The lesson was that when you get a lot of excited people to line up and yell and wave hardware, wonderful things can happen."

Bruce opened his mouth. "The Helicarrier is a decoy."

Emil clapped his hands in time with Kruschev's falling shoe. "Yes! Just a personal touch, a way to involve Morgan in the most catastrophic event of the post–Cold War era. Of course it's a decoy. The bomb is already in place."

"Betty . . ."

"And I'm afraid those trucks they're lining up, and all those things they're going to use to try to keep the blast contained, will be fairly useless. You're been at ground zero on a gamma test, right?"

"Emil," The Hulk burst over the seats, grabbing Emil by the throat, pieces of chairs flying. "Are you telling me there's a gamma—"

Emil coughed, rising to meet the Hulk. "We can waste as much time as you like. But I figure they have about fifteen minutes."

CHAPTER 16

Betty pushed the panel down and peered through the opening. The room below her was one she had not seen, which was no surprise, since this was her first visit to the consulate. She could make out a dark wood interior and, even with the lights off, the room fairly glowed with shiny surfaces. Pushing the panel a little wider to get a better look, she saw a man standing against the wall and froze.

The man did not move. After a moment Betty peered more closely and saw why: it was a suit of armor, or something like it; a dummy dressed in leather and furs. Nearby stood more recent armor, and so on, up to the decorative coats of the army of Nicholas, the last tzar. Betty slid the panel aside and dropped through, landing deftly on the carpet. She surveyed the room in its entirety.

On another wall, near a dart set, was a large, blunt, double-bladed axe, with a handle about two feet long. The metal axe head was nearly a foot long. Perfect. Betty took the axe off the wall and began to walk with it, the weight swinging at the end of her thin but powerful arms.

There were footsteps outside the door to the museum room and Betty got behind one of the suits of armor as she heard the door creak open.

The man who entered was one of the men who had come into the bathroom, whom Selznick had called Kimball. Kimball was about forty, well built, with short gray hair. As he stepped into the doorway, surveying the dark room, Betty realized there wasn't a thing about him that didn't scream *military*.

Kimball surveyed the dummies lined up against the wall and stopped, obviously seeing for the first time the panel in the roof. He moved forward, walking closer to

230

it, and folded his arms, laughing softly. He keyed his radio. "Spacey, she's in the ceiling."

Betty began to move, her eyes on the back of Kimball's head, hands grasping the handle of the axe, now breathing quietly and raising her arms, ready to bring down the axe head. The axe head came up.

Kimball suddenly dropped about ten inches and Betty felt the air fly out of her as a heavy boot collided with her sternum. "Christ, woman," Kimball said as he turned around. "You think I'm an amateur?"

Betty slammed against an end table and felt her shoulder collide with a lamp that was bound to have been expensive, pieces of glass flying. She held fast to the axe handle and paid dearly for it when the weight of the thing caused the back of her arm to slam hard against the table edge. Kimball's radio erupted: "Kimball, you in the museum room?"

"She's here." Kimball had his gun aimed and Betty jumped in the air, dancing across the cushions of an antique green sofa when she saw the silencer flare and a cushion burst on the sofa behind her ankle. She grabbed a crystal vase and hurled it as she jumped behind the sofa. The vase flew, Kimball ducked, the base of the vase connected square with Kimball's temple, and the URSA man's body whipped back, stunned. Betty looked up from behind the sofa, not having been there half a second, saw the momentary daze in the man, and jumped. She sprang up onto the couch and sprang again, hitting the ground behind him and to his left, bringing the axe up as she did so. Thirty pounds of iron smacked against the back of Kimball's head and the gun clattered to the floor as Kimball fell forward. The agent fell headlong, smacking his forehead again against the cushions of the sofa. He did not move.

Idiots. Who did they think they were dealing with? She was the wife of *the Hulk*. She'd spent most of her adult life being shot at, beaten, kidnapped, even transformed into a harpy once. And to top that, Dad had spent many a night teaching her to defend herself, to be resourceful, all that imagine-you're-trapped-in-enemy-territory-with-a-sucking-chest-wound crap. Yeah, he was "Thunderbolt" Ross. But what had he called her, way back then, on that Fourth of July? The boys were shooting targets and she was hunting lightning bugs of all things, pouncing, slapping jars down with an efficiency that made him just a little scared, just a bit (though Dad would never admit it) and put up such a jovial, ingratiating fuss, laughing through that cigar. He knew he'd never control her, could only share her with the world, could only watch as she made her decisions, pounced when she had to. What had he called her? *Chain Lightning. You move just like Chain Lightning, little girl.*

Betty heard footsteps running for the museum room outside in the hallway. Spacey. She grabbed the lamp on an end table next to the door and tossed it across, running the cord under the doorway. Then she dove for the dummies, taking her place once again beside the suits of armor.

Spacey was clearly a runner, wiry frame, about five-foot-three. Not tall, but neither was Alan Ladd, whom he resembled. Spacey turned in through the door at full speed. He hit the cord and his foot brought it up, yanking the door hard into Spacey's face. Betty pounced as Spacey fell forward, twisting to roll free of all encumbrances. Betty kicked him once in the face as the agent brought his gun up at her. She swung the axe once, barely missing severing the man's hand, instead connecting with the barrel of the gun. The metal spun away in the darkened room as Betty brought the axe handle down once more square against the side of the man's head.

Betty breathed then. *Jeez. These guys are teddy bears.* She looked around in the dark, listening. There was a commotion in the lobby. Her shoulder hurt like hell, but she felt ready now. She thought briefly about taking one of the pistols, but decided against it. She was above that. They underestimated her and she had no intention of thinking like them. Betty massaged her sore shoulder and arm as she stepped neatly over the unconscious Spacey, kicking the lamp cord aside.

Betty grinned, the axe swinging on the end of the deliciously sore arm. Like a cat, Chain Lightning Ross moved out of the dark room and into the hall. *Two teddy bears down. Two to go.*

Sean Morgan was starting to regret that he had long since stopped carrying a stiletto.

The colonel cried out in pain as Sarah lunged at him with her razor, a line of red spewing out from Morgan's chest. Morgan fell back and reached for his sidearm, bringing it up. He fired, saw the woman he had known as Jo Carlin catch a slug in the chest and spin around, crashing once more against the panel of Tom's GammaTrac station.

She hit the floor and lay there in a heap, face down, her hand still holding the razor.

Morgan felt the pain in his chest begin to throb. She had cut him rather deeply. Morgan looked around and realized that the emergency alarm was still blaring, and the throbbing in his chest seemed to keep time with it. As he moved, the muscles in his chest sang out in defiance, every motion of his arms and shoulders pulling at the slice across his pectoral. The woman was good with a blade. Morgan turned around, leaning for another moment on one hand, panting. He holstered his sidearm. He hated to admit it, but who was he kidding? He wasn't as good at the physical stuff as he had once been. He was a long way from the cocky idiot that had gotten Darla and Mickey killed in Paris. He hadn't paid that little attention in years, he was more mature, yes, all that. But he had lost a great deal of that wiry fire-escape-jumping bravado.

Morgan began to walk and winced in pain. *Yeah, well. Let the kids jump off the fire escapes.*

He should have known Jo for the mole. He should have made that connection. It was inescapable. But her cover had been the best. Her references were excellent. (*Just like Betty Gaynor's vitae is solid gold. Such things can be arranged.*) What did it come down to? He just hadn't wanted to believe it, choosing to ignore the warning signs until too late, until the flatbed was right on them. *Great*, Morgan realized. *I'm not the cocky kid anymore, and I'm still just as careless. Or I can be.*

Pain. Jeez, that hurts. Morgan stepped over one of his agents as he reached the lift. What could he say? The fact was, he had screwed up, and he had been too caught up going to funerals to see all the signs. He wanted to be harder on himself, but he stowed that. *The fact is, Morgan, you screwed up and that happens. Get over it, and move on.*

Morgan reached the lift bay and pressed a button for the express bridge lift. The door slid open and he stepped inside, slapping the appropriate button, when Sarah Josef slammed into him from behind, sending his sore chest colliding into the metal wall on the other side.

Morgan spun around and dropped, kicking out and connecting with Sarah's right ankle as she slashed at him again with the razor. The lift doors shut and Morgan looked up at Sarah. "Bulletproof vest?"

"The thinnest possible," she smiled, jumping on him, grabbing at his jaw. She kneed him sharply in the solar plexus and Morgan cried out, and Sarah reared back her razor. "I'm taking that tongue first, Andy."

Andy?

The lift doors slid open as the razor came down. Morgan drew up and kicked, hard, and the razor caught him across the chin as Sarah flew back and through the door, spilling out onto the bridge. Sarah fell against a chair and righted herself, holding the razor in front of her.

"All right, Mary Lou," said Morgan, "I've had enough of this." He drew his gun. "I know you don't pad your head. Drop it."

Sarah stood her ground, swaying. "You don't understand, Morgan. We're about to be witness to a very large explosion, and we're just above ground zero. You're going to die. I just prefer to see you dead at my hands. But I'm content enough to know you'll go either way."

"Jo . . . Sarah . . . whatever . . ." Morgan stooped himself. He was being flip, and suddenly he looked at the girl again and realized how wrong that was. "Look, it was—was a different time. I did my job."

"And I will do mine, Colonel Morgan. I'm not interested in your apologies. I lost interest in that when I was a little girl and you took my father from me. It just so happens that *my* job involves you being dead."

"Isn't it splendid," Morgan said, "when you can make personal and professional goals mesh so well?" She moved forward. "Don't. I can kill you very easily, Sarah. I will."

And that was when Bruce Banner collided with the underside of the Helicarrier. As the 'carrier groaned and pitched, Morgan lost his balance, just for a second, and Sarah shrieked, jumping, slashing down and slicing across Morgan's gun hand. The piece clattered to the floor and bounced.

Morgan brought his hurt hand into his chest and shot out his left, catching the woman under the chin, kicking simultaneously, hitting her in the hip. Sarah shrieked in pain and slashed at him again, up and across. Morgan looked down in horror and unmeasurable relief as the blade sliced through the crotch of his finest suit pants and came away having severed only one hundred percent wool.

Sarah dropped and kicked hard at Morgan's shin, and as he fell back she jumped him, grabbing his collar. Morgan felt his back crash against the floor and Sarah's weight pressing his abdomen, pulling against the slice across his chest. He grabbed for her wrist with his gun hand, pain shooting through every fiber of his body, his other hand going up to the woman's hair, giving it a yank. Sarah winced, whipping her head, and Morgan slammed her knife hand against the base of one of the chairs on the bridge. Pain shot through his hand as the pressure reported the impact, pulsing with the emergency sirens through his aching wound. He saw the knife come away and as it did he grabbed for it.

Morgan had the razor. Sarah grabbed for it and missed and brought the empty hand up and clawed his face. Morgan felt sharp nails dig into the flesh beneath his eyes as he brought the razor up in a long arc.

A moment later, Morgan felt a thousand stings. Stings in his chest, his face, his hands. But mostly his eyes, because of Sarah's blood in them.

The SAFE Helicarrier had a cafeteria as impressive as its basketball court, and it was here that the Hulk and the Abomination had pummeled their way before Emil managed to get the upper hand again. The Hulk saw reinforced plexiglass sailing towards his head and winced as he collided with it, spittle flying across the gigantic window.

"Come forth," hissed Emil, and he had Bruce by one arm twisted up behind him, the Abomination's barbed and scaly left leg wrapped around Bruce's right one. Emil twisted Bruce's head and slammed his forehead against the pane again. "Come forth, you seed of *sulphur*." He wrenched back Bruce's head and slammed it against the pane again. One of Bruce's lips split and blood ran over his tongue. Emil rasped into Bruce's ear, the words sliding off his lizard-like tongue. "Sons of Fire! Your stench is broke forth." Bruce looked sideways and saw the burning red eyes. "*Abomination* is in the house."

"Johnson," Bruce said with a pant. "*The Alchemist*."

"Yes," Emil said, clicking his tongue. "Very good.

Look down, Bruce. You see the consulate, don't you?"

"I see it," Bruce snapped, fighting to break free. Emil pulled Bruce's arm a bit tighter upward and slammed him against the pane again.

"I asked you what I was going to make you see—and now you know."

"I've seen explosions before, Emil."

"Don't play stupid," the Abomination said. "I've *seen* you stupid, and this isn't it. You know what you're looking at. You're looking at the end of your little Elizabeth. This is it, Bruce. Don't fight! Stop. Listen. You've got to listen to me, Bruce." The demon spoke almost softly, whispering in Bruce's ear. Bruce stared out the glass, looking for an opportunity. And here the Abomination wanted to talk.

Emil continued, calmly. "We're a different race, you and I. That's why I've placed us here, right at ground zero. We might come through it. We belong dead."

"Speak for yourself. Who are you to say who belongs dead?"

The voice rose violently. "Haven't you been *listening*?" Bruce felt his head slammed against the plexiglass again. These were good windows. "I am the *Abomination*!"

"You're insane."

"And you are a Hulk. What is a Hulk? A beast? A rock? The kind of name given to you, not taken, surely. Let me tell you: a Hulk is a shell. That's what they thought you were when the army first saw you, moving across the desert. A shell. Empty inside. Pure power, pure violence.

"That's the secret to identity, Bruce. People call you what they know in their hearts that you are."

"You're wrong." *And we don't have time for this.*

"No. You're not one of these . . . rodents, Bruce. You're as much an outcast as I am, except that you have, time and time again, refused to listen to me. You play.

You pretend. You take a wife. You ignore what you *are*. And what you are is what I am." He said the word long, slow and slithering. "Abomination, Bruce. I've read your psych profile—your father was a murderer, wasn't he? Killed your mother, beat her senseless right in front of you, didn't he? But even *he* knew that as much of a monster as *he* was, you were all that and *more*."

"No . . ."

"You were different, smart, an intelligence devilish and pounding from your brain that even a scientist like your father knew to be afraid of. A new breed. And with all that intelligence lay a lover in your mind, another half, dark and powerful, bestial, sensuous, dangerous. Unfit for human companionship. *Above* it. *Beyond* it."

"You don't know what you're talking about."

"Oh, I do." Emil whispered in Bruce's ear. "Tell me this. When you get up in the morning in your little condominium and that human woman is chattering away at you, do you ever get mad? Do you ever wish she would just shut up? They do go on, you know. Have you ever seen her chattering at you and realized that she's chattering because she's afraid of you, that she's talking to you because it's a play, and we're pretending that you're anything but *not normal*, *not human*, the Hulk—did you ever look at her, mocking you with her deluded love and her barely masked fear and wish that you could just *smash* her?"

"Shut up," Bruce said. "Can you stop it? The bomb?"

"Smash her, like your father would. He was just an ordinary man, but he had no problem being what he was. Why do you have a problem being what *you* are? Why do you cling to this silly role of humanity?"

"Emil. . . ." Bruce shut his eyes. His father was a monster, swinging bony fists and causing bruises, grabbing Bruce's tiny arm, afraid because little Bruce could take an Erector set and make a skyscraper with working elevators and he was only *three*. *Monster!*

Betty did *not* mock him. Betty was his *partner*. Betty was his *life*. There was a savage beast inside him, rampaging across the desert, and when it saw Betty it saw compassion and love and it saw—even *it* saw—that Betty was his friend.

Then why are you listening to this?

"Emil," Bruce repeated, shaking his head, slowly, the claws holding fast to his neck, "you're wrong. You're so wrong. I'm no more another race than you are. You're not an Abomination! You're just a man, Emil. Just a poor guy who made some mistakes."

Emil roared, "Pity *me?*" He tore Bruce away from the window and flung him across the cafeteria. Bruce slid across eight metal tables, barely missing several sleeping SAFE agents, food trays flying.

"I don't know that I pity you," Bruce said, as he got to his feet. "I think I pity the man that you were. But I don't pity you, Emil." Bruce spoke slowly. "You've gone too far now. But you're still, in the end, just a man. A giant, scaly, green man, but a man."

"I am beyond man. So are you."

"Cut it out, Emil. You keep saying that because you have to prove it to yourself, and I think I know why. I think I understand why you've spent all this time embracing this Abomination role, acting it out, showing all the people that ever wronged you."

"Oh?" Emil grinned. "Tell me."

"It's because you're just not a very good man. And rather than admit that, you'd rather convince yourself that you're a beast. Or a superman. Anything but a sad, failed human being."

"*Liar!*" The Abomination soared through the air, knocking Bruce back, and the two tumbled end over end and collided with the far wall.

"But you're not," Bruce cried, as he and Emil rolled.

"That's just what you *believe*! That's what you're trying to talk yourself out of. Nadia's down there, Emil! Your own wife! Doesn't that mean anything to you?" Bruce swung, hard, knocking the creature back so he had room to talk. "Do you think she deserves to die because you think you're so poor an excuse for a human being? And I thought I needed a shrink."

"She's a haughty traitor," Emil said. "She's forgotten about me. Fooling around with that Greg Vranjesevic, she's forgotten everything."

"She thinks you've been dead a long time, Emil. A long time."

"I'm not dead."

"I—" Bruce shook his head. The worst part was that it was mostly true. Emil was beyond the love of anyone, even Nadia. Bruce firmly believed that. There really wasn't much hope to offer him. "You wanted to punish her, Emil. Punish her, I don't care. All you want. But you don't, you can't want to kill her."

"I have cried . . . day and night . . . before thee," Emil sang.

Bruce shook his head, looking at the bay windows. "You're hopeless. I'm tired of this. If we're hovering here at ground zero," he said, "then it doesn't make any difference. I'll see you in hell, Emil." Bruce began to move, making up his mind, dense green legs pumping, bringing his hands up. Bruce ran and sprang from a cafeteria table like a diving platform, straightening his fingers as he flew for the corner of one of the gigantic plexiglass windows.

Four inches of plexiglass burst and splintered as the Hulk sailed through, out into the open sky.

CHAPTER 17

B y now," came the taped voice of Sarah Josef, "the consulate must have been secured."

Selznick looked around him. Spacey and Kimball hadn't made it back yet with the woman. It didn't matter.

Greg looked up from where he sat. He had been staring in disbelief for six minutes, from the moment he staggered back when the elevator door opened to reveal a large, green bomb, humming away in his home. "My God, is she talking again?"

"Your actions," the voice continued, "of course, are being filmed and recorded at a remote spot. The purpose of this film is so that there will be a record of what happened here."

"Why would she do that?" Greg mused. "If they want the explosion blamed on the U.S.—"

"This tape is being sent to Moscow. It is URSA's firm belief that internal matters should remain internal, that the family should solve its problems without sharing them publicly. The inept, mismanaged government in Moscow will see your deaths and know why URSA has done this. They will see the death of their consul and know it is because of their lack of vision. They will see the deaths of these URSA men and know it is because of our dedication. No one will doubt the loyalty of these brave men, who have chosen to give their lives in service of our cause."

"You've got to be joking," Nadia said, rolling her eyes. "Just let us go. She's not even here, you idiots, why don't we just *go*?"

"Stay where you are, Ms. Dornova," Selznick said, a little too idly. "There's no leaving. All right? No leaving."

242

"And if I get up, right now," said Nadia, "and I walk out that door, you'll shoot me?"

"No," said Selznick.

"Nor will I," Timm said. "But I have it on the best authority that there are snipers all around this place. Some of them are ours. And any head that pokes itself out from behind the front door is going to be shot. So sit tight. Not long now."

"I wish *I* could find such easygoing, blithely suicidal help," Greg muttered to Nadia. "It's like being held hostage by MacNeil and Lehrer."

"You don't understand, Mr. Vranjesevic," Selznick said, reverting to Russian. He folded his arms, one hand still grasping his gun. "Timm and I are at ease because we believe in what we are doing. Do you believe in what you are doing? You're a consulate to a country that no longer knows itself. *We* are a part of an organization prepared to give that country its identity again." Selznick smiled. "I can't imagine a more calming fact. We are relaxed because we have already won, and need only wait. And our names—yours, mine, Timm's—will not go down in history, but the right people will know what happened here, and how much we were willing to sacrifice for an idea."

"It can't possibly make a difference," Nadia said. "Not enough to die for."

"This isn't an isolated incident, Ms. Dornova," Timm said. "At home, there are people already in place who are ready to receive this news and make all the right moves. Bills to be quickly introduced and passed. War to be declared. All of these things have been ready for a long time, but there has been one thing missing." *The time is ticking away*, Nadia thought. Ticking away. "All this kindling but nothing like what we needed. A spark. And today, Ms. Dornova, Mr. Vranjesevic, we will deliver more than that spark. We will deliver an *explosion*."

"It won't work," Nadia insisted.

Greg shook his head. "Oh, but it will. Remember Ockham's Razor, the best explanation is the simplest one that fits all the facts? Our friends here will provide just such an explanation. And it doesn't matter how many people raise questions. It will work," he said, disgusted.

"And now," came the taped voice of Sarah Josef again, "the minutes should be few. It is time for the opening act. Mr. Selznick. You will now kill Ambassador Vranjesevic."

"All in the plan, sir," Selznick said, standing, brushing off his pants. "Glad to be of service."

Selznick had the gun up, the hammer clicking back—
—and then several things happened at once.

A panel in the ceiling over the man fell down, swinging out. Greg Vranjesevic took the moment's distraction to dive behind the couch. He looked up to see a heavy axe come swinging down, its handle smacking Selznick on the back of the head, and a woman uncoiling from the ceiling like a snake: Betty Gaynor or Banner or whatever her last name was. Selznick's gun landed on the ground next to Nadia, and Greg dove for it, grabbing the weapon and coming up, aiming it at Timm. Timm was turning to fire on Betty when Greg fired once, twice, acrid smoke rising in the den. Timm grew an eye on the side of his head and fell violently sideways, his gun discharging as he did so. The bullet was unaimed, glancing off the battle-axe and across the room, tearing the glass face off an antique grandfather clock.

Betty breathed, looking around, holding the axe before her. "That's all of them?"

"Yes," Greg said.

"Then let's go."

"We can't," Greg said. "Snipers, apparently."

Betty chewed her lip. "Never heard of an embassy without a helicopter on the roof. How about you?"

"The pilot's gone," Greg said.

"Not so," Betty said, walking quickly to the elevator.

She dropped to inspect the gamma device that sat there, humming away. She froze for half a second when she saw the timer's digital readout. "Your pilot's right here, Mr. V."

"You fly?"

"About twelve hours in a helicopter, but I'm the best you've got. We have five minutes," she said. "Let's go."

A moment later, Greg, Betty, Nadia, and the other hostages had found their way up the stairs to the roof exit. Betty slammed the metal door open, looking around quickly. She spotted the helicopter and looked back at Greg. "There's no reason for all of us to risk getting shot at once. I'll try to get her started, then you guys come when I do."

Betty sprang out onto the long, flat roof, running across the tar-and-gravel rooftop. Almost immediately, the roof began to explode, echoing a far off *crack!* of gunfire, bits of gravel flying behind her as she moved. Someone was shooting, sure enough.

She had lied about her time in helicopters. Not counting simulators, her time in the air was more like five hours. *One hour for every minute we have left*, she thought. *Okay, girl. You can do this.*

Betty jumped up into the cockpit and took the pilot's seat, surveying the controls. She wasted fifteen seconds trying to remember where to start before she saw the fuel gauge. Empty? Why would they keep it empty? Betty sniffed. She *smelled* fuel . . . Betty stuck her head out the side of the helicopter and saw her worst fears confirmed. A metal tube splayed out the side of the tail, having been torn through with, most likely, a pair of clippers. Dripping off the end was the same amber liquid that now collected on the rooftop in a pool. There would be no flying away.

"No!" Betty smacked the dashboard with her fists. "No!" There was another *crack!* from across the street and something tore through the corner of the chair she was sitting in. Betty jumped, scrambling out of the helicopter and running again. Bullets chased her ankles, gravel exploding and scraping against her.

"Forget it," Betty said, slamming herself against the metal door once she'd shut it and were they all back inside. "It's not going anywhere. And your friends didn't lie—we're being watched." Once they were back on the second floor, she slid down to the carpet in the hallway, her head resting in her hands. "I guess that's it."

And then, the embassy shook from its roof to its basement, as it might if struck by a green, seven-foot-tall, twelve-hundred-pound human missile.

Betty looked to her left and saw her husband crashing through the ceiling, through the floor, and down to the lower floor.

"What in hell?" Greg stared.

Betty raised an eyebrow, getting up, slinging her axe over her shoulder as she stood on the rim of the hole Bruce had left as he moved through the embassy. She looked down below, holding back her hair. "Kind of you to drop in."

Bruce looked up, through the hole, and said, "Betty! I nearly hit you, I'm sorry. It's kind of hard to aim when you're—"

"Bruce—"

"The bomb, its a gamma device. Where is it?"

"Elevator," said Betty, as she and the others ran down below. "Bruce, I don't think there's much time."

Bruce Banner crouched down at the open elevator door and stared at the readout. Three minutes. "You're right." The device was on tractor belts, resembling something like a mesh between a vacuum cleaner and a globe. "It's so tiny," he muttered. "The one I built was two stories high. It needed its own platform." Bruce wheeled the bomb gingerly toward himself as he got down Indian style, curling his gigantic legs underneath him. "This green glass on top. I think this is just a panel." The Hulk cleared his throat. "Okay," he said. "You—you're the ambassador? You think you can find me a screwdriver and a pair of clippers?"

A radio on Bruce's collar crackled and spoke. "Banner? Banner, you there?"

"I'm here, Morgan, but we're in a jam. Listen, there's a bomb here."

"We're stuck in a holding pattern," Morgan said. "Everybody's out and we're stuck."

"I know, I saw. The bomb is here, it's not up with you, it's here. I'm gonna try to defuse it."

There was a pause. "I can get you a team. There's gotta be—"

"No time," Bruce interrupted. "I gotta go. I'll be in touch."

Greg was rummaging through the security desk. "I have a pair of scissors and a dime."

"Screws are too small for the dime, but I'll take the scissors," Bruce said, holding up his giant hand. The scissors landed softly in his palm and he sat them down before him.

"Wait!" Nadia said, opening her handbag. "Here." She drew out a white fold-over plastic pouch. "This is for my reading glasses." Bruce took it and smiled. It held a tiny pair of tweezers and a minuscule screwdriver, both for handling the screws on a pair of frames. "Perfect."

Bruce breathed once, deeply, then took the screwdriver between his thumb and forefinger. He bent down, looking for the screws that held the globe-panel in place.

His hand shook. "Hell!"

"What?" Betty yelped.

"It's just—it's just that my fingers are so *huge* that it's hard to work with normal equipment. Okay. Okay." He bit his lip and controlled the movement of his hand, trying hard to feel the tiny piece of metal that barely registered in the nerve sensors of his skin. He got the first screw, then moved to the second, on the other side of the green globe, moving around, alternating, as he would with a tire.

The truth was, Bruce always hated tools, even though he was very good with them. Perhaps there was something in that. He mastered tools because he needed to use what was knocking around in his brain, but even when he had finer hands, they could never express but bluntly the visions his mind held. Tools were clumsy and unyielding, like his limbs. There was a time when he nearly punctured an artery trying to change a tire in the rain. Tools would never reflect the mind of Bruce Banner, and neither would his clumsy, massive body now, except through a glass, green and darkly.

The clock gave him two minutes when Bruce gingerly lifted the green dome off the top of the device, and he beheld exactly what he expected. Wires.

"Is this one of those which-one-do-you-cut things?" Betty asked.

Bruce sighed. "Sort of." He looked at Betty. "Fact is, though, it's never as simple as it looks in the movies, except the part about cutting the wrong one can make you dead." He surveyed the wires. There were three critical wires running to the detonator, all of them green. Light, medium, and dark. Very funny.

"One and a half minutes." Bruce looked at his wife. "Betty. I can't do this. Get out of the way, I'm going to take it as far away as I can, maybe the ocean."

"You can't."

He shook his head. "I have to. I'll try not to be there when it—"

"You can't move it," Nadia said, standing at the security desk. She was running through Sarah Josef's droning message, now playing a part of it:

"The device is not to be moved. If the device is moved more than six feet once it has been activated, it will explode."

The Hulk was already beginning to stand, his hands around the bomb, and he froze. He couldn't have moved it more than three feet. "Okay." He set it back down. "Okay, then now we have a minute-fifteen, and I have to think." He scratched his chin, then pushed the sweat away from his brow. "Look at that circuitry. Ten years ago I couldn't have done this. It's possible that even if I cut the right wire it won't matter." He was muttering to himself, very fast, not asking for comment and receiving none. The other three simply stood and watched as the behemoth talked to a bomb. "One thing I know is that this is clearly fashioned after my own design. So it should be pretty much the same, just a lot smaller and cooler. Now, my bomb had a trick to it that I put in sort of as a failsafe. The motherboard. Of course! Screw the wires, it was the seventh circuit!"

"What will that do, cutting that circuit?"

"Well, in this case I'll just pull a chip out, but it should just die. It's a bottleneck I put in my design. A place where all the signals travel through, and if I kill that, no more signal."

"Do it," Betty shouted.

"Except I don't have any real reason to assume these guys followed my design that closely."

"*Bruce* . . ."

"Right. Okay." Bruce bent forward, picked up the scissors, then lay them down and picked up the screwdriver again. He leaned in and carefully wedged the flat of the screwdriver against the underside of the chip on the motherboard. "Okay. Here goes."

"Stop," came a voice, slithering and wet. Bruce froze.

Nadia screamed. "Oh my God! That's him, that's that creature that . . ."

Bruce looked at Nadia and at Emil. "We're a little pressed for time here," he said, resisting the urge to call Emil by name.

"And you'll have eternity to regret it if you do what-ever it is you're about to do."

"What?" Thirty seconds.

"Bruce, URSA had a feeling you might try this. I warned them about that, so they reversed your failsafe."

"Reversed?"

"Reversed."

"We're about to blow up here."

The gamma demon crouched down, drawing in close, whispering. "Listen to me. For Nadia. The truth. Reverse your action."

"What the hell is the reverse of *seven*?" Bruce shouted. Twenty seconds.

Betty shook her hands. "Thirteen?"

Greg raised an eyebrow. "Three-point-five?"

Emil sat back, casting a look of disappointment on Betty. "Religious studies instructor indeed." He looked at Bruce. "Seven is the number of God."

"One of them," Betty said.

"The number of the devil is . . ."

"Six-six-six?"

Emil nodded, tilting his head. "That or four."

"Four?" Bruce said. "I never heard that."

"I have," Betty said.

"Really. I promise," he rasped. "But six is bad, too."

Ten seconds. Bruce looked at the motherboard. Six or four. Six or four. "When you set this whole thing up, you got URSA to help with your agenda?" *Why are you here?*

"Yes."

"So," he was whispering between his own words, "they saw the verse, the proverb."

"Yes."

There are six things which are an Abomination unto the Lord. The six-or-seven confusion.

Bruce bent down again with the screwdriver and closed his eyes as he stuck the head underneath the sixth chip and pried it loose.

The timer chirped once. And died, the red light disappearing. No dramatic last readout, it did not read oh-oh-seven, or anything.

Bruce stared for a long moment. Nothing, and nothing happened.

Betty pounced, like a cat, like chain lightning, landing on his chest and putting her arms around him. Bruce was just beginning to breathe.

"I don't believe it," Bruce said. "I don't believe he—"

Bruce looked back, past his wife, who clung to him like a vine as he stood. He looked past the embracing Greg Vranjesevic and Nadia Dornova, scanning the room.

Emil was gone.

CHAPTER 18

The incredible Hulk stood just outside Sean Morgan's office. The Helicarrier was alive with activity, as it should be. There were work crews everywhere, fixing a million broken items from all the pitching and turning of the Helicarrier's adventure with autopiloting. Add to that the gaping hole in the gymnasium floor, and there were a lot of work orders being approved.

Morgan was on the telephone, speaking into a headset, and the sandy-haired man looked up and gestured for Bruce to come inside. The director kept talking, the bandage on his face moving with his cheek, so that it seemed to Bruce that it *had* to hurt for him to speak. One of his hands was bandaged as well, and there was a telltale rise under the SAFE head's starched shirt, the bandages underneath running across his chest, where he had been sliced by the late head of Gamma Team. All in all, though, he was not as much a mess as he might have been.

"Nick—no, Nick. Listen, I have no clue why the ambassador requested the Russians send the tape of the crisis to me first. What difference does it make, I sent it right to you anyway? That's appropriate after all, you're the international types. Uh huh . . ."

Bruce did not like being here while all of the agents were awake, but Morgan had asked to see him, politely no less.

"Altered?" Morgan continued, looking at Bruce for a moment. "Nick, the very idea is not just insulting, it's positively horrifying. SAFE wouldn't alter a tape of international consequence. My God, that's the kind of spooky thing I'd expect from S.H.I.E.L.D., but we're just a bunch of locals with a Helicarrier, here, Nick. I don't even think we *have* a video editor."

Bruce covered his mouth, smiling. Morgan was having

an unmitigated and decidedly uncharacteristic ball. "Uh huh," Morgan continued. "Woman? Yes, yes, Nadia Dornova was there." There was a long silence. "You know, the Broadway woman. *Antigone* . . . What other? Uh huh . . . Look, Nick, reports or not, I've seen every inch of tape from that day and there was no other woman besides Dornova, which is not a real shock, because she's Greg Vranjesevic's girlfriend . . . No . . . No one else . . . No, I have no idea." Morgan coughed. "Yeah, well, I get a lot of that. Yours too. Why, Nick, I have absolutely nothing up my . . . Nick?"

Morgan set down the headset. He composed himself and after a moment took on a grave face, very grave, mock-undertaker grave, even, Bruce thought. "This job," he said, "has few joys."

"He's upset?"

"He's always upset," Morgan said. Now his face took on a calmer tone, began to lose some of its joviality. "Thanks for coming."

"You've had quite a shakeup around here," Bruce said.

"Yes." Morgan nodded, leaning back. "Coffee?"

"Nah," Bruce said. "Betty wants me to cut back."

"Interesting."

"Um . . ." Bruce looked at the headset on Morgan's desk. "If I understood that conversation correctly . . . thank you. I mean that. We failed in everything we wanted to do."

"Hm. How so?"

"KGB didn't get Emil, of course. So you guys didn't get yours back in exchange."

"Well, I'm sorry that the full deal didn't go through. But if you're talking about our little favor to Betty. . . ."

"Yes."

"I wouldn't have it any other way. She captured this man Timm, a double for URSA, who was in the employ of SAFE. That alone is enough to earn our favor. I like to take care of my people, Dr. Banner.''

"I'm, ah, I'm sorry about Jo." Bruce had gotten the whole briefing in short form already, but they hadn't really talked about it.

"I haven't been paying enough attention," Morgan said. "Too much—I don't know. Grief."

"Yes," Bruce said. "But it's useful, I think."

"She could have been me, actually," Morgan said, musing. "She had every right to her revenge, when you think about it."

"You know what?" Bruce leaned forward. "Try not to. All right? Because you'll never make sense out of it."

"Well." Morgan looked out the window. "Well. There's plenty of time for that, I guess."

"Maybe you should take some time off."

"Hm? No," Morgan said. "This is my element. It'll be everything I can do to make sure SAFE doesn't lose its funding after we were so heavily infiltrated. Years of work will have to be redone. So that's what I'll do."

Bruce watched the man, a profile in silhouette against the gray sky outside. "Whatever you say."

"We didn't completely fail, anyway." Morgan looked at Bruce. "We stopped him, didn't we? That bomb could have gone off, torn away half the city. Insane."

"That's something, I guess."

Morgan spun around and leaned forward on his desk. "No," he said. "That's everything."

The Hulk smiled, rising. "Thank you. I guess I'll be leaving you to your work, then." He started to turn and walk.

"Dr. Banner—"

Bruce turned around. "Hm?"

"Thank you for trying to save my son," Morgan said softly.

The Hulk nodded, slowly, clutching the door handle.

"I have nothing to say, Morgan," he managed, "except thank *you*."

"Thank you for deciding to walk with me," Betty said. She snuggled against Bruce as she walked through the Village, listening to the blues clubs through the doorways as they passed.

Bruce grinned a bit. "Well, even this getup won't keep me from being recognized if someone were looking for the Hulk in particular." He wore a wide, dark hat and a coat that could house a regiment.

"I know," she said. They came to a stop at Washington Square, and Betty stepped up on a stone embankment, high enough that she could see eye-to-eye with her husband. "I know, we could be recognized. Our cover could be blown. But every now and then, isn't it nice to walk in the city and just say, to hell with it?"

"Yeah, well, except I feel so . . . old." Bruce looked across Washington Square Park. There were students hanging out, crunchy granola types mixing the past and the future.

"But not like an outsider," Betty said.

"No," he answered. "Not in the way you mean."

She turned around and leaned back against the massive giant in the dark coat, looking at the cold streets, and they both breathed deeply.

"You should know that Morgan protected your secret," Bruce said. "I didn't even have to press him on it."

"You mean I can stay?" She sounded on the verge of crying. "The Faculty Senate isn't going to suddenly learn I'm a fugitive from justice and throw me out?"

"Well, God knows Morgan might ask you for a favor later on. You might wish you hadn't taken his help."

"So, um," she said, looking down. She ran her fingers through a strand of hair that fell from her wool hat. "I can't believe I'm actually saying, 'um.' I'm always getting on my students about that.'' Betty cleared her throat. ''So you're gonna stay, too?''

''The only danger is to you,'' he said, slowly.

''You don't have to ask me how I feel about that.''

After a while he tapped her arm and gestured over his own shoulder. ''Let's get some hot chocolate.'' She hopped off the cement block, once again three-quarters of his height. ''And of course, I'll stay. I like it,'' he said. ''I like it.''

They stopped a block down at a vendor's cart. Bruce hung back about twelve feet, in the shadows, dark entrance of an alleyway between two buildings, while Betty bought the chocolate. Bruce was looking down the alley when Betty whistled, holding one of the chocolates out. He took his and sipped it, letting the hot liquid run over his tongue.

Down the alley, Bruce saw something move. He turned his gaze in that direction in time to see a sewer cover swaying a bit, suspended by a shadowy shape underneath, the metal disk raised up nearly half a foot. Bruce stared at the shadow and looked back at Betty. It wasn't the sewer cover that caught his eye, made him hand Betty his chocolate and apologize profusely, made him begin to move down the alley after telling her to meet him back home.

It was the pair of glowing, blinking red eyes underneath. The cover shut before Bruce even got near, but Bruce wasted no time bending down and wedging his pinky into the keyhole, lifting it. Vaguely, he heard Betty shout something about being careful. He would. He always would.

Bruce landed in the sewer tunnel, his feet hitting the floor of the tunnel with a splat. ''Come on, Emil,'' he said, as he stood there, the surrounding few feet lit up by the light from the alley above. ''I'm tired of this.''

There was movement to his left, about ten feet down. Something stuck its head around the corner, and Bruce

became aware of a torch burning. Then he saw the torch
and the arm that bore it wave, gesturing with the torch.
Bruce moved in that direction, hand running along the wet
brick, listening. He could hear something, breathing, and,
as he reached the corner, he heard—Kennedy?

. . . shall pay any price, bear any burden. . . .

Bruce turned the corner and saw flickering light, then
realized it was still another turn away. He padded down
the tunnel, listening to Kennedy and the dripping of the
liquid in the pipes and the odd, rasping breath of the
Abomination.

One more corner and the tunnel opened up into a wide
section the size of Bruce's living room. On the far end,
the torch had been put into a crevice in the brick and hung
there, lighting up the two long walls. Bruce barely had
time to register that the walls were covered in glass
screens when the living room under the city exploded in
video.

Each wall lit up with pixellated images from damp
ground to cobwebby ceiling. In all, there had to be twenty
screens on each side, and Bruce stood between them,
watching both walls, staring ahead. Across the room the
tunnel shrank down and continued, and Bruce saw a dark
figure crouched there, back in the shadows, rasping, red
eyes glowing, the slithery voice speaking. "Stop. Look,
Bruce. Look. Look what I have to show you."

Bruce watched the screens, all of them, the images
blinking out into static and coming back, one after the
other. Time bent forward and back, swooping close to the
present and zooming back, Kennedy and the blank check,
Khrushchev and his shoe, Ike and the people who liked
him.

"What is character?" the fiery eyes in the dark said.
"What is an individual? Once I thought a man is defined
by what he believes in. But that is not it. That is another
way of saying a man is what he serves. And somehow
that is not right."

There were too many images for Bruce to follow, but he couldn't help his eyes tracking as many as he could, his brain labelling each of them. Andropov, Flight 007 a fireball in the sky, *Sputnik*.

"We are what we are. That's simplistic, isn't it?" Emil said, and on Bruce's right he caught a picture of Emil Blonsky, so large he filled all the screens on that side, young, with dark hair and a royal hawklike nose. And on the left, a young Bruce, a scrawny kid in a lab coat, hair greasy and unkempt, ugly purple cords. He was folding his arms, not looking at the camera, staring instead at a blackboard with a blurred diagram, just another project, maybe. Maybe the gamma bomb. "Here we are. Trapped in time, Bruce. This is us before the gamma wave. This is us before our cells were turned inside out and we were made new beings. We are what we are, so are we still the same?"

Green, suddenly. Emerald and brilliant, flashing hard green and blinding bright, both walls lit up.

The desert, a field of green glass. Then the pictures again, young Emil. Young Bruce.

"I ask you," the figure in the dark rasped, "are we the same? I tell you what I think. I think we are changed, and we change ourselves. But we cannot help what we become. We cannot help being what we have become. Do you understand? I make a choice, it affects me, and I become a new thing. But I must react in the nature of what I am."

"That's an excuse," Bruce said.

"You're not listening," Emil said. "Look at these images, two men, Bruce Banner and Emil Blonsky. And the gamma wave flies over us and we are gone, erased. All our hopes gone, all our dreams burnt to irradiated cinders. We have been made new beings. I am an Abomination. And you are a Hulk. We are not fit for humanity. You know it. Deep inside, you know it, as much as you do not wish to listen to me. We do not belong because of what we are. And we cannot help being what we have become.''

The videos blinked off and Bruce looked back at the crouched figure. The only light in the tunnel came from those two, glimmering red eyes, and the flickering torch, the flames flickering madly off the dead monitor screens. ''Can't we?'' Bruce asked, moving between the dark screens.

The crouching figure did not move. It did not breathe. And as Bruce stepped forward, reaching out, he already knew what was going to happen.

He touched the head, tipping it, and the electric eyes flickered as the stone gargoyle tipped sideways with the Hulk's hand. It fell over, without drama, leaving a trail as it went down, the fins on the side of the head scraping their way down the muck-covered bricks.

''Can't we?'' Bruce asked again, quietly, to no one in particular.

And the Hulk put his giant, green, unwieldy, dense hands in his pockets, in the dark, under the ground, far from the eyes of men. And he listened in his mind to the words of the Abomination and he considered the source, and he questioned their wisdom, and he doubted their truth. And in fear of those words he crouched by the gargoyle and closed his eyes, because he could look at the electric eyes no longer.

And aboard the SAFE Helicarrier, on the GammaTrac, there was not an Abomination in sight.

Jason Henderson was born in north Texas and attended the University of Dallas, where he wrote his first book, *The Iron Thane*, in his junior year. After finishing his JD at the Catholic University of America, Columbus School of Law, in Washington, D.C., Henderson came back to Texas and now lives in Austin with his wife, Julia, an educational policy wonk. His other novels include *The Spawn of Loki* and the *Highlander* novel *The Element of Fire*. He is coauthor, with Tom DeFalco, of the first book of the *X-Men & Spider-Man: Time's Arrow* trilogy, to be published in the summer of 1998. Visit Henderson's home page at http://www.flash.net/~jhenders/JHENDERS.HTM.

Rocketed to Earth as an infant, **James W. Fry** escaped the destruction of his homeplanet and grew to adulthood in Brooklyn, New York. In 1984, seduced by the irresistible combination of insane deadlines and crippling poverty, he embarked on a career as a freelance illustrator. James's credits include *The New ShadowHawk* for Image, *Star Trek* and *The Blasters* for DC Comics, *Spider-Man Team-Up* and *Midnight Sons Unlimited* for Marvel, and Topps Comics's *SilverStar*. He has provided illustrations for several *Star Trek: The Next Generation* YA novels, the Spider-Man novels *Warrior's Revenge*, *Carnage in New York*, and *Goblin's Revenge*, and the anthologies *The Ultimate Spider-Man*, *The Ultimate X-Men*, and *Untold Tales of Spider-Man*. Himself a leading cause of stress-related illness in comic book editors, James's greatest unfulfilled ambition is to get one full night of guilt-free sleep.

SPIDER-MAN!!™